Family, Pack

Michael Jasper

UNWRECKED PRESS

Also by Michael Jasper

The Family Pack series: The Finder Team series:
Family, Pack   *Finders, Inc.*
Hunter's Moon   *Lost & Finders*
The Finder Pack
(a Family Pack/Finder Team crossover)
Augie and Ozzy Take Back the Mountain (a Finder Team prequel)

The Contagious Magic series:
A Sudden Outbreak of Magic
A Wild Epidemic of Magic
A Lasting Cure for Magic
The Last Sorcerer (a novella)

Standalone novels:
The All Nations Team
A Gathering of Doorways
Heart's Revenge
The Prodigal Sons
Unassisted Living
The Wannoshay Cycle

Story collections:
What Was Left Standing
UnWrecked Tales
Gunning for the Buddha

Graphic novel:
In Maps & Legends (with art by Niki Smith)

Chapter One

His new apartment measured no more than seven hundred and twenty-five square feet, and tonight Tommy Roling felt every inch of the place closing in on him.

I can't wait much longer, he thought. *Not tonight. Not here.*

The yellow-and-green linoleum of the kitchen crashed head-on with the faded pink shag carpet of their dining room slash living room. The scratched-up card table he'd gotten from Mom held what was left of tonight's dinner. Mostly greasy wrappers, torn boxes, and a few loose french fries. The stale smell of the fries and the mystery-meat burgers—he'd eaten one too many of them—made Tommy's nose twitch as he paced heavily from linoleum to shag, waiting for Suzanne to get the baby to sleep.

Corinne had picked up a cold again, and her barking cough made Tommy wince every time she let loose with it. So he paced and tried to ignore the ache and tension that had crept into his bones in the past few minutes.

At nearly six foot three, Tommy had to duck every time he walked past the crooked light fixture hanging above the dining area. The weird angles of the apartment made their second-hand black and white couch spill over into the dining area, so the card table couldn't be centered under the light without blocking the path to the living room. The result? Tommy smacked his head on the dangling light at least twice a day, even though they'd been living here for almost a month now.

Us, he thought. *Me, Suzanne, and the baby. Corinne. My girls.*

He froze as Corinne's wailing and coughing from the tiny second bedroom quieted. He swiped at his forehead, standing in the middle of the tiny kitchen like a convict, or a caged animal—he could almost touch both walls if he extended his arms and stretched. This place was all they could afford.

He glanced at the calendar thumb-tacked to the wall next to their ancient wall phone. Over half of the days in January had been crossed out with an X up through today, the nineteenth. Tomorrow, the lunar phase was listed as a perfect O. It was like the start of some crazy, uneven game of tic tac toe that he was already losing.

Tommy gathered up the remains of their supper, grimacing at the loud crinkling sound of the papers and mostly empty containers, and shoved it all into the garbage can. He straightened the piles of bills left on the table and snagged the flier from Northeast Iowa Community College before Suzanne saw it. He shoved the flier with its smiling white faces and bright blue text into his jeans pocket and stood in the middle of the kitchen, his big hands shaking with impatience.

If I don't get out of this stifling apartment soon, all hell's going to break loose. I can feel it in my blood.

"Please be asleep," he whispered. He touched his throat and felt his pulse doing double-time. "I gotta *go*."

But he couldn't leave without making sure Corinne was down for the night.

He let out a cautious breath and checked his pocket for his keys. He had his heavy coat in his hands to protect him from the harsh Iowa wind of late January, though in a few minutes he wouldn't need it at all. The light in the apartment had grown too bright, making his eyes ache.

Gotta go. But first...

Tiptoeing his two hundred and seventy pounds across the squeaking floor, Tommy at last risked opening the door to Corinne's nursery.

Should've turned off the light behind me, he realized too late.

A sliver of yellow living-room light cut into the pink wallpaper and curtains of the baby's room. The light caught Suzanne's eyes where she sat rocking the baby on her shoulder. All he could see of Corinne under the thick pink blanket was the round top of her head, and a wild tuft of strawberry-blonde hair sticking up.

The cold reflection of the light in Suzanne's angry gaze was enough to make Tommy step back. The baby had cried and coughed for almost twenty minutes, and that always made her panicky.

"Marvin's waiting on me," he whispered as an apology, his voice like a croak.

Suzanne's eyes widened as she looked at him, as if to say "Be quiet!"

Then they narrowed, and he caught her nod.

Ever since they started dating, she'd known about how he had to unload trucks for Dad's friend Marv over in Earlville for a couple nights every month. She understood, but that didn't mean she liked it. She hated being left alone with the baby, especially when she had an early shift at the restaurant the next day.

"Love you," Tommy whispered. Then he closed the door as quietly as he could with hands that now quivered with bottled-up energy.

He nearly ran the three steps across the pink carpet and one step over the yellow linoleum. The only thing that stopped him on his way out the door was the barking cough of his six-month-old. The sound tore at his hammering heart. He paused, hand on the cold knob to the door leading outside.

I can't keep doing this. I'm going to fall apart.

Tommy stood there, waiting for another cough, waiting for his heart to slow down. After half a minute, neither happened, but he'd take that.

Finally, he pushed open the door with shaking hands, closed it silently behind him, and ran down the steps into the cold night toward his car. It was going to have to be side roads and pedal to the metal all the way to Westhoff's land.

Nobody better try to stop me before I get there.

O f course, when you go for a drive in the town where you've lived for all but one of the twenty years of your life, you can't help but get noticed by *everyone* in that town.

As soon as he pulled out onto Main Street, Tommy saw Mickey's rusted-out blue pickup ahead of him. Despite his best efforts to stay back and avoid their rearviews, both Mickey in the driver's seat and Krunch in the passenger seat stuck their hands out to wave at him, and then give him the finger. Tommy did the same back to them and kept driving.

When they pulled over to talk, he didn't look over at them. Instead, he hunched low, blinking sweat out of his eyes, and gripped the steering wheel tight.

I haven't hung out with them in forever, he thought. *Wonder if they still have those weekend-long PlayStation marathons at Krunch's house.*

Tommy kept his driver-side window rolled down, sucking in the cold air, and then he stuck his entire head out the window for a painful, blinding, sobering second.

Slow it down. You're almost there. There's still time.

Two more turns and he hit a gravel road. The back wheels of his Grand Am spun, pulling the little car into a swerve that he drove out of without even having to think about it. He goosed the gas pedal and kept pressing it until the little six-cylinder engine hit seventy. The car's revving drowned out Tommy's tortured breathing.

Above him, the night sky opened up with a blanket of stars almost bright enough to drive by without headlights. The turn for Westhoff's back acres was lit up like a movie theater entrance to Tommy, though all the colors now bled into white, black, and gray.

His vision was going wide on him, the world opening up to him, coming clearer and fuller, as his eyes—always the first thing to change—drank in the moon fat and white overhead.

He slammed the car into the turn without slowing, and rocked down the half-mile dirt lane leading to the fifty unused, overgrown acres of old man Westhoff's land. His nose was full of metallic sweat, burning oil, and toxic exhaust.

As soon as the car was parked and the engine killed, Tommy rolled out of the door, pulling at his clothes and wheezing like a dying man. His shirt ripped and his socks came off in tatters, but he was beyond caring. He exhaled, and then inhaled the terrified scent of three, maybe four deer running away from him, half a mile away.

His fingers were clawed and his breath plumed in front of him like a semi's exhaust, the air chuffing in and out of him as he nearly hyperventilated from his efforts.

I tried to hold off the change for too long, he thought. *Can't keep doing that.*

And then his clothes were off and his blood was on fire.

All thinking, all worries, all fears disappeared, and under the wide-open sky and glowing moon, Tommy let out a full-throated laugh and *ran*.

When he opened his eyes, the world was gray, and unknown hours had passed. The dark blonde fur that had sprouted like weeds from his skin—keeping him utterly warm despite the twenty-five-degree temperatures outside tonight—was gone. He lay naked in a clearing, his belly round and full, legs and back aching, with the sharp taste of copper in his mouth and his own salty-sweat scent filling his nose.

And he was freezing.

Corinne, he thought as he watched the stars glowing down on him. A hint of color crept into the night sky down toward the eastern rim of the horizon. *My little girl will be waking soon.*

According to Mom, Corinne was a dream baby, already sleeping through the night at her age, but Tommy felt like the little girl still got up way too early in the morning. If she wasn't up by six a.m., Suzanne would wake in a panic and tiptoe into her room to check on her. Which of course would do the trick and wake Corinne up, anyway.

The freezing air and the memory of Corinne's barking coughs ripped from her tiny body got Tommy moving despite the aching of his exhausted body. His arms felt like useless tree limbs attached to his armpits, and his thick legs still twitched and spasmed from all his running.

I'm so out of shape it's pathetic. What would my coaches think if they saw me now?

He'd banged up a couple toenails tonight, too. He felt his gorge rise as he sat up, but he swallowed hard and closed his eyes for a few seconds. Mom always said that only wimps tossed their cookies after a wild night of running.

After a few more deep breaths of icy air, he felt better. Despite the repeated attempts of his buddies Mickey and Krunch, he'd never gotten completely drunk, despite many opportunities at parties and nights at his friends' houses to do so. But this must be what it felt like afterward: no memory what had happened in the past few hours, a nasty taste in your mouth, and shit in your gut that you'd been too out of control to stop from putting in there.

Not to mention the sick certainty you had that you did something really bad while you were drunk.

"Just hope I didn't kill an' eat Bambi this time," Tommy mumbled as he got to his feet at last. A giddy laugh escaped his lips, followed by a resounding belch that made him laugh even more. All that running had felt *good*.

Tommy liked having it in him. Even if it was just two, maybe three nights a month, when the moon was fat overhead. Despite all the lying and sneaking around and stress it caused, Tommy wouldn't change his condition for the world. Having it in him was a blessing, not a curse like Mom made it out to be.

The only drawback was coming back to reality. He was going to have to snag some Red Bulls on his way to work today to stay awake at the call center. Nobody was going to buy a subscription from a guy who was mumbling and yawning in their ear for the ten or so seconds he had their attention.

Getting back to his frosted-over car took him a good fifteen minutes. Usually he tried to stop running close to where he'd parked his car, but last night had been an out-of-control one. He'd woken in a clearing not a hundred feet from the muddy creek that ran down the eastern border of Westhoff's land.

Too close to the border, really. A couple deer hunters had set up tree stands and a round shack made of tin on the other side of the creek. Tommy didn't want them getting a look at him when he was hunting as well. Just his luck they'd think he was a big old buck and take a shot at him, right in his own marked-off territory.

As he walked over the frozen ground speckled with patches of old snow and headed up the gentle slope that led back to his car, Tommy was grateful for the dark. He was less embarrassed of the blood on him than the jiggle of his gut and his fat white ass exposed here out in the middle of nowhere.

He knew he'd let himself go in the past year, ever since he'd quit the football team and given up his scholarship at the University of Northern Iowa. The coaches and scouts had been all over him when he was just a sophomore in high school, after the summer of his growth spurt. He'd hit his current height then, and putting on weight had been easy. Soon he was going both ways, playing defense and offense, a varsity starter as a sophomore and then as a junior and senior as well. And the college coaches started calling and emailing him.

But two things stopped his football career. The first was timing—his fourth college game was a night game, and it took place under a full moon. As a freshman, he'd just won his starting position at defensive tackle, and he couldn't control himself. The change came over him, just partially, just for a few seconds, really. He'd broken through the line of blockers and sacked the quarterback hard enough to put the kid in traction. Someone said the guy was now in a wheelchair.

And the other thing, of course, was Suzanne.

Few girls had ever paid much attention to him before, but now there was this cute redhead driving up from Dyersburg to Cedar Falls with her friends and spending the occasional night with him in his dorm room.

After the full-moon game, he didn't want to play football anymore. He quit the team and gave up his scholarship. He was back home for good when he learned that Suzanne was pregnant, leading him to drop out six weeks from the end of his freshman year.

But now he was done with all that college bullshit, and he was a father. A dad. Who needed a fancy football scholarship? Who had time? He figured he'd be lucky to get a degree from the local community college. Forget about playing ball, ever again.

When he finally cranked the engine and jammed the heat and defrost on high, Tommy could barely feel the tips of his fingers or his ears. His toes were already numb from the frost-tipped grass.

At least he'd kept to the territory he'd marked out years ago, as a kid, while he was running wild in the night. Otherwise he might end up in someone's barn miles from here, chewing on one of their pigs or something. The fifty acres of rough land here owned by their old family friend Joe Westhoff was perfect for Tommy's needs. After over fifteen years of coming here, he knew every acre like an old friend.

Tommy tried not to think about anything but his little girl as he toweled off the blood from his face, hands, and chest. He did his best to get the mud from his battered feet before putting on a new pair of socks and his size fifteen shoes.

I hope she didn't cough all night, he thought with a sharp surge of panic. *What if she was really sick? What if she was dying? How would I know?*

Nobody taught you these kinds of things—how to know you were doing the right thing with your kid. Mom always said not to worry, that instinct would take over. But lately he'd started doubting most of the advice she'd given him over the years.

Back in his clothes once more, he dropped heavily into his car. The shocks complained noisily in response. The heat from the vents blasted him in the face until he notched it down. Utter exhaustion fell over him as he put his car in gear and began driving home in the weak light of dawn. He could still taste blood on his tongue.

It wasn't until he turned off the car outside the apartment he shared with his girls that he even noticed the bloody gash in his side.

Chapter Two

Muscle turns to fat after less than a month of inactivity. Tommy learned this the hard way. Firsthand. He hated the feel of his own body, and rarely looked at himself in the mirror with his shirt off anymore. Even back in his football days, he'd never had that ripped look that some of the guys on the football team had, the skinny ones whose bodies were slowly turning to muscle. But after a couple months of weights and practices, he'd gotten pretty solid in his senior year of high school and the start of his freshman season with the UNI Panthers.

Now, easily fifty pounds overweight despite his big frame—Mom and Dad were both tall and, as Mom called it, "well-proportioned"—Tommy had love handles at the age of twenty.

One of which he brushed his hand against as he killed the engine to his Grand Am, back in the small gravel parking lot next to their apartment.

And his hand came away sticky with warm blood.

"Oh God." The pain hit him then as the last of the animal adrenaline left him. Like being stabbed in the side with a dull knife, being pushed farther in with each breath. "Oh shit, oh God."

He didn't want to lift his shirt and look under it, but he had no choice. Hands shaking, scared now that he'd mortally wounded himself, Tommy flicked on the overhead light and pulled up the wet bottom of his black Nickelback concert shirt.

He saw a six-inch slice in his side, just under his ribs. Blood still oozed from it, slowly. Bright red against his pale skin tinted with blue from the cold, the blood now dripped onto his gray car seat.

He turned off the light and wiped his sticky hand on his jeans. Sitting in the fading darkness that was being chased away by the lone street light a block away and the approaching sun, Tommy tried not to panic.

Where do I go? To the ER here in Dyersburg? Mom might be there working the nurse station. If I go to Dubuque, they won't know me. But I might bleed to death before I get there. And we can't afford doctor's bills.

And Corinne...

Tommy took a deep breath, the pain in his side doubling almost enough to make him cry out. And then, his baby girl's pinched face in his mind, he forced himself to get a grip.

"She needs me," he whispered. "I can handle this. Keep it... under... control."

As he muttered to himself, much the same way he'd talk lowly to himself before a big game to psyche himself up, Tommy looked through the windshield until he found the moon, just a tiny disk peeking out above the leafless oaks surrounding the houses and apartments next to the parking lot.

"*Control,*" he whispered.

He closed his eyes and thought first of Corinne, her soft blue eyes looking up at him as he gave her a bottle of formula.

My blood in her, mixed with Suze's. A better version of me. Containing all my hopes and dreams.

Tommy breathed faster, senses heightening. He smelled the Peterson's cats through the car windows. They'd been digging in the garbage again, along with a brave owl not more than five minutes ago.

The darkness disintegrated, as if the night was turning itself inside out.

He tasted fur and felt bits of bone on his tongue, mingled with blood. Rabbit fur. And something else, something sweeter.

"I can... do this..."

Panting now, Tommy let go of the steering wheel before he bent it. Grateful of the shadows from the trees and the big fence in front of him, he felt his muscles clench and tighten. Sinew built in him. Bones stretched too fast to feel, and his elongated head brushed against the roof of the car.

"*Do this*," he growled, snout snuffling cold air.

His jeans ripped and his shoes split open. His T-shirt stretched, skin-tight now. Fur tickled every inch of his body as it sprouted out, thick as grass. He could barely fit inside his car now, legs jammed in the well of the driver's seat, neck bent awkwardly.

And the fiery pain in his side subsided. Dwindled.

Tommy kept his eyes closed tightly, vision going red, and then flashing white behind his lids. He focused only on the change. He'd held it off earlier, but he didn't know until now that he could bring it back like this, at will. He'd always been too afraid to try. To lose control.

Soon the change would be complete, and he'd break loose of the car on all fours. Instead of letting that happen, Tommy relaxed instead. He wasn't sure if the gash in his side was completely better, but once again, he was out of time. This would have to be enough—Mom said to never change unless it was night, full dark.

Coming back into his normal body was, as always, a disappointment. He not only felt like he shrank, but he also got the sense of jumping into a pool of warm Jell-O. He missed the muscles and high tone and strong lungs that came with the change.

Tommy exhaled and opened his eyes at last.

First things first. He lifted up his shirt, prepared for the worst. But his side no longer bled. Only a long scratch remained, already scabbing over.

He let out a billowing sigh. No trip to the ER this morning. Thank God.

He looked to his left and saw that the windows of his car were steamed over, and in some places the steam had already turned to glistening frost. Pale blue daylight the color of Corinne's eyes glowed on the other side of the windows.

Tommy swiped at the window next to him with a shaky hand. As it cleared, he saw someone standing on the other side of the window, bending down to look in at him, eyes wide.

"Jesus!" Tommy said as he jumped back.

It was Suzanne. His heart did a weird leap, as if it wanted to bust free of his chest. For a bad half-second, he hadn't recognized her.

How much had she seen?

He'd managed to keep his secret from her for over two years. He wasn't ready to share that with her just yet, and especially not today.

Mom would've said that was a mistake, too. She was good at those kinds of reminders.

"You gonna come inside or what, big daddy?" Suzanne shouted through the window. She gave him a bitter smile. "Baby just started crying."

Corinne's cough wasn't doing much better when he got back inside the cramped little apartment. Tommy had already come up with an explanation for not just the blood on his shirt, but his torn pants and ruined shoes—one of the boxes he'd been unloading for good ol' Marv over in Earlville had slipped out of his hands as he was putting it on the skid loader, and he'd gotten snagged.

But Suzanne was in such a state about Corinne being sick and up early on the day of her double-shift at the restaurant that she didn't even notice his bedraggled appearance.

As she went into the nursery to get the baby, Tommy slipped into their bedroom and changed quickly, reminding himself to toss the clothes after Suze left.

"Your turn," Suzanne said as she passed the screaming baby to Tommy.

He felt a twinge in his wounded side as he reached up to grab her, and then he forgot about the pain from his wound, his heavy limbs, and his lost hours under the full moon. Suzanne gave him a quick kiss on her way past him to the shower.

Corinne's ragged crying and coughing subsided after he'd made about three dozen circuits of the kitchen, dining room, and living room with her in his arms.

"That's what I'm talking about," he murmured, bouncing her softly and inhaling her sweet baby scent mixed with the tang of wet diaper and spitup. Tommy loved all her odors, good and bad.

He'd fix her a bottle and change her diaper later. Right now, it was chilling time.

He flicked on the TV, put the volume on low, and rocked Corinne in Dad's old recliner as the Cedar Rapids news station began their morning show. He had until ten before work started, and if he was lucky, he could get a bit of rest with the baby and squeeze in a quick shower while little Cory took her morning nap.

Every day was like this—thinking with two brains, one for him and one for the baby. The clock was always ticking in his head, reminding him of all he had to do and when it had to be done. It tired him out. And it *never* ended.

Ten minutes passed. In the recliner, Tommy almost drifted off to sleep, but the baby's body-wracking coughs would wake him every thirty seconds or so. He wished he could rest his big hands on Corinne and absorb the violence of her coughs so she wouldn't feel them, and eventually this nasty cold would just go away.

As the weather guy on TV droned on about an approaching snow storm, the third "biggie" as he called it for the season, Tommy closed his eyes and pictured his little girl healing herself in much the same way as he had done that morning in his frosted-up car.

Maybe she had it in her, too, and all she needed was me to show her how.

He grinned as he thought of his six-month-old covered in strawberry blonde fur, baring her newly grown-out teeth, sharp as knives. Knowing Corinne, she'd be growling and feisty as a hellcat. And she'd never get sick again. Never get hurt.

"That would be so awesome," he murmured.

I'll take her running, he thought, savoring the weight of his sleeping baby daughter on his chest, held tight in his sore arms. *Soon as she's old enough to—*

A cool hand touched his forehead, and Tommy nearly leapt up out of the chair.

"Whoa," Suzanne said, standing next to him and smelling of her rose-scented perfume and strawberry-tinged shampoo. "Relax. Don't toss the baby through the TV, okay? So tell me. What would be so awesome?"

Should've heard her coming. That's the second *time today.*

"Nothing," he said. "Just talking to the baby."

His stomach churned, and he tasted something acidic, almost metallic on his tongue. Nasty.

"Call the doctor for me, wouldja?" Suzanne said, already moving away to the kitchen. "See if Cory-baby needs to get on meds again. Can't believe she's frickin' sick again."

Tommy looked at Suze's new jeans and her tight-fitting blue sweater. She'd lost some of the baby weight in the past half-year, but like him, she was still heavy. That sweater didn't used to be so tight, though the guys in town wouldn't complain.

He felt a surge of jealousy at that, along with a pang of sadness. Suzanne looked good with her makeup and her nice clothes. They hadn't gotten a chance to just hang out lately. They couldn't really afford to go somewhere nice for dinner these days, unless they put the meal on one of their almost-maxed credit cards. So they were usually stuck at home. And at home it was either baby or chores or falling asleep on the couch while watching some dumb show on TV.

"Need to do the bills today, too," Suze said, running a hand through her long hair, which was the same reddish-blonde color as the sleeping baby on Tommy's chest. "Do you have time?"

He nodded, blinking his sore eyes in the bright light streaming in from the kitchen blinds.

Don't know when, he wanted to say, *but I'll get to it.*

He could never say no to Suzanne.

"Gotta go, babe," Suze said. She gave him a quick peck on the mouth and pulled on her heavy powder-blue coat. She looked like she was about to say something else, then stopped herself.

"See ya," Tommy said. "Try not to slam—"

The door banged shut behind Suzanne, and Corinne jumped in his arms. Her blue eyes opened, widened, and he felt a scream welling in her tiny chest.

"Shh," he said, rocking madly and aiming dark thoughts at his departing girlfriend.

Corinne relaxed and dropped her head again, and Tommy glanced up at the TV. His skin suddenly filled with goosebumps as he looked at the graphic in the right corner of the screen, floating above the somber-looking blonde anchor in her dark green blazer.

Mystery Death in Dyersburg.

Reaching for the remote as carefully as he could, careful not to rouse the baby again, Tommy tapped the volume button three times.

"—Investigators and area volunteers have been searching for additional clues as to who the man was, and just what may have caused his fatal injuries. We were able to talk to the local man who knew the farmer who found the body near the gravel road west of the small town of Dyersburg. He said his friend claimed that the victim's extensive wounds reminded him of someone he'd once seen after a black bear attack. Yes, you heard that right. Black bear attack. The Dyersburg police department had no comment this morning about the victim's identity or cause of death. We'll keep you posted here on KIOW News First as the story unfolds on this patch of land owned by the Joseph Westhoff family."

The camera switched to a wider shot of the anchor and her cohort, another well-dressed person in a suit. He was grinning wide with his too white, perfect teeth as she finished her report.

"Until then," her male stand-up comic wannabe sidekick said, "keep your pepper spray handy, and stay out of the woods, okay?"

"Sound advice, I'd say," the blonde anchor said, shaking her head with a crooked smile.

"Safety first," he said. "And now in sports news, the Hawkeye basketball team had another nailbiter of a game last night in Iowa City, and..."

"Idiots," Tommy muttered as he tapped down the volume. The remote fell from his numb hand when he saw the black dirt jammed under his fingernails. He'd been spacing off at the end of the report, but now her final words came back to hit him.

Land owned by the Joseph Westhoff family.

Oh shit. That's where they found *this guy, some guy they couldn't even* identify, *for Christ's sake. Maybe he didn't have any ID on him.*

Or maybe his wounds were so bad they could no longer see his face or even get fingerprints on him.

"Those are my woods, damn it," he said to the TV.

He was breathing fast again, as if he'd been running. The walls of the tiny apartment felt too close all over again. And his arms were still coated in goosebumps.

Tommy had to take a shower, but Corinne was already starting to squirm. She needed a new diaper and a bottle and fresh clothes. And he still needed to call the doctor before he got to work—no personal calls were allowed at the subscription center. Better do that before heading over to Mom's. Maybe the doc could squeeze her in for a quick check-up this morning. The shower was going to have to wait.

He clicked off the TV in the middle of another weather update. High of twenty-two today. Like that was even news anymore. Cold and snow and wind.

He paused for a moment with his hands full of pink clothes, diapers, and wipes, and wondered what he'd be doing right now as a college student—studying? Sleeping off a hangover from a frat party? Waking up next to some hot girl from the suburbs of Chicago? Heading off to the gym for a workout with my teammates?

Tommy rubbed his eyes and started getting his daughter ready for her day.

Dream on, Wolf Boy. You're not going anywhere. *Not unless something impossible happens.*

Chapter Three

That night, after visiting the doctor and then the drugstore, followed by an endless day of talking to strangers on his squawky headset and pushing subs of *Highlights* magazine, then a quick dinner of mac and cheese and nuked chicken nuggets, and topped off by an early bed time for both Suzanne and the baby, Tommy went running again in the woods outside Dyersburg.

Mom can't rag on me about tonight, he thought, his hackles up now that he was out of the car and into the cold, moon-lit air. The night smelled of manure, mulch, and distant chimney fires and car exhaust. His blood burned.

According to Mom's rules, this was Tommy's sole night to run. She said they only got one night for each full moon. Any more than that and they could hurt themselves, or worse—get caught.

Tommy hated Mom's rules.

What's it to her if I take a couple extra nights along with it? She doesn't need to know. I even made sure to avoid the state trooper spending the night at the Westhoff's, keeping tabs on things from up there.

Stripping off his clothes and kicking out of his shoes, he started jogging. He was ready for the change to come over him. Last night he'd wasted too much energy holding it off; tonight he needed it to get here faster.

Why the hell couldn't it just happen when I wanted it or needed it? Like this morning—I made the change come over me to heal my side.

But he knew he had no real control over it. Nobody had taught him *that*.

He sucked in a sharp, cold breath and pushed himself faster down the path. That was the best way to get it kick-started, as painful as running was in his flabby, normal, unchanged body.

Inhaling in short gasps, he ran harder, heart thumping, blood rushing, vision going crystalline with clarity. The bark on the big oaks, crawling with tiny bugs. The wet slurp of the cold mud under his feet close to the tiny stream. The mad scamper of other animal feet through the undergrowth—squirrel, rabbit, gopher, mouse—fleeing his huffing, puffing approach.

Above it all, the wide-open, unfettered night sky of eastern Iowa, opening up like a black book filled with stars instead of words. And the moon, a white ball of perfect roundness, smiling down on him, whispering words of power and life into his waiting, cocked ears.

Frozen sticks snapped like bones under his feet, and he dodged bare tree limbs reaching for his eyes as if he could hear their approach.

Tommy knew this route so well he could've closed his eyes to run it. Good thing, too—once the fire in his blood took over, he'd have no control over his thoughts or actions. He'd just be animal instinct.

A memory hit him then, more like a series of images flashing through his expanding vision, of the night Mom had first taken him out here. He was barely three years old, the night less cold than this one, and nowhere near as clear.

That haziness had annoyed Mom, he could tell. He would learn soon enough that she always liked to have everything her way.

Tommy had wanted to cry when they left the car parked on the Westhoff's lane, took off their shoes and socks, and started walking. Mom had long blonde hair, curly, the prettiest woman Tommy had ever seen. She was wearing just shorts and a halter top, and he had on shorts and a T-shirt.

Shaking from both the cool summer air and the secrecy of their late-night outing, Tommy followed that mane of hair, focusing all his attention on it as she began jogging once they were inside the trees. She just *left* him. In the woods, in the dark. At some point she must've taken off her clothes.

Forgetting all about crying, the blood thumping now in his ears, a smile stretching his face, Tommy ran, too. Mom bent low, running hard now, covered in blonde fur. Tommy pursued her. Fear melted into anger, then anger became pure, unbridled bliss as he went from two legs to all fours.

It was all he could do to dodge the trees and bushes and keep from tripping as he ran, panting, the world rushing past as he went lower and lower, feeling his toes and his fingers dig into the hard, cold dirt, smelling six kinds of shit and tasting five flavors of fur, with the constant, maddening taste of blood coating his tongue.

And then his memories stopped, and he went wolf.

Next thing he remembered was Mom waiting for him at the end of the trail, at least three miles from where she'd parked their car. Mom was laughing, sweat steaming off her glistening body, and she'd picked him up and engulfed him in the biggest, longest hug of Tommy's life. She kept saying how proud of him she was, all the way back to the car, and he just basked in her praise.

Tommy crossed over a clearing of dead grass, his shadow a brief partner, then pursuer in the sharp moonlight. He sniffed one of those flavors of fur—rabbit—and toyed with the idea of pursuit.

Mom had stopped taking him on runs when he turned ten. Something went out in her eyes during that time, and looking back on it now, as he felt the burning in his limbs on the sharp incline leading to the end of the trail, Tommy guessed something had happened between her and Dad. Of course, nobody had said anything about it.

Not my problem, he told himself. His chest was aching now, the cold air burning in his lungs, the good taste of life in his mouth going sour.

If Corinne has it in her, I'll bring her here, too. Can't wait. And I'll explain *what's going on to her each step of the way, and not leave her in the dark.*

If *she had it in her*, he thought, and then the moon took over, and he knew nothing more.

When he got back home at three a.m., Tommy couldn't sleep.

The little apartment creaked with the cold, but that was the only sound other than the dull tick of the cheap owl-shaped clock on the kitchen wall. He peeked in on Corinne, listened to her raspy breathing for long enough to tear another hole in his chest, and then tiptoed back to the kitchen table, avoiding the creaky places in the floor.

Suzanne had conveniently left all the bills and the checkbook sitting there for him, held down by her beloved cell phone.

"Great," he grunted on his way past the table to the junk drawer. He needed band-aids for his side before he ruined another perfectly good black T-shirt. He'd opened up his wound again on his run tonight.

After wiping away the last of his own blood from under his shirt, Tommy plastered his side with over a dozen bandages. All they had were the narrow, three-inch-long ones you used when you nicked a finger. They'd have to do for now. At least the stupid cut had stopped stinging. He wished it would just hurry up and heal.

His wound care complete, Tommy hit the power button to boot up Suzanne's noisy little laptop, one of the leftover machines his older brother Burt had donated to their cause. Burt always had the newest gadgets and computers and video games. One of the perks of living at home, Tommy assumed.

Still waiting for the laptop to rev up, he looked over at the muted TV. A map of Iowa now showed on the screen.

"Oh great," Tommy said, reaching for the remote. He left the laptop on the table and walked over to the TV to hear the news update without turning it up so loud it woke the girls.

"...This town in the heartland of America has watched the family farms in the area get bought out by corporations, seen two factories close their doors and move the work to Mexico, and suffered along with local businesses during the economic downturn of the past few years. The town seems almost frozen in time—people still wave at you as you drive past, whether they know you or not, and the diner downtown serves breakfast all day long, for less than five dollars with tip. Into this pocket of Americana comes a mysterious, violent death. And the people here are unsettled."

They were blaming the man's death on a wild animal attack—the Dyersburg police felt strongly that it was a pack of wild dogs. They advised locals to take caution. Tommy snorted. Nobody in town could possibly believe that. And by taking caution, they'd just pack a hunting rifle in the trunk of their car and blow away any wild dog that got close.

People here knew better—that's why Tommy had to be so damn careful about where he went every full moon—but he figured the cops were just trying to quiet the story before it killed the town for good.

Tommy muted the TV again. With another jab in his wounded side, where his strip of band-aids pulled at his skin like suckers, he headed for the stack of bills on the kitchen table again.

On his way to the kitchen, he looked at the old PlayStation console, also a hand-me-down from Burt, and felt a wave of regret that surprised him in its intensity.

Can't remember the last time I played a game on that. Before Corinne, for sure. Burt and I used to play all the time, along with Krunch and Marty and the other guys from high school. Before everything changed.

Tommy touched his injured side, wincing at the pain.

As a kid, he never could understand why his big brother never got to change like he did. For some reason, the werewolf gene hit each family differently. They had second or third cousins up in Wisconsin where all three kids in the family had it, but Mom and Dad never visited them. Then there was Aunt Melanie down in Iowa City, who had it, and crazy Uncle Carl, who most certainly didn't have it, and their two boys. As far as Tommy knew, neither Tyler nor Trey had it in them.

It was spotty like that. He'd asked Mom about it a long time ago, back when Burt was in the hospital again for pneumonia when they were in grade school. She said the bloodlines had gotten weak over the years.

"It's a generational thing," she said, "ever since our great-grandpa came over from Germany, the line's gotten weaker. Harder to predict who's gonna have it in them." She glanced over at skinny little Burt in the hospital bed to make sure he couldn't hear them. "When you learn about the survival of the fittest in school, you'll understand. And that's why you have to keep an eye out for your big brother when you get older. You're already bigger than him, and he'll need your help, I'm sure. Okay?"

On that day, Tommy remembered wondering what it must feel like to have a cough as loud and harsh as Burt's. He'd never been sick like that, ever. The worst he'd ever felt was a touch of a fever on the nights when the moon was out and Mom didn't let him outside. He'd had to bounce around in the locked playroom down in the basement all night, not sleeping a single wink.

Now that he was a father, Tommy sometimes wondered what Dad thought of all this. He'd once asked him what it was like, not being able to do what he and Mom could do, but Mom had stepped in quickly to change the subject. Dad's own shortcomings in his blood didn't seem to bother him, so long as he got to drink a few beers after working at the shop all day and watch whatever was on ESPN that night.

Tommy tried to calm his swirling thoughts by looking at the sobering facts of his and Suzanne's finances. With his paltry income and her tip money, they barely made enough to pay rent and buy groceries. Being able to buy a new toy or some clothes for Corinne was always an excuse to celebrate.

I just hope Corinne can tell that I love her, he thought, doing some creative financing to stretch this week's check until Saturday, when they had to get groceries. *Dad never told me, but somehow I could tell. I'm not sure how he did that.*

Tommy set down his pen and pushed away the checkbook, envelopes, and receipts spread out in front of him. He blinked his sore eyes and stretched with a jaw-popping yawn. His arms, low back, and legs all ached from the exertions of his run earlier. And the stinging in his side had slowly turned into a throbbing.

I'm like an old man, he thought, pulling himself up to find some Tylenol.

He washed them down with an airplane bottle of whiskey Burt had bought for him. The burning of the Canadian Club killed the taste of blood from Tommy's mouth at last. His nose felt too clogged for him to smell anything.

He fiddled with the paperwork on the table for another ten minutes before the liquor and his own fatigue hit him.

Let me take a break here for second, Tommy thought, resting his chin on his hands.

Which led to flattening his arms on the table like a pillow so he could rest his head on them and close his eyes. He was dead asleep in ten seconds.

J ust put the money in the bag and nobody gets mauled."

The bank teller, Lisa Schnelling, a brown-headed girl just a few years out of high school herself, just stares at me with a half-smile on her face from the other side of the counter.

She thinks I'm joking. I look down at my right hand. It's not shaking, and the claws jut out from my fur-lined fingers. It's just in my hand, nowhere else, and when I raise it up to show her I mean business, it's enough.

"Hold on. I'll get it, Tommy. Just don't—"

"Stay calm," I tell her. "Under control. And no one will get hurt."

Lisa fills a bright red bag full of cash so fast I can barely see her little pink hands move. Nobody else notices. This is going to work.

When I grab the bulging bag that Lisa nearly tosses over the counter with a whimper, my right hand is normal again. I smell metal, suddenly, and nervous sweat.

And then the lights go out in the bank, and somebody is shooting at me.

I spin toward the door, smelling my way in the blackness until the door is a pulsing pink rectangle leading outside into what's now night time. I charge through it, the bag of money tight to my chest like a football, and look for my car.

I parked it right next to the bank entrance, but it's gone now.

The car had Corinne in the back seat, strapped in, and the engine idling. She and I are making our break from Dyersburg, leaving it with a bang.

But the car's gone, the streetlights are out, and I can't pick up her scent. I can barely see the gray outlines of the bank behind me and the other cars parked out front.

Another shot rings out from inside the bank, and I run, casting my muzzle around madly for Corinne's scent. The night fights against me, though, and none of my heightened senses cooperate. All I can smell is the stink of gas, and the cold, polluted air numbs my ears and coats my lung with tar.

I let someone *take* her.

As I run, bundles of money slip out from the bank bag, and I let them drop. Someone's after me. I can hear and smell them. Someone small and fast like a deer.

I'm running and running through the dark streets of Dyersburg heading south out of town. No car lights, no street lights, just blackness. The moon must be new, hiding from me. At last I stumble into a clump of trees.

Westhoff's land. I made it. My territory.

As soon as I stop running, I feel a sharp pain in my side. Blood oozes from the spot where the bullet passed through me. The security guard—or was it Smith from the cop shop two doors down from the bank?—must've tagged me, the bastard.

While I stand there, trying to catch my wheezing breath, a pair of red eyes comes at me, low and fast.

At that moment, the moon breaks free of the cloud, a big yellow ball almost as bright as the sun. And I see who's been chasing me all this time.

Baby Corinne, her face distorted into a mouth of sharp teeth, red eyes, fur the color of strawberry blonde. Her tiny, furry hands reach up to me, fingers curling, claws growing out of her fingertips, reaching for me, grabbing—

Tommy ripped himself out of his dream with a cough that nearly knocked him out of his chair. He sat up and had to pry the fingers of his right hand off his left forearm. His fingers left bright red marks in his arm.

Red...

Something red, like in his dream. He couldn't place it, though. His arm hurt, and his neck was all out of whack from sleeping hunched over on the table.

What he *could* remember was Corinne. Holding her that morning as she coughed. Her tiny ribs under her skin. Her red face. Her ragged breathing that smelled like sour sickness whenever he caught a whiff of it.

The line's gotten weaker, Mom said all those years ago.

So, did Corinne have it in her? Was there any way to really tell?

And what, he thought as he cautiously touched his side through his still-dry, unbloodied shirt and felt the layers of Band-Aids holding firm beneath it, *what would I do once I knew for sure about her?*

He planned on finding out, soon enough.

Chapter Four

Sleep. Work. Try to stay awake. Make calls. Leave work. Pick up supper at Subway. Drive home to his girls. Eat.

Talk. Keep the nightmare images away. Hold Corinne tight.

Wait.

Wait for the right time.

Tommy felt like he spent all of his days since leaving college *waiting.* Always holding his breath, checking the clock.

When he could wait no more that night, at twenty minutes after ten, Tommy walked over to the couch and kissed Suzanne on the forehead. She'd fallen asleep there again, watching TV, her cell phone on the floor next to her. Tommy told her he was going to take the baby for a ride to try and get her to sleep. He'd worked hard to keep Corinne awake this long after her nighttime feeding.

"Oh hey," Suzanne called out groggily as he was changing Corinne's diaper before bundling her up for the cold. "How many did you sell today?"

"Seven subscriptions," he said, smiling down at his daughter and pitching his voice higher, "so I'm twelve away from this week's bonus. Yes I am, Corinne Marie. Cuz your daddy rocks the phone lines. Yes I *do.*"

"Nice," Suzanne said. "Maybe Corinne and I can go out and do some clothes-shopping this weekend, when you get paid."

"Sure," Tommy said with a shrug, only half-listening as he tucked Corinne into the bucket of her portable car seat, which she was quickly outgrowing. He was thinking about the woods out by Westhoff's, and the state trooper car that had been gone from the front of the Westhoff farm house that afternoon.

"Say bye to Mommy," he said to both daughter and girlfriend. "Tell her we'll be back in half an hour or so, and you'll be all asleep then."

"Bye, sweetie," Suzanne called out, glancing up from her cell phone, already texting one of her girlfriends, no doubt. "See ya soon."

The door closed behind Tommy and Corinne.

"You're welcome," he muttered, his breath puffing out around him in a cloud. He hurried to the car to snap Corinne's infant car seat into place in the back seat. She didn't even make a sound, despite the cold and the wind.

The car started on the third try, and he clicked off the metal thrash music he'd been listening to on the way home from work. The car barely had time to heat up before they arrived at the turnoff on Westhoff's dirt lane. He was pretty sure nobody had seen them arrive.

"Sh-shit, it's cold," he said after shutting off the car. The wind always managed to find its way through the gaps in his old, banged-up car, whistling like a dog owner for a lost pooch.

Tommy put his left hand on the icy door handle, then let go of it.

I must be nuts. Do I really need to get her involved in this too? So soon?

He toyed with the idea of calling Mom, just to talk this through, but he was pretty sure she was at work tonight, doing a 7p to 7a at the Dubuque hospital. No way would she discuss any of this at work, where anyone else could overhear. And then he'd have to explain to her what he was doing out late, the night after a full moon.

Tommy shivered, feeling something pressing down on the top of his head, like the palm of an oversized hand.

He slid open the sunroof cover and peeked out at the moon, which had been completely full as of 9:21 last night.

He'd checked online today at work. Already starting to wane. It was close enough to full, though—it had to be.

"Okay," Tommy said at last, wriggling out of his jacket, then his shoes and socks. "Enough farting around."

He turned and leaned way back to peek at Corinne, sitting in her hard plastic seat facing the rear window. Wrapped up in her fuzzy pink blanket, she caught his gaze and gave him a big smile. He could see both of her front teeth poking through her pink gums. My girl. Getting so big already.

"I hope you show me what you got in you *fast*, little girl, yes I do," he said in his babying voice on his way out of the car.

Wearing just jeans and his black Seether T-shirt, Tommy gathered up his daughter, leaving her pink blanket behind. He could feel his pulse quickening, the change itching to begin. Corinne squirmed and squeaked from the cold.

He jogged as best he could while still holding her safely in his big hands, until they were inside the whispering trees and out of the worst of the wind. After finding a spot where the brilliant, life-giving moonlight could cover them both, he stopped.

He breathed in Corinne's sweet baby smells one last time. Then he took off her cap, her sleeper, and her diaper.

Already feeling the change flowing into him, his hands shaking, legs quivering, breath coming fast now, Tommy stepped away. Stripped off the last of his clothes. Breathing in low growls now.

Hunching almost on all fours, he tensed, ready to *run*. But he had to know about his little girl.

Would she come running with me if she could?

His mouth felt suddenly full—too full—of teeth as he opened it to call out to her.

Her name came out as a growl, low and mournful.

Because the only change coming over Corinne was a wicked blue hue spreading over her normally pink skin. Her wispy, strawberry-blonde hair fluttered in the wind. She took one look at Tommy as he crept closer to her and sucked in a long, terrible, rasping breath.

Corinne screamed, an ear-splitting shriek that knocked Tommy back into himself, ending the change.

He grabbed her off the ground, holding her to him as his fur receded and panic set in. Still holding her tight to him, skin to skin, he gathered up his clothes, smelling her fear and pain at the cold wind on her bare skin.

What if I'd done this last night? I never could've come back from the change. And she would've frozen to death while I ran and fed, completely out of my brain.

Corinne screamed so hard she couldn't get her air.

"I'm so fuckin' stupid. It's okay, baby, I got ya. *Daddy's got you.*"

He covered her up in his shirt and jeans, grabbed her hat, sleeper, and diaper, and stumbled back to his car. Now the moonlight burned in his eyes, along with hot tears that crowded his vision.

He felt exposed and vulnerable out here, in the place where he usually felt insane with power and muscle and energy.

I fucked up. Again. I totally fucked this up. My baby. My lucky baby.

My normal *little girl.*

"I'm sorry," he whispered, again and again. "I'm so sorry."

Getting his screaming daughter back into her diaper and sleeper, and then strapping her into her car seat, took what felt like an eternity, but was probably closer to ten minutes.

Something skittered through the darkened woods, a deer or some rabbits, maybe. Tommy's back stiffened as he thought of those red eyes from his dream last night. He flicked on the car engine and cranked the heat for Corinne. He closed all the car doors so the car would warm faster, and so he wouldn't have to hear her screaming. The moon slid behind the clouds, and his toes had gone numb.

He dressed himself as fast as he could, skin crawling the whole time. If a cop found him like this out here, after the dead man was found in this area, there'd be all sorts of questions and issues. Something out there was watching him, he could feel it.

By the time he got back into the car, Corinne was still crying, as if she'd been deeply insulted. The girl had a temper.

As feeling slowly returned to his fingers and toes in the idling car, Tommy felt everything inside him that he'd been holding tight to in the past few months start to let loose. He bit down the urge to start screaming at Corinne to stop crying.

The job. Moving out of Mom and Dad's place. The hand-me-downs in his baby's nursery. His frustration with Suzanne. The ache in his side as his wound split open once again, fresh blood leaking out of him.

Everything was crumbling.

And he had to wait another month—twenty-nine days of counting down and *waiting*, two things Tommy was always doing—before he could put any of it back together.

Chapter Five

12:05 a.m. Somehow he and Corinne had spent over half an hour out there in the clearing, under the yellow, less-than-full moon. Now it was Friday morning instead of Thursday night. And Corinne just kept right on crying.

Tommy drove slowly through the silent town, and his car was the only thing moving on the streets. He saw Smith, the town cop, parked in his black-and-white at the intersection of Sixth Avenue and Main. The blue-green glow of his interior lights gave his bearded face an unhealthy glow as he watched Tommy approach. He held up his left hand and pointed at his watch meaningfully.

Tommy tried to smile and give him a "what-can-you-do?" shrug, and then he cocked his thumb at the wailing baby in his back seat. Hopefully the cop would see Corinne's little fists waving in the air. Smith gave him a wave and a nod, and then Tommy was past him, breathing so fast his interior windows fogged up.

I don't need Smith pulling me over for a bad headlight or running a stop sign. Not with the bloody towels in my trunk. Not in the state I'm in. I'd probably just hit the gas and tear-ass out of here if he tried.

A few blocks later, in no hurry to get home with Corinne whimpering and occasionally coughing in the back seat instead of screaming, Tommy's cell rang. The loud ringtone set her off all over again.

"Hello?" he said with a wince, his voice all muzzy from fatigue and cottonmouth.

"Hey, Tommy!" a familiar voice said. In his tired state, Tommy couldn't place the person behind the deep, too-cheerful voice. "Glad you're still up. Had a feeling you might be. It's Uncle Carl! And is that Miss Corinne I hear in the background, saying hello?"

Tommy swiped at his eyes, making the moonlight flash across his vision like lightning.

Should've let it go to voicemail, he thought, too late.

"Um. Yeah. Uncle Carl? You sound... different. Your voice is all weird."

"Well, it's just my cell, I guess. But listen, Tommy. I know it's been a while since we visited, but I remember how hard those first months are with a new baby. I think I can help. Are you sitting down?"

"It's *late*, Uncle Carl."

"I know. I'm sorry for calling at this ungodly hour. But sometimes, you just have to act on the old impulses, y'know. This is one'a those times." Carl paused. "You okay, kiddo? I hear the little one just a-hollering back there."

"Just trying to get her to sleep by driving her around."

"Ah. Sorry to bother you. But this—something just, well. Something big just came up."

He sounded drunk. Tommy turned at the Lighthouse Restaurant on the eastern edge of Dyersburg and started back through another loop of town, passing the town's tiny golf course and catching a whiff of manure from the Wuchter's hog farm on the other side of the 9th hole. He'd heard stories about his crazy uncle Carl. The guy could pound the beer and liquor.

"Okay, look," Carl began. "A friend of mine has a proposition. Something for you to think over. And the way I look at it, it kills two birds with one stone. Because I know," Carl's voice went low, and Tommy had to hold the phone tight to his ear to hear him over the baby's squalling, "I *know* what's been going on up there, how you got roped into moving in with that young lady, and how you're doing so much for the little one. How you had to give up pretty much everything for them. Football, college, your scholarship. And how you're having trouble these days, financially."

"Uncle Carl," Tommy said, slowing for the turn to their apartment. "What are you talking about? You're drunk, aren't you—"

"Twenty-five fricking thousand dollars," Carl almost whispered into Tommy's ear. "That's what I'm talking about, son."

Tommy let his foot off the brake and let the Grand Am drift past his apartment.

"What do you mean?"

"Someone wants to adopt your baby. Someone who knows how these things work."

"What the hell?" Tommy's car swerved on a patch of black ice, and he nearly dropped the phone. "Look. Call me tomorrow when you're sober."

"Tommy. Shut your damn face for a second and listen to this. Twenty-five grand. Do you know how far that kind of money would go in Dyersburg? And it can all go to you, if you play your cards right."

"She's not up for *adoption!*" Tommy hissed into the phone, trying hard not to yell. He was driving aimlessly now, and as luck would have it, he was coming up on the spot where Smith's cruiser sat again.

Idiot, he thought, not sure if he meant Carl or himself.

He had no choice but to keep on driving and wave at Smith again. The cop nodded at him, after a long second of just staring at Tommy.

"Just listen to me for a second, Tommy-boy—"

"Don't call me that."

Tommy gritted his teeth and made sure he made a complete stop at the next block down from Smith's car. A wisp of exhaust curled into the night air at the rear of the cruiser, like a crooked finger.

"Sorry. Tom. Look. These are good people, and smart people. The guy's a techie, and he can get all the documents in order to make it legitimate. Just think about it, okay? A guy your age, you've got things to do with your life still. Maybe we can do the right thing for *everyone*. It's not too late."

As he drove past the two ten-story steeples of the Catholic Church, Tommy looked in his rearview. Corinne had finally fallen silent in the back seat. He got a glimpse of her closed eyes in the little rectangular mirror he'd installed over the backwards-facing infant seat. A reflection of a reflection.

His chest loosened, the tiniest bit.

"How long you been out of a job now, Uncle Carl?" Tommy asked as he turned up his street.

There was a long pause. Tommy smiled a bitter grin at that, but then started to feel a twinge of fear creep up his spine. Like he'd gone too far.

"Yeah, you're pretty smart, Tommy. Don't miss much, do ya? Going on a year now, buddy. And yeah, I do get a small cut on this. But I'm hoping you'll see what a great deal this could be. I heard the baby screaming and coughing. A baby's a lot of responsibility, and a whole hell of a lot of expense, believe me. Is this what you want to be doing with your life right now? At your age? Especially," Carl added, "someone like you. With your history."

"What's that supposed to mean?"

Back home at last, Tommy had just put his car in Park when he saw a flash of red in his rearview mirror.

Smith had followed Tommy and Corinne home, and he kept his cherries on for just a few seconds longer. Tommy had no idea how long the cop had been tailing him while he was listening to his uncle's insane, drunken plan.

Uncle Carl kept right on talking in his ear, like a mosquito buzzing.

"I know you've got to think about this. Just be careful who you talk to, is all I'm saying. I don't want to have to get anyone else involved, you know?"

Tommy watched his breath steam around him as he spoke. Behind him, Smith opened his car door. His face was red in the glow of Tommy's brake lights, though he'd thankfully turned off the cruiser's spinning lights.

"Are you *threatening* me now?" Tommy whispered.

"Look, just think about it, okay? And this is all between you and me. This is our deal, man-to-man. Think about it, don't speak about it, you know?"

"Yeah, sure" Tommy said. "I'll talk to you later, Carl."

Tommy killed the call and shut off his car, hands shaking. Smith walked up the side of his car, flashlight in hand, his bearded face now hidden in shadow. He was doing that slow cop walk, probably getting off on this whole scene.

Still can't believe crazy Uncle Carl said all that, Tommy thought, cranking down his window with a numb hand. Smith looked down at him, face serious and unsmiling.

"Hi, Mr. Smith," Tommy said in a shaky voice.

"Tommy," Smith murmured. "Get the baby to sleep?"

Tommy nodded and kept his mouth shut tight before he started babbling nonsense about his uncle and illegal adoptions. Smith would lock him up faster than he could say "Wolf."

"I hate to bother you, son," Smith began. "With the baby and all. But there was that, ah, *difficulty* night before last, and we got orders to question everyone out at night. Just to be sure. So..."

Tommy's mind went into lockdown mode. He could hear Corinne starting to stir behind him. Smith's cheap aftershave and coffee breath attacked his nose. And he couldn't stop thinking about the mess of bloody clothes and towels stuffed into his trunk. And Carl's voice, echoing in his ears: *our deal, man to man...*

"Tommy?" Smith's black beard, streaked with a couple threads of gray, was a foot from Tommy's own chin. "Son, you okay? You ain't been drinking, have you?"

Tommy blinked and flinched at that.

"No, sir. I'm just tired. The baby's got me worn out. I should really get her inside, unless you needed me for something else?"

Smith moved back and gave Tommy a long, somewhat odd look.

"No," he said after a long pause. He tapped a gloved hand on the window frame of the car door, twice. "Don't need nothing more. Just... be careful out there, son. We don't like strangers in this town, but we like it even less when they show up dead. Don't need a mess like that here. All those news people, asking questions. You know what I mean?"

Tommy undid his seat belt with a loud click and nodded at Smith as calmly as he could. The cop didn't step back to let him open the door. Something flashed in the older man's eyes, in the darkness.

"You'd *tell* me if you saw anything weird tonight, wouldn't you, Tommy-boy?"

Tommy met the cop's unblinking, almost dead gaze. He felt a growl forming deep in his throat. He choked it back, fast.

"Yes, sir, Mr. Smith. You know I keep out of trouble these days. I don't want anything bad to happen 'round here, either. I got a family of my own to take care of now, you know? I'd better get her inside."

Smith nodded at that. He said goodbye and clomped back to his cruiser without a single look back.

With his breath catching in his throat, Tommy grabbed his coat and unhooked Corinne's car seat from the base in the back seat. Smith was driving off when he closed her car door.

"Go find the killer already," Tommy muttered, his breath steaming in cold air he could scarcely feel. "Instead of bugging innocent people like me."

He hurried inside, grimacing at the creak of each step on his way up to their second-story apartment. He fumbled with the lock and nearly bit through his lip at the rattling noises he made.

But Corinne was quiet at last, sleeping the sleep of the utterly exhausted. She'd had a rough night, too. He'd almost forgotten about their fruitless trip to Westhoff's clearing.

His pulse was almost back to normal as he carefully unstrapped and pried his sleeping daughter out of the bucket of her car seat.

Twenty-five thousand dollars. For a baby. My baby. My poor, normal baby.

As good ol' Smith would say: "Don't need mess like that here."

Tommy winced at the stab of pain in his injured side as he lowered Corinne into her bassinet—a gift from Aunt Melanie and Uncle Carl, he remembered now—and slipped out of her tiny little bedroom. He walked past the table with its untouched pile of bills, and headed for the couch, suddenly exhausted even though he'd done no running tonight. Not the kind of running he needed to do, that is.

What the hell was Carl thinking?

And then Tommy had to sit down hard on the couch and clamp both hands over his mouth as a wave of coughing tore through him. He was barking out a lung much like his little girl was earlier today. And his forehead felt hot.

Just what I need, he thought. *Getting sick.*

Tommy leaned back on the couch, chest aching from the spasm of coughing, and closed his eyes. He didn't want to think about that phone call anymore, but Carl's voice kept echoing in his worn-out brain.

It's not too late.

Twenty-five thousand dollars.

When he opened his eyes again, his face was warm and wet with tears. Tommy didn't even know how long he'd been sitting there, crying and starting to wheeze. But it wasn't Carl's crazy deal that had him weeping like a five-year-old.

It was the image he saw every time he closed his eyes: his tiny little girl lying on the ground, naked and defenseless. And how he stood hunched over her, waiting for something that never would happen. Not in his lifetime.

Corinne didn't have it in her, he thought. *I'm all alone.*

Chapter Six

Early the next morning, Tommy woke with a fever. Stretched out on the couch, he'd sweated through his jeans and the two layers of shirts he'd put on at one a.m. last night. His neck ached from sleeping with his head on the unforgiving armrest of the couch. H could barely smell anything from his congested nose, but he could tell that his sweat smelled like metal. His mouth tasted like b.o.

As soon as he sat up, his head spun, and he got the shakes. He was still sweating, but he now felt cold. Freezing. He grabbed an old knitted blanket from the floor, a heavy brown one, but even with that over him he couldn't warm up.

Better eat some Tylenol for breakfast, he thought, shivering in the gray dark of early morning.

The events of last night—with Corinne in the clearing, on the phone with Uncle Carl, and in the parking lot with Smith—all felt like a bad dream that was already breaking apart. He couldn't quite muster the energy to go to the kitchen to grab some aspirin, so he stretched out as best he could on the too-short, lumpy couch, and promptly went back to sleep.

As much as he hated to do it, when he woke again at a quarter past seven, he called in sick that day from work. He could tell he wouldn't feel any better by ten, when he was due at work. He was paid hourly, so there went seventy-two bucks, before taxes. Not to mention any possible commissions he might've gotten.

After Suzanne left for Mom's house to drop off Corinne, both girls in bad moods, Tommy turned off the TV and his phone. He couldn't bring himself to look at the budget stuff on the kitchen table or any of his community college fliers he'd been picking up lately. He went back to the couch to sleep the morning away in a big, shuddering ball, buried under every blanket he could find.

He tried to contain his coughing, because once he started, he felt like he was going to break his lungs, pop them like balloons. The cut in his side was more or less healed, but it still ached if he moved too fast, and sometimes nasty pink stuff would ooze out of it. And every time he got up, his head would swim, so he stuck to the couch and his blankets.

That was his Friday. Sleeping and sweating and coughing.

On Saturday he ended up staring at a lot of TV and watching the baby as best he could while Suzanne ran errands and went shopping, and then Suzanne went out to eat and to see a movie with her girlfriends on Sunday. At least Corinne's cough had started to go away, thanks to the medicine that Suzanne's health insurance had helped pay for.

Got no choice but to get better, he decided on Monday as he hauled himself out of bed after Suzanne had left for work, toting Corinne with her once again. She was angry at having to drop off the baby with Mom.

"Shitty way to start my day," Suze had said, "having to deal with your bitchy mom. The way she talks to the baby but is actually talking to *you*, cutting you down. I hate that. Thanks *so* much for getting sick, Tommy."

Tommy answered with ten seconds of barking coughs. Suzanne watched him, and her tone softened as she kissed his sweaty forehead.

"Get better, okay?" she whispered, and then she and Corinne were gone.

Instead of forcing away the cough and fever through sheer willpower, though, Tommy ended up calling in sick again on Monday.

Determined to get his act together, he made it to the shower for the first time in days on Tuesday. He only had two bouts of dizziness in there, but when he stepped out of the shower, his head ached so bad he could barely see straight.

As much as it hurt, he called in sick for a third straight day. He wasn't going to be any good on the phones today—his voice was all scratchy and weak. He felt like he was floating five feet above his body, arms and legs numb, everything a gray blur.

And then, after a few hours of staring blankly at the TV from under his blankets, the whole time feeling like the walls of their tiny apartment were inching closer, Tommy did something that he never would've done in a healthy state of mind.

He called his older brother Burt and invited him over.

G ood God, you look like shit!"

With a start, Tommy woke from his half-doze on the couch to see his brother's skinny face floating above him like a vision from a nightmare.

"Thanks," he said with a cough that took all his feeble strength to contain. "Knew I could count on you to make me feel better."

Burt brayed his loud, donkey-like laugh and flopped into the recliner. He flicked his shaggy brown hair out of his eyes and crossed his bony arms over his canary-yellow Iowa Hawkeyes T-shirt.

"Just doin' my job as a big brother. It's the only job I'm good at, ya know? But you really should go see a doctor, man. How long you been sick?"

"Couple days," Tommy said, and then groaned. Sitting up straight had given him a mother of a headache. "I'm almost over it."

"Riiiight. Well look, I brought over medicine. *My* kinda medicine, ya know."

Burt popped up from the chair, moving too fast for Tommy to follow. Turning his head to look over at his older brother in the kitchen made his head hurt even more. His tongue stuck to the roof of his mouth, dry as sandpaper.

"I got the best meds of all," Burt said, his voice giddy with enthusiasm. "Three of the best first-person shooters ever made. Plus some new games I've been working my way through. I've got the gun accessories and cheat codes, too. And of course—" Tommy heard the dull clink of cans of pop "—plenty of gaming fuel. You look like you could use some of this, bro."

Tommy couldn't stifle the cough that slipped out of his mouth when he saw the towering pile of game boxes stacked on top of his kitchen table. Next to the boxes sat a six pack of Mountain Dew, each can a different color and flavor, and an economy-sized pack of jelly beans. A grocery bag stuffed with joysticks, plastic guns, wires, and remotes now rested on top of Tommy's checkbook and piles of bills.

Burt grinned at him like a kid and offered him a can of room-temperature pop.

"Lock and load," he said, carrying the bag and the stack of games over to the TV. Tommy caught a whiff of Burt's smoky scent, a mix of aftershave and cheap cigarettes. Burt chattered happily as he set up all the gaming accessories next to Tommy's TV with a practiced hand.

"Can't remember the last time we did this. Glad you called, man. This should be fun. Beats playing all alone back home, or playing online with the weirdos on the Net. Bunch of freaks who don't have a life, ya know?"

As Burt prattled on and fired up the dusty video game console, Tommy felt himself fading. He was floating again, and his older brother made him feel ten or twelve again. Growing up, Burt had always tried to take care of him, even when Tommy grew taller and thicker than him. Even when Tommy demanded he stop.

"Turn the volume down," he muttered, his voice thick. "Baby's still sleeping."

Holding a pair of white plastic rifles, Burt stopped to give Tommy a wide-eyed look, as if really *looking* at him for the first time all day. Shaking his head, he plopped onto the couch next to him. He landed a bit too close, and both boys instinctively slid farther away from one another.

"Wow. Mom said you were sick. But she didn't say you were *this* bad."

"What are you—" Tommy began, his voice weak.

"*Mom's* watching little Corinne, ya delusional goober. The baby isn't here. Now let's blow some shit up like good American men. Here's your gun."

After three games, Tommy remembered why he didn't like playing video games with his brother. Burt spent so much *time*—something Tommy no longer had these days—playing each game that he knew how to beat you three dozen different ways.

To make things worse, Tommy's fever made everything on the screen morph together. At times he truly felt like he was in the middle of this war game, launching grenades from his gun or spattering the landscape with bullets. Each explosion made him flinch. He couldn't seem to catch his breath, and he tasted copper every time he coughed.

When Burt snuck up on him and shot him in the back to end another round, Tommy could feel the bullet shatter his spine and rip into his lungs.

Why did I think this would be a good idea?

He could hear the wheeze in his breath every time he exhaled. He'd downed three of Burt's syrup-like sodas, but they'd done nothing to perk him up. They just made his headache worse.

"One more round?" Burt said with a grin. The skinny little guy was practically bouncing up and down on the couch next to him, cackling softly over his latest win. Tommy was having trouble recognizing him.

"Let's play—" Tommy began, then paused for a few seconds to stifle another outburst of coughing. "Let's play something else."

"Sure." Burt hopped up and began flipping through game boxes. "I was getting tired of that one anyway."

Tommy closed his eyes for a moment as his stomach rumbled. He hadn't eaten much in the past few days. Maybe half a sleeve of crackers and a small bag of chips, all told. He knew he should be drinking water, but his throat hurt too much to swallow.

He wondered if he could just spend the rest of his life right here on the couch, sleeping his life away. Here on the couch, he wouldn't have to work so hard, taking care of Corinne and rushing off to work and doing the bills.

Didn't sound like such a bad idea. I could just sleep and let people take care of me for a change. It'd be a lot like Burt's life, pretty much, come to think of it.

Then he thought of little Corinne in his arms, her body close to him, sharing his body heat and resting her sleeping head on his shoulder.

My little girl. She was priceless.

Wasn't she?

Not according to Uncle Carl. In his sickness and fever, even as he and his brother blew up alien spaceships in every color of the rainbow—Tommy hadn't been able to put Carl's offer out of his head. Not so much the dollar amount, though that was hard to forget. But the *idea* of it. That Carl thought Tommy would agree with his messed-up plan and just give up his baby, for money.

As if that would solve all my problems.

"What's that?" Burt said next to Tommy.

Tommy sucked in a sudden breath and opened his eyes. Next to him, Burt stared at the TV, chewing on his lower lip with concentration and madly pressing buttons on his controller, almost at random.

"Huh?" Tommy said, the best response he could come up with.

"You said something about solving all your problems. Let's hear about that, man. I could use a little of that kind of thing, ya know? Going on half a year now since I had a job."

"Dude. Don't listen to me. I'm outta my head."

"What else is new?" Burt said with a laugh, hitting buttons and maneuvering madly. At some point the spaceships had gone away, and Burt was now playing some sort of brightly colored game filled with spinning cylinders and saw blades.

Tommy set his controller on the floor. He'd had enough of these games.

"I got a weird call the other night," he found himself saying between wheezes. "From our crazy damn uncle."

"Oh, Uncle Carl. That old drunk. I don't know how that chubby dude managed to snag a hot number like Melanie. Maybe he tricked her into marrying him, huh? Fooled her into thinking he's loaded, with his nice car and all. He's been out of work for a while now, too, hasn't he?"

"About a year," Tommy said with a cough.

Yeah, you're pretty smart, Tommy. Don't miss much, do ya?

Watching Burt trying to maneuver the tubes around the floating saws onscreen, he regretted ever bringing it up. Carl had sounded drunk on the phone, and weirdly... *adult*. There was no joking around on the phone, no friendly chitchat. Just business, and then anger when Tommy didn't agree. That shook him up.

"So..." Burt said as he paused the game. The screen went white, and he turned on the couch to look at Tommy. "What did he want?"

Tommy thought about blowing off his brother's question, brushing aside the conversation. But the look in Burt's eyes, an unexpected intensity there from a guy that most people in town never took seriously, surprised Tommy into talking.

And, he had to admit as he took in a crackly breath before diving into his story, it felt good to actually *talk* to someone about this. About anything.

"He said he knew a way to make everything better for me. As if he's all that interested in my life. When's the last time he came home to visit, right? So he calls me on my cell last Thursday night, after midnight—""

"What? He had to be three sheets to the wind, calling that late. Man..."

Tommy swiped away the fresh sweat from his head. Talking had made his head swim all over again. Even as the rattling furnace kicked on in the apartment, he itched to wrap himself up in the blanket next to him. But he didn't dare, not in front of his older brother. Guys didn't do that sort of thing.

"Yeah, I think he was a bit wasted," he said. "Anyway, he started talking about how much I had to sacrifice for Suzanne and Corinne, and then—"

"He's right about that," Burt said in a low voice. "You could've gone on to play three more years of college ball, ya know. And maybe the NFL after that."

"Anyway," Tommy said, hurrying to finish the story while he still had the energy. "Uncle Carl said he wanted to fix my problems by taking Corinne away."

Burt dropped the game controller he'd been fiddling with as Tommy talked.

"*What?*"

"Said it was like some kind of adoption scheme. That he knew some people who had money and had the paperwork and computer stuff to make it all happen."

"Oh man, this is so messed up. You've got to tell Mom."

Tommy's chest tightened up immediately, and before he could tell his brother "No," he was coughing again. Each explosion felt like it would tear apart his chest. His fingers went numb, and black dots swam in his vision.

"Don't tell anyone," he tried to say between coughs, but the words got stuck in his throat, along with his last breath. He heard himself make an awful gagging sound as the room went dim.

"Tommy."

The little apartment turned cold as he fought for air. He felt himself sliding, down and down, like he was losing control of who he was and slipping into his true self, the one that went running and feeding every full moon.

"Tommy!"

The lights went dim, then turned red as his chest spasmed for lack of air. His body had taken too much, he knew it. And now it was giving in to the sickness running through it. He was falling.

He tried to raise a hand to his mouth or even his throat, but a sharp pain in his side kept his arms glued to his side. He felt the rough strands of the shag carpet against his cheek, like tiny tree roots out on Westhoff's farmland.

The last thing Tommy saw before his vision went from gray to black was the blurred rush of red eyes, coming out of nowhere and growing big as basketballs.

Then they disappeared, and the blackness of a moonless night covered him.

Chapter Seven

As much as it hurts to run like this, I run anyway. Lungs burning. Bare feet slapping the cold, slick floor. She needs me. They both need me.

I stop at the nurses' station and yell for someone to come help. But my mouth doesn't work. I can't even open it. I pound on the cheap counter with both fists, sending a metal clipboard and a plastic cup of pens flying with clatter.

I'm breathing fast through my nose, and I sound like a train puffing uphill. All I can smell is my own sweat, salty and bitter.

Finally a nurse shows up, dressed in dark blue scrubs and smelling like bleach. I grab her cold hand and drag her to the room, which seems miles away. We find Suzanne lying on the bed and crying like a child. Like a baby.

"Help me," Suzanne says, both hands on her huge, round belly. "I can't make it *stop*."

The nurse breaks free of my hand and pushes me out into the hall. She's much stronger than me. I can't seem to get my feet to work. I just fight for traction, spinning my wheels, and the nurse succeeds in pushing me around.

Suze screams inside the room: "I can't do this, I can't I can't—"

And then I hear the cries of my baby girl. At last, I'm able to charge into the room, like breaking away from a double-team of blockers.

All around the bed, there's no blood, though I can smell it everywhere. Blood.

But I'm not asking questions. I just need to *see* her. All I can make out is that tiny little body, wrapped up in a white blanket that makes her skin look even redder in the nurse's hands. My baby's crying. One of her hands breaks free of the blanket.

I reach for that hand, for Corinne.

I try to call her name, to say it to her for the first time. But nothing's working. The nurse gives Corinne to Suzanne, and my words are stuck in my throat. I can't get any closer—each step takes me farther away. I can't make sense of any of this. I'm panting like a dog from running. But I can't get any damn closer, and I can't hold my little girl.

When I pull my gaze away from Corinne's little head, with its tiny tufts of strawberry-blonde hair, and look at Suzanne, my girlfriend's eyes are red, and she's smiling at me with teeth that glisten in the white light of the room.

My hands ache for my baby, but I can't reach her.

I run toward her, but I go nowhere.

I run, and my heart wants to explode.

I run, but I never make it to Corinne. She's been taken from me.

She's *lost*.

Tommy's empty arms ached when he finally opened his eyes. The sharp smell of bleach made his nostrils burn.

The sensation matched the raw feeling of his throat and the inside of his chest. He closed his eyes on the unexpected brightness.

Where'd I go? Was I out running?

This wasn't his bed in their dark and messy bedroom back in the apartment. This place was all bright fluorescents reflecting off shining white walls. He felt the cold metal arms of the bed frame on either side of him. Along with the stink of bleach, he could smell his own sour body odor. His fingers and toes tingled with pins and needles. He caught a whiff of cigarettes from his right.

"Burt," he croaked, and the word sent another slash of pain down his throat. His head still felt light, but he didn't feel half as feverish as he'd felt back home on the couch. Despite the pain each word brought, he spat, "What did you *do*?"

"I called 911, man. You weren't *breathing*! You were coughing like a mother, then you just stopped. What was I supposed to do? Let you frickin' *die*?"

"They charge you like five hundred bucks for a ride in an ambulance." Tommy opened his eyes wide, groaning at the brightness, and saw the IV line running into his numb arm. "And I'm sure they're pumping me full of drugs, too. Oh, God."

"Tommy-boy," Burt said, stepping closer. "You had a fever of a hundred and five. You coulda died, ya know? Doctor said you might've gotten brain damage if you hadn't come in. You should be frickin' *thanking* me, not yelling at me. Man..."

"But it's going to cost—"

"Your insurance'll cover this, man. Chill out and enjoy the drugs and wait for the nurse to give you a sponge bath. Marcy works here now. She graduated with me, remember. One hot number."

"Insurance," Tommy muttered. "Ah, shit."

Burt hit him lightly in the shoulder with the back of his hand.

"What?"

"I thought I was still on Mom and Dad's, but they dropped me when I moved out. I think Mom told me. I kinda forgot."

"Oh God. I didn't know. I'm... I'm sorry. I didn't know what else to *do*. You weren't breathing. Shit."

Tommy wanted to say something to Burt, but words failed him, and talking hurt too much. And what was the point? He was tired all over again, and the thought of all the debt he'd suddenly acquired in the past few hours made him want to throw up.

Probably a couple thousand bucks, if not more, and it was adding up every minute I lay here on my ass. I'll be paying for today for years. If not the rest of my life.

"Hey Tommy," Burt began, talking low and flicking his gaze at the open door. "Something weird happened to you—I mean, even weirder than you coughing yourself into unconsciousness. Back at your place."

A feeling of dread quickly replaced Tommy's misery like he was flicking on a switch. As far as he knew, Burt never knew about the differences in their blood. Mom had made sure of that.

"You were on the floor, not breathing, and I'd called 911 and did all the things Coach Kilburg had taught us in PE class all those years ago. And I was trying to figure out if you'd swallowed your tongue, and I was reaching for you..."

Tommy swallowed with a clicking sensation. It hurt.

Burt was whispering now, his light blue eyes squinting down at Tommy in a way that made Tommy want to move away from him. Burt wasn't usually like this.

"I touched your arm. And it was covered with—don't laugh at me, but I swear to you, it was covered with fur. The exact same color as the scruffy stuff on your head. *Fur*. Not kidding, man. And you were making this noise. Not a choking noise or a coughing noise. It was like you were frickin' *growling*. Like you had it—"

A quick knock at the door stopped Burt cold. He straightened up and snapped his mouth shut. He stepped away from Tommy, eyes wide with guilt.

Rescued, Tommy thought as a young, brown-haired nurse poked her head inside. Marcy Deppe from Burt's graduating class, as tall and pretty as he remembered her from study hall his sophomore year.

"Hi Tommy. Hey Burt. Sorry to interrupt."

"Hey Marcy," Burt said, pitching his voice low.

Tommy didn't know when he'd put both hands up to his face, but he dropped them now.

"The doctor wants to take a look at your side again," Marcy said, organizing some vials on the counter on Tommy's left. She smelled good, like lilacs. "And I have to give you a shot,

I'm afraid. The infection you had going on there was pretty nasty."

"He was hoping for a sponge bath," Burt muttered, pointing at Tommy. His nervous laugh felt fake and forced.

"You can leave whenever you want, Burt," Tommy said, and then promptly began coughing again. He hurt all over again.

"Fine," Burt said. He grabbed his coat and walked out the door without another word. "Enjoy your hospital stay, bro."

"O-kay then," Marcy said, holding a syringe with a needle so long that Tommy wanted to groan. "Don't worry. I know he's just giving everyone a hard time. That's Burt for ya."

Tommy nodded and felt his eyes ache suddenly with unspent tears.

It wasn't Burt's fault that I didn't have health insurance. And he did *save my life. Even if he ruined it in the process.*

"And one, two, three," Marcy said. She pushed the needle into Tommy's shoulder. The pain was shocking, just for an instant, and then it was over.

No, Tommy thought as he wheezed and watched the IV drip into his arm while Marcy stuck a Band-Aid on his shoulder. *Burt didn't ruin my life. I'd already done that job to myself in the past year and a half.*

When Mom came in and woke Tommy from his doze a few hours later, she held a copy of this week's Dyersburg Commercial in her fisted hand like a club.

"They say that guy last week was from Minnesota, and he was bitten to death. *Bitten!*"

She tossed the paper at Tommy, but instead of slapping onto the bed the way she probably wanted it to, the pages scattered in the air like a startled bird and fell on the floor.

Either the drugs had finally kicked in to break Tommy's fever, or he just didn't care anymore about what Mom thought, because he didn't flinch at all at her arrival.

"I'm *good*, thanks, Mom. The ambulance got me here safe and sound, thanks for asking. And it seems like the brain damage from my fever wasn't too—"

"Oh, quit it. There's no brain damage—no more than you had already, that is. I know all I need to know from talking to the doctors here."

Mom had her long blonde hair pulled back into a tight ponytail, and she had on too much foundation—Tommy could see a faint line of color running up both sides of her jaw. She was still wearing her scrubs, and her breath smelled like coffee.

She must've been working when she heard I was here. Guess she finished up with her patients first, before coming to see me.

"The whole hospital knows you're here. Probably the whole damn town. You couldn't just come in and get some antibiotics before it reached this point?"

Tommy refused to say anything.

Mom sat at the foot of the bed and patted his foot.

"You *sure* nothing happened last moon?" she asked, her voice deceptively soft. He'd almost spilled everything to her before he realized it.

Sitting there, feeling trapped, Tommy felt the wound in his side twinge the tiniest bit. He kept from touching it through sheer force of will. The stupid thing should've been healed up and gone already.

Finally, he gave up trying to keep his mouth shut.

"Mom," he said, the word sounding alien to his ears, as if his voice was someone else's. "Do you remember all the things you do when it comes over you? When you're full of it?"

Tommy let out a barking laugh that turned into a cough. Mom looked at him with alarm at first, and then gave him half a grin as he waved her off with one hand and rested the other hand on his aching side.

"I didn't mean it like that," he chuckled once the cough subsided. "I mean, yeah, sometimes you *are* full of it, Mom," he grinned, and to his everlasting shock, Mom grinned back.

She liked teasing and giving people a hard time, he remembered, from way back. "But I mean when you're all changed over. Going wolf."

"I can't afford to let myself go like that," Mom said, still whispering. "I told you all this. It's all about *control*. You lose it, and you not only risk your life. You risk everyone in the family."

The pack, Tommy wanted to say. *You mean the pack. Not the family.*

Mom kicked at the pages of the newspaper on the floor.

"Forecast is calling for snow tomorrow. You'd better hope we get a pile of it, a big old blizzard to take people's mind off the dead guy in Joe's field. Chewed up. Bitten to death. No wonder you're sick. Eating some drifter from Minnesota who happens to get lost in your woods."

"Mom!" Tommy fought the urge to kick at her until she fell off his bed. "Is that what you think happened? What would some guy be doing out in Westhoff's field in the middle of winter? It was probably fifteen degrees that night."

Mom hopped off the bed and brushed the seat of her scrubs, as if Tommy might have been shedding on the bedspread. She gathered up the scattered pages of the newspaper and dumped them in the wastebasket.

"That's what has me worried," she said, turning back to Tommy with her eyes narrowed. Her whispering voice was loud as a scream to Tommy's ears. "If he wasn't some drifter looking for a warm barn, I worry he was out there in the woods, like you, *hunting* for something."

Chapter Eight

Tommy left the hospital AMA before nightfall. "Against medical advice," they called it, and he'd heard horror stories from Mom about the so-called "idiots" who left the hospital before they were healed up and fully recovered.

But being cooped up in that antiseptic-smelling room without windows, with hardly any air to breathe, was worse than being stuck in his apartment had been the other night. Just lying there, waiting for a nurse to poke her head in on him or stick him with another needle. And all Tommy could think about, with his aching head and sore throat, was the dollar-by-dollar flow of more money out of his pocket. Money he didn't have.

Finally he called Burt and told Marcy the nurse he was leaving. She passed him some prescriptions from the doctor for his infection, and he left. Walking out into the cold late-January wind, Tommy sucked in an icy breath and stumbled on his way toward his brother's beat-up brown Camaro parked next to the sidewalk.

He was shaking his head as soon as he pulled open the door with a loud creaking sound.

"She's punishing me," he said to Burt, who was wearing a black Iowa baseball cap and ridiculous mirrored aviator shades, even as the sun sank behind the hospital. "That's why she never visited me. I'm in there half the day, and Suzanne doesn't even call?"

"Hmm." Burt pulled away and cranked up his radio. Soon Tommy's fillings were aching from heavy-metal guitars.

The silent treatment. Burt was still mad about how I'd reacted back in the hospital room. Great.

"Look," he said to Burt after twisting the radio's volume down a few notches. "Sorry I freaked out on you in there. It was just the money, and being sick, too. But I don't want to think about the hospital bills right now. And hey... Thanks for bringing me in. You probably did save my life."

"Yeah?" Burt lit a cigarette and cracked the driver's window to let out the smoke.

"Must be your ninja-like reflexes from all those damn video games. You probably pressed 911 faster than anyone else in the world ever could've. And they say video games are bad for you."

When Burt finally cracked and let loose with a quick chuckle, Tommy laughed along with him until he started coughing. It hurt, but it felt good, too.

"Ninja!" Burt said, grinning. He did a quick air-guitar move in time to the rocking music just before turning onto Main Street, nearly dropping his cigarette in his lap, and Tommy knew that all was well between him and his brother. Simple as that.

"So where we going? I should get home, with the baby and all."

"Don't worry 'bout it. Mom's got ya covered. She figured you needed the rest."

They rumbled past the church and a couple bars. A few blocks later, Burt tweaked his horn at some teenage girls walking out of the library. Everyone waved at Burt, people in cars and people on foot. For some reason, he always made people smile.

"So where—"

"Wait," Burt said, his eyes hidden behind his oversized shades. He put the cigarette in his lips and snaked a bony arm into the back seat, fumbled around, and after a clunk of ice on metal, handed Tommy a can of Busch Light.

"Slap a coozie on that, bro, and chill out for a bit. I want you to meet some friends of mine," Burt said. "We'll be there in a couple minutes."

He wouldn't say anything more as they turned again and began driving out of town. Soft, silent flakes of snow began falling as they drove west, chasing the setting sun. Tommy found a Dale Earnhardt coozie on the cluttered floor and slipped it around his can of beer. Finally, he snapped open the can and took a sip.

"That's what I'm talkin' about," Burt said, exhaling smoke out his window as the wind streamed past. "Chug a lug, man. You deserve it after your shitty day."

After a couple more sips of the cold, bitter beer, Tommy gave up and took a long swig that nearly emptied the can. His head immediately started to swim, a familiar feeling from the past few days, but one that felt good for a change.

This, he thought, *is what guys my age are* supposed *to be doing. Not changing diapers and worrying about insurance.*

The sky had turned black by the time Burt made it to the entrance of the ethanol plant ten miles outside of Dyersburg. Tommy had been enjoying the easy feeling his now-empty beer had given him, and he was daydreaming about a night of no responsibilities for a change.

Maybe we'd go cow-tipping. You never know.

So when Burt's car slowed to a stop at the razor-tipped fence outside the small brick building in front of four six-story white tanks holding ethanol, Tommy let out a surprised laugh.

"You running out of gas?"

Burt pushed down his shades and looked at Tommy. His eyes were a bit wide, like he'd been smoking pot and getting paranoid. He looked scared, just for a second, and that unnerved Tommy.

Then he grinned and tooted his horn three times, fast. Someone in a thick blue coat with the hood up scurried out of the little building to unlock the gate and slide it open with a rattle.

"They're in back," the guy called out as Burt's car rumbled inside. "Behind tank 2. And put out your cigarette, man! Jesus."

"Burt," Tommy said, blinking fast as he tried to focus on what was happening.

I am such a lightweight. And all this ethanol in the air's giving me a headache.

"Relax," Burt said, smashing his cigarette into his overflowing ashtray. He parked next to one of the tall tanks holding the fuel made from the cornfields all around town.

They got out of the car and went into a long, low shed made of metal painted light blue. Tommy rubbed his throat, which was still sore, and breathed through his mouth to avoid the harsh fumes all around him. One side of the shed was filled with pipes, tubing, and a variety of small machines that looked alien to Tommy. The other side had a trio of electric golf carts.

Four men bundled up in winter coats and stocking caps watched them walk inside. They sat in metal folding chairs around a metal desk sitting crookedly on the dirt floor. Only two of the four guys were familiar—Tommy's freckled buddy Krunch and Krunch's dad, both of them looking pissed, for some reason.

The other two were about Tommy's age, and *big*. Tommy was used to being the biggest or tallest guy in the room, but even sitting down, he could tell that these two had him beat. He felt like he was playing football again, sizing up the other team across the field after checking heights and weights on the roster.

The first stranger had his tight black cap pulled down to his eyebrows, while the other reached up to scratch his brown, buzzed hair. The guy with the black cap glared at Tommy for a second, and then he got to his feet.

Damn, Tommy thought with a sinking feeling. *Definitely taller than me.*

And then they were shaking hands and Big Krunch was introducing everybody.

"Tommy, this is Mark and Luke Callahan. They're from up north. Minnesota. They're, ah, friends of the family."

The bones in Tommy's right hand ached after shaking both brothers' hands. He missed lifting weights, being in shape.

"Thanks for coming," Krunch's dad continued. "Why don't you and Burt have a seat?"

Krunch, who still hadn't said a word, got up and grabbed two folding chairs leaning against a riding mower. He almost looked apologetic as he handed the chairs to Tommy and Burt. He had alcohol on his breath, reminding Tommy of the beer now going sour in his own belly. Usually you couldn't shut Krunch up, but now he was silent as a mourner at a funeral.

Feeling panicked now, Tommy looked over at Burt, who was definitely the skinniest, most frail guy in the room. Burt looked surprisingly calm, and he gave Tommy a playful elbow to the ribs.

"Chill out, man," he said as everyone sat down. "I got your back."

One of the brothers—Tommy couldn't remember if his name was Mark or Luke—snorted out a harsh laugh at that.

"Sorry," he muttered to a glaring Big Krunch.

One of the fluorescents behind the two brothers flickered and went out with a loud buzzing sound. Mark or Luke put an elbow on the crooked desk and stifled a yawn.

"Heard you had a rough afternoon, today," Big Krunch said to Tommy. "Sorry to hear it. Never a good time to get taken to the hospital in the ambulance." He kept talking, not giving Tommy a chance to do anything more than nod. "These are hard times here in town, you could say. Strange times. And Burt tells me you might know something about these, ah, weird things going on here in town."

So that's what this was about. It was like he was being questioned by Smith all over again. But now there were these other dudes glaring at him like a criminal, too.

"Does he *talk*?" the brother with the elbow on the desk said to Krunch's dad.

Tommy ignored the jab and looked instead at his own brother. Burt was chewing his lower lip like it was a steak, with his eyes focused on the dirt floor in front of the other men. He had to know Tommy was looking at him, but he didn't return his gaze. The first two fingers of Burt's bony left hand tapped a silent beat on his knee.

Right. I'm on my own here. Fine.

Tommy looked at Krunch's dad, focusing on the older man's squinted eyes under his thick gray eyebrows.

"We're talking about the dead guy, right?"

The big guy with the buzz cut stood up fast enough to send his metal chair flying back onto the dirt floor. He took a step toward Tommy before his brother snagged his coat and held him in place.

"Slow down, Luke," the other brother—Mark—said.

"Don't play stupid, boy," Luke spat, pointing a big finger at Tommy. He shook loose of his brother's grip. "That dead guy was our brother."

"What?" Tommy blurted out. "Um. I'm sorry. I just don't understand—"

"Matthew," Mark said, rubbing his face and pulling his cap down even lower. "His name was Matthew."

Tommy had a mad impulse to start laughing, thinking of his six years of Catholic elementary school with the nuns and their Bible lesson. Was there a younger, 'roided-up brother named John, too?

Luckily, he was good at hiding his emotions, and not even a hint of a smile touched his face.

"These guys," Big Krunch said, "are here to help the cops find out what happened. And do some detective work of their own, without Smith's, ah, help." He looked over at Burt. "Can you and James go wait outside, son?"

"*What?*" Krunch said. "You make me come here, then you kick me out right when things get good? Why'd you even bring me along, Dad?"

"Get your ass outside, James. *That's* where I need you. Now."

Burt gave Tommy a quick glance and a pat on the shoulder as he followed Krunch toward the exit. The metal door clanged as Krunch slammed it behind them.

His dad was going to kick his ass for that, Tommy thought, as he watched a weed-eater next to the door fall onto a metal barrel with a loud clang.

When he turned back to the others, Krunch's dad had toppled backwards over in his chair, and the two huge brothers had disappeared.

Two man-sized wolves with dark brown fur, yellow teeth, and blazing red eyes now stood in front of the desk, and they were coming for Tommy.

Chapter Nine

As he jumped out of his chair, Tommy tried to get his lips to form the words to Krunch's dad's name, but all that came out were a few spits of air. Part of him wanted to ask where the two brothers had gone, but he knew all too well what kind of change had come over them. As if to remind him of that fact, he saw that the wolf on the left still had the tattered remains of a once-tight black hat on its furry, triangular-shaped head.

He took a step back, inhaling the musky animal scents of the two beasts creeping closer to him. Their red eyes went wide, and their mouths seemed to be cracked into permanent smiles.

Other than Mom, Tommy had never seen another werewolf before. He couldn't believe how big they were—seven feet long, easy, and wide as a doorway.

Is that how I look, too? he wondered. *These bastards are huge.*

Before he could move back any more, something horrific touched his ears. A gargling sound, mixed with growling, all of which somehow formed crude, recognizable words.

The first wolf was *talking* to him.

"You... act all... surprised..." it said, panting. A long sliver of drool fell from the side of his tooth-crammed mouth. "Don't play... dumb with... us."

"How," Tommy began, his voice a raspy whisper. He coughed, sending pain shooting down his battered throat. "How are you able to do that? Moon's not full."

If there was a worse sound than a werewolf talking, it was a wolf's sarcastic laugh. Both of them burst into barking laughter.

"You... country wolves... so clueless."

Impossible, Tommy thought, inching away from the two panting beasts. He felt dizzy, followed quickly by a wave of nausea. *This was impossible. Everyone in my family told me the change only came once a month. Had they been lying? Or has our blood line gotten* that *weak?*

The first wolf—Mark, the one with the ruined black hat—bared his teeth at Tommy, less than three feet away.

"Looks like... we got to... teach you."

The Mark-wolf leaped. The movement was fast and unexpected, and Tommy was barely able to get his arms up to keep the wolf from tearing out his throat. He twisted as the wolf hit him, sending it spinning away with a yelp. Tommy didn't know who made that noise—him or Mark.

Panting for air, he backed away from the two wolves, one on either side of him. He nearly tripped over Big Krunch, who was still on his back on the dirt floor, with a big knot on his forehead. Somehow one of the wolf boys had moved fast enough to knock the big guy out earlier.

Both wolves approached, taking their time, laughing their knowing, barking chuckles. Tommy smelled everything: bitter gas and dead oil, raw dirt, sweaty fur, and above all, blood. His nostrils burned from all of it.

It's in my *blood*, he thought.

He felt like he had it in him for an instant, that the change would come over him as if the moon was fat and yellow overhead, instead of half-full and draining power by the minute. All he could smell now was the foul reek of the Callahan brothers' wolf breath.

"Now he's... learning."

Tommy knew what would happen if he didn't change, had time to marvel at the sudden appearance of thick blonde fur covering his arms. If he was to believe Burt's story, it would've been the second time that day he'd changed. The second time he'd lost control.

It's in me.

Mark's muzzle shot forward, aimed at Tommy's belly. Luke's clawed front paw reached for Tommy's back. Heart racing, vision widening, Tommy threw himself forward, out of the reach of their claws.

He thought of the full moon and little Corinne writhing in its cold, unforgiving light. He grabbed that feeling and ran with it, though his feet never moved an inch, except to burst through his socks and shoes. Yellow claws emerged where his toenails once were.

In me. In my blood.

"Let's do this," he said, his words a gurgling growl.

The change complete, and he now stood on all fours next to both brown-furred wolves, his newly grown tail brushing the metal wall behind him. His breath hissed from his nostrils. Most of his clothes dropped in tatters to the dirt below him.

Backed into a corner, he got in a couple hard blows to Luke's face and slammed his head hard into Mark's mid-section before both wolf brothers overpowered him and took him down to the dirt floor.

Too bad you never played football again, man. You handle yourself all right. For a fattie."

"Screw you," Tommy said, spitting blood onto the ground, though he felt a small surge of pride at Luke's blackening eye and Mark favoring his sore belly. His nose and arms ached, and he could feel at least two teeth that had come loose after the fight. He still couldn't believe that any of the events of the past ten minutes had been real.

"Cut it out, boys," Big Krunch dad said, still sitting on the ground next to his broken chair. His voice was a bit groggy and weak after getting knocked out. "Let's go, before the security guy drops in and gives me hell for staying here so late and messing up the shed."

I could kill Burt for setting me up like this, Tommy thought.

He swiped blood from his swollen nose, and felt fresh pain in his side as he walked toward Big Krunch to help him up. At least Mark was walking with a bit of a limp. They probably would've still been hammering on me if Krunch's dad hadn't started to come to from where he'd been knocked over in his chair.

When they saw the older man move again, the Callahan brothers had backed off Tommy immediately, and they switched back into human form in the wink of an eye. They had most of their clothes back on and straightened long before Tommy pulled himself together. His shoes and jeans were ruined, just hanging together with a few threads.

"I ought to kick your tails for hitting me," Krunch's dad said as he let Tommy pull him back up to his feet, holding his head. Tommy felt something tug in his side. A few seconds later, he felt the warm ooze of blood from his poorly healed wound just above his waist, in his right love handle.

"It was an accident," Luke said, doing a bad job of hiding his smirk. "Mark and Tommy here wanted to tussle. One of 'em must've elbowed you in the noggin while they were throwing their weight around. Happened so fast. Punks."

Big Krunch dusted off his John Deere cap and put it back on at an angle to fit over the fresh knot rising up on his forehead. He looked up at Mark and cleared his throat, almost nervously.

"So. Did you talk about your brother at all, or did you just fight?"

"Mostly fight," Luke said with a barking laugh, before Mark could answer. The brothers began heading for the exit to the shed.

"Didn't want to talk to him about Matthew," Mark said in a low voice. "Not yet."

Tommy could've sworn he heard Mark add, "He's not ready," but he couldn't be sure, because Big Krunch had grabbed him and pulled him to a stop a few feet from the exit.

"Hold up," the older man said.

The brothers stopped as well, moving in front of the metal door leading outside.

Tommy realized he could've overpowered Big Krunch, easily, just by turning into his other form. The thought sent a shudder through him.

"Tommy-boy," the older man said, almost whispering. "You have to know that this wasn't my idea. But when Burt called me today, and Smith told me you'd been out late the other night, right after their brother was... Well, it all kind of added up. We need you on our *side*, you see? I mean, I'm just a regular guy. I don't, ah, have a badge or a gun. I just have connections. Just like your brother. And I owe this to your dad. He and I go way back."

Tommy held a hand to his still-bleeding nose. He felt a range of new aches and pains coming from nearly every inch of his body. He also felt a creeping sensation come over him, like the sudden chill from a just-opened window.

The way Big Krunch looked at and talked to the Callahan brothers made it seem like the older guy was afraid of them. Not just afraid, but *terrified* of what they were. Tommy guessed that Big Krunch knew exactly why Luke and Mark's clothes were ripped and their eyes were now bloodshot. But he'd never admit to it.

"Okay," Tommy said at last, nodding at the two guys standing there watching them. "So what do *you* think happened to their brother, then?"

Big Krunch glanced at the wolf boys for a long moment before answering. Another fluorescent light flickered deeper inside the shed, giving off a loud buzz before going dark. Tommy realized he couldn't smell a thing with his banged-up nose, and it made him feel dizzy as a result.

"That was no bear," Big Krunch said. "We've got something worse than a bear or two here in Dyersburg. Maybe another cult, like the one over in Earlville back in the early '90s, or some sort of sick gang-related murder from Chicago that went haywire. Cops are hoping it was just a freak, ah, one-time thing. I'm trying to make sure that it doesn't—"

A loud banging on the inside of the door cut him off. Tommy hoped the wolf brothers didn't see him jump at the noise. He'd been leaning close to Big Krunch, barely able to smell the whiskey on the guy's breath thanks to his clogged nose.

"Time to *go*," Luke said from the doorway. "Got more detective work to do back in town. Starting at one of your pubs."

Stepping back into the cold and the wind made Tommy feel like he'd been slapped in the face with reality again. The fog of ethanol filled his nose, cutting through the congestion in his head and making his eyes ache.

"We'll be in touch," Mark called out on his way to his dented and dusty pickup parked next to one of the huge tanks of fuel.

Luke smacked a meaty fist into his palm and cackled at Tommy. Their truck roared to life, and with a spray of gravel, the Callahan brothers were gone.

"Now that," Burt said, leaning on the hood of his Camaro in the shadows, "must have some chat, bro."

Tommy felt a surge of anger at the sight of his older brother lounging out here.

You bring me here, he wanted to say, *and then abandon me, like it's all part of some big plan?*

"I need to get home to my family," he said, glaring at Burt and daring him to return the favor. "Let's go, already."

"Right," Burt said. Keeping his eyes forward, he slipped into the driver's seat.

With a honk, Big Krunch and Krunch drove past them, headed for the gate as well. The booming of an engine and a squealing of tires on the highway let Tommy know that the wolf brothers had left the building, most likely heading back into town to raise some more hell.

Tommy stood outside the passenger door to Burt's car, sucking cold air in through his mouth. The night sky did its best to slip through the bright glare of the spotlights aimed down at the grounds of the ethanol plant. Tommy could barely see the moon, only half-full tonight and hanging low like a thrown rock, right before it lands.

"Can't believe it," he muttered, his words lost in the rumble of Burt's idling car. "Can't believe I was able to make it happen, just like that."

He pressed two fingers to the side of his nose that wasn't bleeding, leaned over, and blew hard from his battered nostril. He was glad it was too dark to see what garbage shot out his nose and onto the ground.

He also didn't want to think about how *fast* those brothers had changed, from human to wolf and back again. They'd had years of practice, made it look easy. While Tommy had struggled with all his willpower and muscle to make his change happen.

"Nice farmer's blow, man," Burt called from inside the car in a jokey but tentative voice. "Don't be getting any on my car, though."

Tommy ignored him.

But if I can change whenever I want, he thought, *why would Mom force me to just let it happen once a month? When I could've been doing it whenever I wanted?*

As Tommy got into the car at last, with the smells of ethanol and car exhaust and Burt's cigarettes flooding back into his nose again, he knew exactly why Mom would do such a thing.

Control. *The woman was a control freak, and she'd been running me all my life. Denying me the full range of my abilities. Turning my gift into a curse, really.*

That was all going to change. Starting now.

Chapter Ten

After they left the ethanol plant and headed back through the darkness toward town again, Tommy almost felt thankful to Burt for bringing him there.

At least, he thought, *I got to learn I'm able to do—what I've been able to do all my life, but never knew 'til now.*

Gripping the steering wheel so tightly his hands were white, Burt whistled softly under his breath, careful not to even give the hint of turning his head to look in Tommy's direction.

Smart move. The way I feel right now, I'd probably rip your head off if you tried to crack a joke about what just happened.

Another thing he learned, something that was just now starting to sink in as his pulse returned to normal, was this thought: *I'm not alone.*

There are other guys like me out there. I'd always thought I was the only person like this anywhere, besides Mom. Sure, there was Aunt Melanie, but she was twenty years older than me, and she lived in Iowa City. And her two boys, Trey and Tyler, were probably going to end up like sickly little Burt over there, trying to act all cool and unaware and okay with the world, when they had no idea what really went on. Just like I was clueless, before tonight.

And just like little Corinne would be, too. Clueless and normal.

The thought of his daughter nearly brought unwanted tears to Tommy's eyes. The cold air streaming in from Burt's partially open window made his vision blur for a moment. He felt like he hadn't seen her in weeks. He thought about the nasty dream he'd had while he was in the hospital, how he'd tried and tried to get to her. How badly his arms had ached to hold his little girl. And how she needed her daddy's protection. Always would.

Mom had been caring for Corinne while he'd been sick and Suzanne had been at work. They had a crib at their house, so she was probably sleeping over there again, most likely. That was Mom for you. Keeping things under control, as usual.

We were going to have a little talk about that, too, Mom and me. Real soon.

Burt turned on some heavy metal music, and then clicked off the radio again. He fumbled for his pack of cigarettes on the dash, sending two cancer sticks flying onto the floor.

"Sorry," he mumbled.

Tommy let the word hang in the air for a while. While he was still pissed at Burt for taking him there without any kind of explanation, he felt a shred of sympathy for the guy, too.

Maybe he really thought he was doing me some good.

Thirsty, but not really wanting another one of Burt's beers, Tommy reached behind him anyway. He pawed around inside the cooler until he'd found a loose beer inside the melting ice and plastic bottles of Mountain Dew.

"So," he said, cracking open the beer. He gazed over at his brother, whose angular face was lit up with the green-blue light of his dashboard. "What do you know, Burt?"

The Camaro swerved a bit on the deserted two-lane as Burt risked a look over at him, just for a second.

"Huh?"

"Tell me what you know," Tommy said. "About *everything.*"

Tommy reached over to crank down the heat and open up the vents to the outside. Usually Burt freaked if you messed with his car, but he didn't even budge as cold air blew in on them from outside. Tommy welcomed the frigid wind. It perked him up and sharpened his tired, dulled senses.

"Let's start with today. Why the hell did you call Krunch and his dad?"

"Oh, man," Burt began. "I don't want to—"

"Get to it, man. Before we get back to town. Talk."

Burt smacked the wheel with the palm of his hand, a dull slapping sound.

"All right. Fine. People have been talking, you know? And I can't help but listen to 'em. Especially when they start talking about family."

Tommy blinked at that as he swallowed more watery beer. He never went out, never hung out with any of his old friends anymore. He'd been out of the loop since Corinne's birth, if not longer.

"*Who's* talking?"

Burt shrugged, and the car shuddered a bit as a result. The wind had picked up tonight, blowing across the plains like an angry spirit.

"I was down at the Side Entrance the other night. Friday. All the usual suspects where there. I split a pitcher with Krunch and Mickey, and they were askin' about you. Wondering what you were up to. Then Smith comes over with Krunch's dad, and they send Krunch and Mickey packin' for being underage. So I get the whole pitcher to myself while these two give me the third degree. About *you*."

Tommy exhaled, feeling a tingling sensation fill his tired limbs. He patted his nose with two fingers, trying to feel for broken bones and cartilage.

"Great," he said. He took a long drink of beer.

Burt kept talking as they went through the viaduct a mile from town, the wind disappearing instantly for a couple of seconds as the car went under the railroad tracks, then returning with a vengeance on the other side.

"So Smith's there, sipping his tonic water with lime, telling me how he saw you cruisin' town the night before around midnight, with the baby in the back. How he stopped you, and how odd you were acting. Not your usual friendly self. He said something 'bout how I should be keepin' an eye on you. What with the dead guy being found the night before, and all."

Any other time, Tommy would've laughed out loud at that—*Burt, looking out for* me?—but he didn't tonight. He felt too nauseous, thinking about Smith keeping tabs on him.

"He told you all that?"

"I know," Burt said. "People *talk* to me. I guess it's cuz I listen."

Tommy exhaled, and his breath came out frosty in the cold interior of the Camaro.

"What else?"

"So I was sticking up for you, telling them you were toeing the line now that you had a baby and a real job. Then those two big dudes showed up. The guys from tonight. Big Krunch introduces them, and they were real interested in hearing about you—they must've been eavesdropping. Said they'd heard of you, back from your sports days. They wanted to meet ya. Bad."

Tommy couldn't finish his beer. His nose was aching now. It felt like Luke or Mark's paw was still there, pushing against it, hard. He needed about a dozen aspirins.

And he kept thinking about the way Big Krunch had looked at those two big thugs. Like he was expecting them to claw him to death at any second. With the knot on his head Mark or Luke had given him, Tommy figured the old guy had good reason to worry. Those Callahan goons were up to no good in town.

And with them sniffing around, nothing was safe here anymore. Tommy was going to have to burn all the clothes and towels he'd left in the trunk of his car. He usually got rid of the stuff right away, got everything all cleaned up and normal-looking, but the past week hadn't been a typical week.

"This is messed up."

"I know," Burt said, slowing from sixty to forty as they passed by the first few houses of town. "So that night at the bar, I left pretty soon after they got there. Didn't tell 'em anything about you. And I wasn't going to do anything about calling Big Krunch, but then... Well. You pissed me off today in the hospital, yelling at me like that. So I called Little Krunch, told him to call his dad and set up the meeting tonight."

Burt gave Tommy another sheepish grin as he rolled through a stop sign.

"Did I mention the fact that I'm sorry 'bout that?"

Tommy punched him in the shoulder, but pulled the punch at the last minute. He was thinking about the fight tonight, and something else Krunch's dad had said: *That was no bear.*

They never asked me about their dead brother. They just wanted to mess with me. Maybe they already knew how their brother died. Or, more likely, they think I'm *the one who killed him.*

With a shiver, Tommy looked at the dark houses sitting back from the road, behind lawns still dotted with patches of gray snow.

Maybe they were right, too. I'd never remember it, if I did tear him apart. But that made no sense, especially if he was a wolf, too...

"Feel free to kick my ass," Burt said, interrupting Tommy's increasingly paranoid thoughts. He gunned the Camaro's engine as they rolled over the bridge leading to the two blocks of downtown. "It's my fault you got yours kicked tonight."

"Wasn't all that bad," Tommy said, and then added, "I had some help."

Burt grinned and slapped the steering wheel again.

"You turned, didn't you? Or whatever you call it. You changed, just like you started to do up in your apartment this afternoon. I fricking *knew* it!"

Tommy felt his breath catch. He almost asked Burt what he meant, but it was obvious Burt was in on the big secret. No sense in playing dumb with his big brother, not now.

"How long have you known?" he asked Burt instead.

As they idled at the town's lone stoplight, waiting for the green, Burt grinned at Tommy, like he was glad to finally be able to share all his secrets.

"I suspected something was up since I was ten or so. But you and Mom never talked about it, so I never asked. You know how it is with Mom and me. She barely tolerates me."

You and me both, Tommy thought, but he knew that wasn't true. *I've always been her favorite, while Burt was Dad's son, for whatever that was worth.*

"Didn't you ever want to tell anyone?" he asked Burt. "Or do anything about it?"

"Who would've believed me?"

Tommy nodded and looked out the window next to him. Already, at nine p.m. on a Tuesday, the Side Entrance was full. He couldn't see an empty table inside the dimly lit bar at the corner of First Avenue and Main Street, with half a dozen big guys in sweatshirts and jeans huddled around the pool table in the back. Then the scene blurred as Burt punched the gas. Green light.

I'd never really thought about Burt's side of things. How life must've been for him, knowing a secret like that, but being left out of all of it. How shitty was that?

Still feeling awkward, Tommy pulled out his phone to have something to do with his hands and checked for voicemails. Nothing. Not a single one from Mom or Dad, much less Suzanne.

Did nobody care what happened to me today, for Christ's sake? Not even a follow-up, how's-it-going-tonight call?

Burt cruised past the old, darkened, movie theater with its empty marquee and made a right turn, away from Tommy's apartment.

"Say," he began. "Mister Tommy..."

"Oh boy," Tommy said, rolling his eyes. He'd heard that tone in Burt's voice a million times in his life. Now a million and one.

"Got a favor to ask of you. Don't have to do it right now, of course. Just want you to think about it."

"What?"

Tommy thought Burt was going to hit him up for money—which was a joke, as Tommy was always broke—but Burt's face had gone stony and serious. His eyes glowed with reflected light from the streetlights outside.

"Next full moon maybe," Burt began, "could you, you know. Bite me?"

Tommy nearly slid down out of his seat. He looked hard at Burt to see if he was full of shit or not.

"*What?*"

"Infect me, man. Give me the wolf virus. Or whatever it is you inherited from Mom. Give it to me, too. I mean, look at me. I'm like a stick, can't gain weight if I tried. A stiff breeze knocks me over."

"Burt..." Tommy began, shock getting replaced by anger. "I don't..."

Uncle Carl. Suzanne. The baby. Everyone wants something from me, he thought. *Now my big brother, too? If I'd ever agree to such a crazy-ass thing, I'd probably kill him. Bite off his head by accident while I was in wolf form.*

Some of the fire had gone out of Burt's eyes, most likely due to Tommy's long silence. He turned left and stopped in front of Tommy's apartment. Tommy felt like he'd been in this cigarette-smelling, cold car for hours.

"Just think about it," Burt said. "All I'm asking. I won't even make you pay me back for gas after I've been hauling your ass all over town today. It's on me."

"Right," Tommy said, pulling himself out of the car. He was about to storm off without another word, but he remembered where his temper in the hospital had gotten him with Burt.

Don't underestimate him. And anyway—he's your brother.

"Hey," he said, leaning back down through the open passenger door to look at Burt's tired eyes. "Thanks, bro. For everything."

"Right."

"I mean it. Thanks. Okay?"

"My pleasure," Burt said with a laugh, gunning the engine so the passenger door swung shut fast. Tommy had to pull his hand away to keep his fingers from getting caught in the door. Heavy metal music banged out of the Camaro's speakers as Burt peeled out of the parking lot and roared away.

"Bite me?" Tommy repeated, standing there until he could no longer hear Burt's car rumbling out into the night.

It didn't work that way. That was just a myth. Wasn't it?

"He must've been adopted," Tommy muttered as he made his way across the parking lot, past his dusty car, and up the steps to his apartment.

When he unlocked the door and walked inside, the place was completely deserted.

Chapter Eleven

All seven hundred and twenty-five square feet of the apartment remained dark and silent as Tommy crept around the place, looking for his girls.

As far as his spotty memory could tell of that afternoon, nothing seemed to have been touched since his abrupt departure earlier that day. The paramedics had knocked two of the kitchen chairs over as they hauled him out of there, and all the bills on the kitchen table now littered the linoleum. The TV was still on, flickering an abstract red and green screen saver from Burt's abandoned video game.

After righting the chairs and scooping up the mail, Tommy checked their bedroom a second time, and then Corinne's room again. He caught a welcome whiff of his daughter's scent in there, which made him relax for a moment, and then her smell filled him with sadness.

I miss her. I could've died today—twice—and wouldn't have seen her again. And Suzanne never called once, much less tried to visit me in the damn hospital.

He peeked into the bathroom, saw his swollen nose and the blood on his sweatshirt, and quickly flicked off the light again.

What a night, he thought as the apartment returned to darkness again.

He flopped onto the couch and grabbed the remote to click off the TV. He listened to the wind rattle the shutters outside, once, and then the world went quiet.

Slipping a hand under his shirt, Tommy felt the long horizontal scar a few inches above the waistband of his jeans, wrapping around his side. The wound was still tacky. The Callahan brothers had made it open up again.

I've let people push me around too long. Maybe I was brought up that way by Mom, just to keep me from getting too angry. Because if I did lose it, I'd change. *Just like the Incredible frickin' Hulk. Forget the full moon, just punch me in the face a few times, and I'd be your wolf man.*

"Good thing the baby *doesn't* have it in her," he whispered, his voice gravelly as an old man. "Maybe the family curse will end with me."

With a grunt that turned into a growl, Tommy wriggled the phone from his jeans pocket. He punched the button for his one and only speed-dial number.

Time to get some things straight in my life, he decided.

"Tommy?" Suzanne said after the third ring.

"Where are you?" he whispered into the phone as soon as she spoke.

"Oh my God," Suzanne said. "I heard all about it. Are you okay?"

"Where *are* you," Tommy repeated, refusing to get distracted by her question. "And where's the baby, Suzanne? You're not watching her, are you?"

After a pause, during which Tommy could only hear distant country music and other muted voices coming over the phone, Suzanne exhaled into his ear.

"She's with your mom. I just couldn't take care of her tonight. She's been there all day. She's safe, okay?" Another long exhale. "Aren't you going to ask about me? About how I am?"

Tommy checked the clock on the wall—almost ten now, so Corinne would be sleeping for sure now. He hoped.

And Mom never called or left a message for me about any of this. Just great.

"You sound like you're doing just fine with your girlfriends," he said at last into the phone. "Tell Keri and Tamara and the others to have a drink for me, too."

That did it. Suzanne sucked in an exasperated breath and let him have it on the other end of the line. She ranted about how hard things were for her, going to her crappy waitress job all day, coming home to their crappy little apartment, and caring for a baby who was always sick and going to the doctor. Tommy almost started nodding along with her out of habit before catching himself.

Instead, he held the phone away from his ear and thought about his last football game, over a year and a half ago. He remembered it like yesterday.

How it felt, breaking through the offensive line, throwing elbows and shoulders into the other blockers. Feeling them fall away like tackling dummies. The fire in his belly heating to an inferno as he zeroed in on the quarterback.

The quarterback never saw him as Tommy took him down to the cold ground with a shoulder pad planted into the base of the kid's spine. He remembered seeing red as the QB crumpled to the ground.

Sack. What a perfect word for what Tommy had just done. Turned him into a sack of potatoes.

Was the moon full that night?

Mom said it was, but Tommy was too devastated in the days, and then weeks, after the game to check. Everyone told him it was a clean, fair tackle, that Tommy hadn't done anything wrong. But the kid had to be taken off the field in a stretcher, and from there into an ambulance. The flashing truck lit the night in flashing red light that perfectly matched the blood in Tommy's vision.

"Tommy!"

He'd taken his helmet off after that play and refused to put it on again. Ever.

"Tommy-boy, you'd better say something!"

Tommy looked at the phone in his hand, emitting Suzanne's harsh voice, and almost tossed it across the room. He was breathing fast, holding the phone in a death grip as he paced around his apartment. He stopped walking in circles and closed his eyes.

"I'm here," he said. His voice was so calm it shocked Suzanne into silence. He opened his eyes and watched the skin of his own arms turn to gooseflesh. "And I have something I need to say to you. *My* turn, Suze."

"What," she blurted, though it didn't come out sounding like a question. More like the belch of air you make after getting punched in the gut. Tommy had heard Mark Callahan make a similar sound like that earlier tonight.

"You have to own up to what you've done," he began, his voice still freakily calm and deep. "That child of ours isn't going anywhere. We can't take her back, like returning a pair of shoes to Payless. And she's not a dog—" Tommy felt his throat tighten up at that, as an image of Corinne screaming in the clearing under the full moon flashed into his head "—that you can just drop off at the kennel when it's convenient. I know you're busy with work, and it's not fun, having to be all grown-up all the time, but you should've thought of that before you stopped taking the pill."

Oh man, Tommy thought, *swallowing hard. Now I've said it. Can't stop now.*

"Wha—" Suzanne began again, but he cut her off. He could imagine the dazed look in her brown eyes right now.

"We're in this together, Suze. I need you to be tough. Strong. You can't flake out on me. We have a *baby* together. A *life*. I'm working, doing the best I can. You have to, too. Do you understand?"

Tommy exhaled and looked at his hand, expecting to see it shaking. Instead, it was rock steady. It was also covered in a thickening layer of blonde fur.

Oh hell, he thought.

"Why are you talking to me like this?" Suzanne whispered.

"I'm talking to you," Tommy said, forcing himself not to yell, "like an adult. That's what we *are* now."

"I don't have to take this," Suzanne whispered on the other end of the line. "I don't know what's come over you, Tommy-boy," she spat, getting up a head of steam now. "But I'm guessing it's your brother and your mother, talking smack about me. Again. I do *plenty* for Cory. Way more than you. You didn't have to carry her for nine awful months. You never had people stare at you like an unmarried slut with your belly out to here. You never—"

"*No*," Tommy said. This time his voice was almost a bark. He could feel his tendons stretching as the change crept into him with each pounding beat of his heart. He spoke slowly, though his body changed and stretched on him with each word. "No, I never had to deal with any of that. You sacrificed a lot. I know that, Suze. But it didn't stop when she was born. Neither of us are done sacrificing for that little girl."

"I don't have to take this," Suzanne whispered, and then the line went silent.

Call Ended! his phone flashed cheerily.

Tommy closed it with a hand that now sported five two-inch-long claws, bleach-white and razor-sharp. He dropped the phone on the couch and used his claws to slit his torn clothes the rest of the way off his fur-lined body.

"Sack," he muttered through the elongated teeth now filling his snout-like mouth. "Like a sack of potatoes," he added, and then laughed. He tottered on his back paws, off-balance now, top heavy.

This time, the sound of wolf laughter didn't disturb his ears one bit. Ears that now poked up from the top of his long head and brushed against the flaking plaster of his apartment's ceiling.

The floor squeaked in protest as Tommy clumped heavily from the dark living room past the kitchen table. He dodged the pesky light hanging off-center over the kitchen table without even thinking about it.

His nose no longer ached with pain, though the assaulting smells from the apartment—old food, baby powder, dust, dirty clothes, spit-up—filled his snout with a new kind of ache. Like feedback.

I can't stay like this, Tommy thought, somewhere inside his animal brain. *Have to control it. Before I go out running. Before I try to* feed.

But first, he had to see something.

Still struggling to get his balance, Tommy ducked into the bathroom. Getting his big head low enough to look into the bathroom took more effort than he'd expected, and he felt a jab in his wounded side that nearly sent him into a rage.

And then he was looking into a pair of glowing greenish-blue eyes, pupils wide as black holes as the irises grabbed every last shred of light to see in the dark. Too far apart, those eyes. But they *had* to be far apart, because a furry snout a good six inches wide had replaced the nose that had once held the spot between his eyes.

Tommy whimpered at the sight of the rest of him. The grinning mouth, not so different from the Callahan brothers with all its bright white teeth, including the crooked one he'd injured falling down the steps when he was eight. The ears that framed his oversized head. The fur covering every inch of him.

He panted and licked his lips with a tongue fast and pink.

"Who are you?" he whispered in his gravelly wolf voice.

"*What* am I?" he asked his reflection.

The smile never left his wolf face.

And then, Tommy simply started laughing again. The sound was terrible—worse than the frenzied barking of the biggest dog in the neighborhood, and he knew the neighbors below him could hear it—but Tommy couldn't stop.

Control, he told himself, over and over, thinking not of his mother this time, but his daughter. He lost his balance and dropped to the floor, almost cracking his oversized head on the toilet on the way down.

You owe her, he told himself, just like he'd told Suzanne earlier.

"Control it," he said, and this time, he said it out loud, with his regular mouth and voice. He opened his eyes, not remembering when he'd ever closed them in the first place, and looked around him. He was cold and naked, sitting on his bare ass on the linoleum, his back against the cold tub, with the toilet at his right elbow.

He wiped his face and his hand came away wet. At first he thought it was blood, and his pulse quickened all over again. But when he got up to turn on the light in the bathroom, he saw his pale, squinting face was covered only in tears.

He snapped off the light as fast as he could. With a low moan, he staggered into his bedroom and fell face-first into bed.

The world goes dark for a second as I rub my aching eyes. Need about ten more aspirin to get through this day.

I look around at the row after row of chairs, only a quarter of them with students in them. Everyone looks as unprepared as I do—wide eyes, fumbling for pens and little blue books, nervous laughter mixed in with the sounds of pages being turned and backpacks dropping to the concrete floor.

"I can't believe," I say to the pretty brunette with the tight red sweater sitting two chairs away from me and chewing on her pen cap, "that they make us write this out instead of letting us type on our laptops."

She gives me a big smile, but doesn't say a word. She nods instead at the front of the room, where our ancient professor with his gray sports coat stands in front of his podium, glaring at me and holding his stack of test questions like a shield in front of him.

I give him a wave and pull out three pens from my bag. Trying to act all cool, except I forgot all about this damn Western Civ exam. Didn't study at all this past week. Not after the big win last week. The past few days were one long party. Coach is talking bowl game, somewhere warm in December instead of snowy Iowa. Why *shouldn't* I celebrate, man?

At last the pages with the essay questions come shuffling down each row. I get mine and forget all about our ten and two football season and the curving chest of the girl next to me.

I am dead.

The black words of the ten essay questions run together on the white page perched on my tiny wooden slab of a desk. A desk I barely fit into.

None of it makes any sense. I don't recognize the letters, much less the words. I feel like I'm diagramming plays for our football team's offense, but I'm a big dumb defensive lineman. I don't do *plays*. I just hit, break up blocks, and tackle. And in two to three years, the NFL is going to pay me big bucks to do that every season.

So why am I messing with Western Civ?

The air in this old lecture hall, in one of the oldest buildings on campus, smells like dry rot. A mummy would love it here. But my throat's closing up, and my nose throbs. I'm going to just walk out if I don't get a hold of myself. Why the hell didn't I even crack open a textbook this past week?

I breathe through my mouth and stare up at the ceiling to calm myself. I never noticed the big wooden beams up there, painted black. They meet and cross and spread over the gray plaster ceiling like a net, or a web made by a spider bigger than the capitol's dome. Cracks spread out from the beams, the ancient plaster chipped and in need of replacing.

As I stare skyward as if looking for inspiration, I feel the professor's eyes on me, but I can't look away. Something's *moving* up there.

The building shifts, as if we were in southern California instead of a college town in the safe flatness of eastern Iowa. The cracks widen, and with a roar of thunder, the beam right above me snaps. Plaster and slivers of wood rain down. The thundering continues as the chain-reaction of the roof's destruction picks up speed. More beams crack and pop like gunshots. I feel plaster hit my cheeks and rain into my hair.

And I'm the only one who notices. Everyone is bent over their blue books, scribbling away.

I force the rotting air into my lungs through the tiny straw that my throat has become. I stand up and throw both arms in the air, waiting for the broken beams and the wedges of plaster to begin falling. Maybe I can catch them all, prevent any more damage and destruction.

The professor sees me and pounds on his podium, a dull thunking sound, but that is soon drowned out by the crunch of the ceiling disintegrating.

I don't catch any of the falling debris. It clobbers the kids around me instead, squashing them with evil splattering sounds, and not once do any of them look up.

Just like a quarterback I once sacked, they never knew what hit them.

Through the newly opened hole in the roof, the night sky pokes through. Black as ink and dotted with razor-sharp white stars. I think, just for an instant, that the devastation will stop. That I'll be able to keep the rest of the roof from dropping, just by sheer force of will.

But then I see the thin yellow line of the crescent moon through the broken roof. It smiles down at me with a cruel heartlessness. At last, the fire alarm begins blasting out, and everyone throws down their pens and blue books and runs. I just stand there, arms held up like a priest in front of a congregation running for the exit as the church disintegrates around us.

The hint of moon keeps right on smiling down on me, without a shred of mercy, as if it knows all my secrets. With the fire alarm still wailing, the last beam gives way, and the roof of my college dreams comes crashing down on me.

* * * * *

Tommy woke with a panicked howl trapped behind his tightly closed mouth. His pulse thudded like one of Burt's heavy-metal bass lines, while a passing night train whistled a three-second goodbye on the tracks four blocks away.

He gazed around the cool bedroom, at the dresser with its crooked middle drawer and the floor with the dirty clothes strewn across it. The living room was dark through the open bedroom door, though he could see a trace of faded yellow light from the streetlight, filtered by the cheap plastic window blinds.

Nobody else was there.

Tomorrow, Tommy thought, running a hand through his hair to make sure there wasn't any bits of plaster in there. *Tomorrow has to be a better day.*

Because really—how could it get any worse?

Chapter Twelve

On Wednesday, the day after the hospital and his fight with the Callahan boys, Tommy woke aching and dry-mouthed from snoring all night. His banged-up nose remained clogged. His side ached, and the nasty vision of himself in the mirror from last night haunted him from the moment he woke up. He was tempted to go back to sleep for the rest of the day.

When he finally managed to get out of bed at half past seven, though, he made up his mind to get himself back on track.

"This is what I can control," he said to himself, plotting out his day.

He'd work the phones like a maniac and make as many good calls as he could to get caught up from his four sick days. He'd eat better and get more exercise. He'd stay the hell away from Burt and his new buddies.

But first he had to stop by Mom's to check on the baby. He knew he'd have to explain his swollen nose and get lectured by Mom all over again about not taking responsibility for the baby.

And he was right. Mom was on him as soon as he walked in, yelling at him without ever once raising her voice, directing all her questions at baby Corinne just to get under Tommy's skin. She didn't care if he'd been in the hospital or not. With Mom all up in his face, he was tempted to throw all that he'd learned last night in *her* face.

At no point in her crabbing session did Mom mention Suzanne. Which was a good thing, Tommy thought eight and a half hours later on that long Wednesday, after he'd sold a grand total of two subscriptions and had pretty much worn out his voice talking to so many people on his cold calls.

Because Suzanne wasn't there when he brought Corinne home. And not once did she pick up her cell that evening, despite the calls he made every half hour before giving up at last.

He was a single parent all night. Mr. Mom, fixing supper—ground-up veggies from a jar for her, a peanut butter and bacon sandwich for him—and then Corinne's bath, followed by a bottle of formula to help her off to sleep.

He wasn't sure who fell asleep first as he rocked her in the glider in her bedroom. He opened his eyes from his doze and saw that hers were closed, at last. Tommy slid her into her crib, and, after checking voicemail one final time, he stumbled off to bed as well, exhausted.

My plans for taking charge of my life, he thought just before falling asleep, *will have to wait 'til tomorrow.*

The next day started long before dawn, with a crying baby who needed a diaper change and a bottle. That rough start was followed by another fruitless day on the phones. Not a single sale.

And then, after work, Tommy had a near-miss as he was hurrying out of the call center's parking lot. Some idiot in a beat-up old gray pickup pulled out of a handicapped space right in front of him, and Tommy had been forced to slam on his brakes to keep from T-boning the truck. His car slid half a dozen feet sideways in the gravel before stopping.

The driver stuck a big left hand out his window to wave at Tommy as the truck's back wheel spat gravel onto the hood and windshield of Tommy's car. Cussing and spluttering with rage, Tommy saw the face of Luke Callahan through the back window of the truck's cab before the truck motored away.

Luke was shaking his head and laughing at Tommy. Judging by the wide shoulders of the driver, that had to be

Mark behind the wheel in a new black cap. And crushed between them, not daring to look back, sat none other than big brother Burt.

Tommy straightened his car and cruised out of the parking lot, hands shaking and breath pluming fast into the cold interior of his car, fogging the now-dusty windshield. He wanted to follow them and see what they were up to with Burt, but by the time he'd gotten to the highway, the Callahan's truck was half a mile away, heading west, away from town with a fading roar. He'd never catch them.

And what would I do if I did run them down? Fight with them again, and lose?

Heading toward town and home, Tommy rubbed his sore eyes and wondered what the hell Burt was doing with those two goons.

"Hope he didn't arrange for one of them to bite him," he muttered.

Burt was the worst at picking friends. Not that Tommy had any room to talk—he felt like he was about out of friends lately himself.

Even at work, he felt like everyone had avoided him all day, as if he had something contagious. And he'd known most of these folks since kindergarten. At lunch, people seemed like they had better things to do or someplace else to be when they saw him in the break room eating lunch.

Screw them, Tommy thought. *I don't need any of them. They probably heard I wasn't making my quotas and didn't want my negative vibe to rub off on them on the phones. In this crappy economy, it was every man for himself in the call center.*

He picked up Corinne, dodging Mom's questions about Suzanne as he glanced at the headline about the dead guy in the latest copy of the Dyersburg Weekly: "Mystery Surrounds Unknown Dead Man."

Mark and Luke's big brother.

Tommy didn't want to read any further.

With Corinne in tow, he headed home to an empty apartment. That night was a repeat of the night before.

Suzanne never showed, and Tommy's anger grew all night, simmering to a slow boil as he watched Corinne rolling over on the pink shag carpeting, from one side of the living room to the other.

But there was nothing he could do, because he couldn't leave the house to go track down Suzanne. He had to stay there and take care of Corinne.

He was at the mercy of his girls. Trapped.

On Friday, he sold just one subscription, and then found out why everyone had been avoiding him for the past few days at work following his sick-day absences. At ten minutes to five, his manager gave him his final paycheck and a small cardboard box for packing up his stuff.

"Sorry," Janie said. "This wasn't my choice, Tommy. But the economy's still in a downturn, and we had to make some tough decisions. Four other people got cut. It's all based on seniority and productivity. And you just had a bad run of weeks."

Janie patted his hand. She and Mom had gone to high school together.

"Send me an email in a month or so," she added, "and I'll see if we have any openings then. Okay, sweetie?"

Tommy trudged out of the call center with his paltry box of personal belongings from his cubicle: three photos of Corinne in plastic frames, some pens, a half dozen Tupperware dishes with food remnants permanently stuck to them from past lunches, and a couple old issues of *Highlights* magazine that he'd meant to bring home to Corinne one of these days.

Looks like today was now one of those days.

The contents of that box and his last paycheck were all he had to show for the job he'd held for the past year, ever since leaving the university.

This check better last for at least a month, he thought as he drove away from the call center for what felt like the last time, ever.

The fun continued. The next day, the afternoon mail brought Tommy's first hospital bill, something he hadn't been expecting for another couple of weeks. The number at the bottom of the third page made him fall into a wooden kitchen chair hard enough to break it.

Five thousand, two hundred and thirty-six dollars. Plus another bill for $500 for the ambulance ride.

Fifty-seven hundred dollars. Tommy sat on the floor, stunned, with the ruined chair's broken pieces jabbing him in the back and ass.

No way I'll ever be able to come up with that. I don't even have a damn savings account. And what's in checking is just enough to cover groceries, with a little left over after my last paycheck.

That last bit echoed in Tommy's head: *My last paycheck.*

I am so screwed.

Devastated, he took Corinne and the bills over to Mom and Dad's. He didn't know what else to do—that huge amount printed on the first bill just made his brain go blank.

Mom was at work, to Tommy's relief, so he ended up talking for an hour with Dad while they watched a Hawkeye basketball game and Dad held the baby in his squeaky recliner. He'd forgotten how nice it was to just hang out with Dad, even if he always had a beer or mixed drink at his side. His skin was looking kind of bad, Tommy noticed with a strange sinking feeling in his gut. Gray, and a little sweaty. Like Dad wasn't getting enough fresh air or something.

Dad offered to watch Corinne the rest of the afternoon and overnight. Once he learned that Mom would be done with her day shift in two hours, Tommy was happy to cooperate. By seven thirty, thanks to all those beers and mixed drinks, Dad would pretty much be stumbling around the house, and no good to Corinne.

Burt never showed his face the whole time Tommy was there. Tommy was too stressed about finances to care if Burt was out drinking with the Callahan brothers or at home, hiding out in the basement and avoiding him.

At seven that evening, Tommy got back into his car, alone. Snow had started falling, fat and lazy flakes. It was a Saturday night. He should've been headed to Dubuque with Suzanne to catch a movie, some dumb action flick (his choice) or a romantic comedy (hers) that would slip out of their heads as soon as they got back in the car to get something to eat for the drive home. Spending money and eating—that was a typical date for them.

Not any more, though. Dates were a thing of the past.

Feeling strangely nostalgic and lonely, Tommy drove through the snow and headed north out of town, aimlessly, just taking in the scenery as the fields turned white and the trees gained a white coat of snow. Driving, not thinking, not worrying about money or babies or absent girlfriends or anything else.

Before he stopped for gas almost two hours later, he was thirty miles from the Minnesota border and panting as loud and hard as if he'd been running instead of driving his car. He hadn't been able to outrun the stress, as hard as he'd tried. His chest seemed to tighten the further he got from home.

Grudgingly, he turned the car around and headed back home, though he took back roads and detours to extend the drive.

I've got nothing to return home to, so what's the rush?

* * * * *

On Monday, Suzanne came back home.

Tommy heard her key scrabbling in the lock at ten thirty in the morning. She was shocked to see him at home; she must've come at this time of day because she knew he wouldn't have been home.

"Should've checked the parking lot first," he said instead of saying hello. The baby was napping, and he was full of piss and vinegar after his crappy weekend.

"You got *fired*, didn't you?"

"Let's not go there, not yet." Tommy felt that weird calm fall over him again, and it felt good instead of the constant worm of fear and uncertainty he'd felt all weekend. "Tell me where *you've* been."

"With some friends. And," she gave him a sheepish glance, "staying at Mom's."

Tommy almost went over to her, then, to give her a hug— he did miss her, sort of like the way you'd miss a co-worker or classmate who'd been on a trip for a week or two. He didn't feel any of the wild surge in his heart that he felt when they were first dating. All of that affection had drained from Suzanne and diverted to Corinne in the past half year.

"Yeah, and Mom had some good advice, for me, actually."

Tommy watched her flip through the bills, and then stop on his two bills from the hospital. He reached for them, but it was too late.

"Oh my God," she said. "Why didn't they send that to your insurance company?"

"It's a long story," Tommy began. "I don't—"

"No insurance? Didn't I tell you to get signed up before your birthday last year? Oh God. Mom was so right about you. No job, no health insurance, nothing. You do *nothing* for me, Tommy!"

Tommy had his mouth open to say something just as ugly and mean back to Suzanne, but his ears—hyper-sensitive to every sound the baby made in the past few days—caught the sound of a sniffle and a bump from Corinne's room. Suzanne's loud voice had woken her too soon from her nap.

Within five seconds, Corinne was screaming.

"Oh, my baby," Suzanne said, dropping the bills and making a move for the bedroom. "Let me get her."

Tommy's face went tight, and he felt the urge to grab her by the shoulders and push her back. He caught himself at the last moment before he could touch her, but Suzanne flinched and sucked in a loud breath at his sudden movements.

"No," he said, and an angry part of him relished the look on her face. "You don't go near her. You abandoned her, Suzanne. I'll get her."

"Tommy!" Suzanne took another step back, standing in the spot next to the table where the now-broken chair had once sat. He heard her sniffle, but he didn't look back. He left her and hurried into the baby's room.

By the time he'd gotten Corinne settled down somewhat and brought her out into the kitchen again, Suzanne—along with their checkbook and the extra cash they'd kept in an old coffee canister in the cabinet next to the fridge—was gone.

A strange thing came over Tommy after Suzanne left and didn't come back that night. With the money gone, he didn't expect to see her again anytime soon. He just didn't care any longer. Trying to keep up with the baby and worrying about money and the future had left him feeling exhausted and numb. His last words to Suzanne had taken the last of his energy.

He walked Corinne around the apartment until she fell back to sleep, the whole time thinking, *So this is what it feels like to hit rock bottom.*

Each time, he'd look down at Corinne and tell himself, *No. Not rock bottom.*

The next morning he tried to call Mom to see if she could watch Corinne while he did some job-hunting, but she wasn't home. Dad said she was picking up a day shift for another nurse, and Dad was just leaving for work as well. There were no other babysitting options on such short notice.

He wished he could go to work to get away from the constant demands of his little daughter—she still wanted him to hold her almost every minute she was awake. His temper grew shorter than a lit fuse, and he was starting to worry that he'd lose his temper and do something really bad if he didn't watch it.

Finally, when she refused to go down for a nap that morning, he took her for a drive to see if she'd nod off. But as soon as he'd pulled out of the parking lot of their apartment, he saw the hood of a gray pickup fill his rearview mirror. Mark Callahan was back there, gesturing at him from the driver's seat to pull over.

He thought hard about making a run for it—*who was this guy, acting like he was a cop, pulling me over?*—but instead he slowed to a stop. He realized he'd been waiting for this for about a week now. Expecting another confrontation.

Corinne was still fussing in the back seat, so Tommy let the car run and turned up the heat before he stepped outside into the cold. Mark's face was dark up in the cab, and he pointed at the passenger seat.

Tommy shook his head. *No way am I getting in there, not with Corinne here.*

"You are one anti-social guy," Mark said when they were both standing outside. He wore a grin that never touched his dark brown eyes. "We've been trying to talk to you again all week. Don't you even leave the house these days? What's your boss think of that?"

"Why you hanging around my apartment like some sort of detective on a stakeout?"

Mark's eyes glowed red for a second, as if irritated. He'd left his truck idling as well, and the choppy engine gurgled and popped.

"Someone's got to keep an eye on you. You don't know what kind of power you have. Might attract the wrong kind of attention."

"Ah, so it's out of the goodness of your heart. Very nice. But you can knock it off, okay? I can take care of myself."

Mark stepped closer and turned to face Tommy. He leaned his right hip against the Grand Am hard enough to make the car rock. Corinne squeaked from inside her car seat, and then began to cry.

"But," Mark said, leaning closer, "can you take care of her, too? 'Specially if she's inherited your special, ah, *skills*. Know what I mean?"

Tommy grunted at that and leaned back. Mark's breath smelled like roadkill. And Tommy hated having to look up to meet the other guy's gaze.

"Don't you guys have a killer to find? Or did you forget about that? Drinking every night with my loser brother will do that to you. Kills brain cells, big time."

"Are you asking about Matthew out of the goodness of *your* heart?"

"I'm just ready for you guys to go. My brother has enough drinking buddies from here in town. Guys who are—" he leaned closer, despite the foul odor coming from the bigger guy's mouth "—*normal*. Know what I mean?"

Mark hit Tommy upside the head so fast Tommy was down on one knee with his vision going gray before he knew what had happened. When Tommy's head cleared, all he could see were the glowing red irises of Mark Callahan's oversized eyes. The guy was turning right here on the street.

"Watch yourself," Mark growled, pulling Tommy to his feet. He smelled like rot and wet dog, and his wide face was dark with brown fur. "You have blood on your hands. We're close to putting it all together. You're at the top of our shit list, country wolf. You watch yourself," Mark said again, backing up, his eyes back to normal, his face furless. "And we'll be watching *you*, Tommy. You and that baby girl of yours. Your little bastard pup."

"Screw you," Tommy said, but it was lost in the thunder of Mark's truck, revving up and backing up in a reckless U-turn. Then the Callahan boy was gone.

"Screw all of you," Tommy whispered, and then he dropped back into his car. In the back seat, Corinne was quiet and staring intently at Tommy from her little mirror.

"I know, little baby-girl," Tommy said. "*Language*. Sorry 'bout that." His hands shook as he put the car in gear. "What do you say we go back inside for a while, okay?"

Three more days passed, and Suzanne didn't come back. When Mom said work was picking up, and she could only watch the baby four hours a day from now on, Tommy hit the wall. He spent all day Friday in the apartment with Corinne, holding her and rocking and waiting for his cell to ring.

Suzanne wasn't going to come back. This was how it was going to be, from now on. And the Callahan brothers had stopped by twice in the past day alone. He'd almost turned wolf on Luke and launched the bigger guy down the steps leading to his apartment before Corinne's cry from inside had brought him up short.

I'm going crazy, Tommy thought, over and over, as he clicked through the five channels that came in on their TV and peeked out the window every few minutes to see if anyone was out there waiting for him. *If I'm not already there, that is.*

The clock on the kitchen wall crept closer to midnight on Friday. The moon was just a tiny fingernail in the cold night sky, with exactly two weeks until it was full again.

Tommy had barely slept in the past forty-eight hours. He kept waiting for someone to throw something through a window or kick in his front door. He turned off all the lights and leaned back in the couch, trying to sleep.

Backed into a corner, trapped like an animal, Tommy finally gave up. At eleven thirty, he picked up his cell phone, clicked through the recent calls until he found the number he needed. He hit a button and sunk into the couch, eyes closed, the stale air in his apartment thick as cotton in his nostrils.

"Okay, Uncle Carl," he said as soon as the other line connected. "I have to know. Is the deal still on the table?"

Chapter Thirteen

Five minutes after the Lincoln Town Car rolled off, Tommy still stood outside in the mid-February cold in just his black T-shirt and gray sweatpants. His eyes burned from lack of sleep and the wind slapping him in the face. He registered none of the discomfort. He just leaned into the wind and felt his empty hands shaking at his sides as the night deepened around him.

At last, when he heard the streetlight next to the parking lot for his apartment flicker and buzz itself to life, he looked away from the empty road in front of him and clumped up the steps to the apartment.

Inside, his breath caught in his chest. The place was empty.

All mine now.

"God damn it," he rasped as he grabbed a sweatshirt and his beat-up tennis shoes. The words were as soft as the exhale of a dying man. The place felt smaller than ever, too close to even breathe.

And her *smell...* it was everywhere. But she was gone. He'd let her go.

The door slamming behind him as he fled the apartment was as loud as a gunshot.

Tommy threw himself forward, gasping for air, nearly tumbling down the steps. He didn't bother locking the apartment or going for his car. With the dark of night falling around him like a hood over his head, he felt the ache in his eyes and smelled his own sour sweat.

I could go after them, he thought. *Chase drunken Uncle Carl down in his rusty old boat of a car and get her back.*

There was still time.

But then he remembered the packs of twenties wrapped in rubber bands and stuffed into a plastic grocery bag, which he'd hidden under the unmade bed he'd slept so fitfully in the past few weeks. Blood money. Money that would buy him a better future, and hopefully give Corinne a real life as well.

He stared up at the fat white moon above him. This was the last night of the full moon. He hadn't gone running in weeks.

This empty feeling will go away, he told himself as he searched the white orb above him for the profile of the woman in the moon. He found her at last.

The ache in my chest will fade. I'll get over this. It's for the best, for all of us...

With a growl, Tommy pulled his gaze away from the traitorous moon. It took all his strength. Angry energy flowed into him, and he began to jog. He didn't want to drive to the acreage tonight. He just *ran*, his feet pounding against the pavement until he was out of town. He didn't plan on coming back here, ever.

He ran and ran and ran. And when he got to the trees of Westhoff's land, he let the change take over him again and went down to all fours. He shrugged out of his sweatshirt, pants, and shoes. The cars and houses and stink of town faded away, leaving him with only the loamy odors of nature. With his snout low to the ground, snuffling as he ran on all fours down the path, far from any prying eyes, Tommy fought the urge to howl, thinking of his baby girl.

She would never know this feeling. She was cursed with being normal, and she was gone now.

She didn't have it in her, and she didn't deserve the poor excuse for a life he'd try to give her.

She had a new life now, a better one. A life Tommy could never give her, not in a thousand years.

Corinne, he thought, and this time he did howl.

Long and loud, until his throat hurt and his chest scratched him from the inside out.

And then, at last, leaving his shredded clothes behind in the woods, Tommy ran. His breath grunting in and out of his flared nostrils, his four sets of claws chewing up the frozen ground in great clumps.

As he ran, he waited for his heart to burst and coat his dark blonde fur in blood. He refused to stop until it did.

T he handoff had been smooth. Easy. Way too easy. Tommy couldn't believe how simple it could be to change your life, completely.

Uncle Carl had set the date for two weeks after Tommy had called him, in mid-February. Not a full moon, but two days after.

Two weeks seemed like an eternity to wait for Carl to come get Corinne, and Tommy was convinced it would all fall through. That Carl would mess up, or the family that was "adopting" her would chicken out. Or Tommy would slip up and tell Mom or Burt about what he was planning on doing. Or Suzanne would come back and break it all up.

But Mom never had time to watch Corinne lately, and the days grew crazier as the baby caught another cold. Tommy took her to the doctor again and took care of her on his own, as best he could. He had no time for anything else.

It all happened too fast for Tommy to process. One day he was drowning in bills and paperwork from his ride in the ambulance and his hospital stay. The next day, he was packing up all of his baby's clothes and waiting with her, strapped in her car seat on the landing outside of their apartment, waiting for Carl to show up with the money.

During that time, he felt himself pulling away from Corinne. He usually talked to her non-stop, hoping she'd be able to tell he cared for her with his babbling and attention. But while changing her diapers or bathing her or simply putting her to bed, Tommy found few words to share. They felt trapped inside his belly, like so much undigested food. He'd lost the energy to entertain and educate her.

Plus, he had to admit, he didn't want it to hurt so badly when she was gone. So he was preparing himself for that time in the days leading up to the handoff.

And now, with less than ten minutes from the designated time Carl was supposed to pull up with his grocery bag of cash and empty back seat for Corinne's car seat, Tommy found himself talking to his baby girl for what was going to be the last time.

"You're going to like your new family," he whispered to Corinne, wrapped in her pink blankets and clutching her Dora the Explorer pacifier. "According to your great-uncle, these folks have a big house down in Iowa City. They're smart, with good, good jobs, unlike your dad here. Your room will probably be as big as our shitty apartment here, altogether. Sorry. Language."

Tommy rubbed his big hands together, hating the feeling inside of him—it was like the anticipation before a big game, a mix of fear and excitement, knowing big stuff was about to go down.

Corinne squinted at him in the wind, her blue eyes sparkling in the fading light. She gasped as a gust of cold air took her breath away, and then smiled with her two top teeth and red gums up at him.

"We should be waiting inside, I know," Tommy continued. The chattering kept him from thinking too much and worrying about Smith showing up to botch the whole deal. "But it's too stifling in there. Maybe all this fresh air will help you sleep on the way there. You've got about an hour and a half of riding ahead of you, so you'd better be good. Okay?"

As he talked, Tommy rifled through the contents of the diaper bag that Mom and Dad had given them at the baby shower last year. Suzanne had conned him into going to the women-infested party, and this had been the only present he'd gotten to open. He winced at the bright Hello Kitty logos all over the outside of it as he made sure the formula and diapers and bottles were all in place. Carl had assured him he didn't need to pack anything like that, that the new parents would have everything that Corinne would ever need, but Tommy had to be sure.

"Best thing about all this happening now, when you're still so little, is that you won't remember any of this. You'll never know you were born in this tiny little town in the middle of nowhere. You can start over, get a fresh start. And you won't have to grow up with a dad who doesn't know what the hell he's doing. And messing you up along the way, so you end up doing the same stupid shit as—"

The rev of an engine stopped Tommy in mid-sentence. A big brown Lincoln Town Car slid up the street, and then hit the brakes to make the turn into the apartment parking lot.

Uncle Carl had arrived.

"If I smell beer on his breath," Tommy whispered as he picked up Corinne in her car seat in one numb hand and her diaper bag in the other, "this whole deal is off."

The big car hummed to a stop near the bottom of the steps from Tommy's apartment, but the walk there felt like it took forever. Tommy watched Carl get out of the car, wearing a plain black sweater and new-looking jeans. His eyes looked clear, and as Tommy got closer—still walking slow and heavy—he couldn't smell any alcohol on his uncle. First time for everything.

Carl had a plastic grocery bag in his hands. It looked a lot less full than Tommy had expected it to look.

"Tommy-boy," Carl began, smiling nervously as he looked up at him.

"Don't start," Tommy said. He brushed past Carl and clawed at the back door. He pulled three times, the last time almost snapping off the handle.

"Sorry," Carl said. He leaned back into his car and hit a button. The locks on the other three doors shot up in unison.

Tommy was panting now, and he couldn't stop himself. Get her strapped in, get her safe, get her out of here. That's all he could think about. If Carl said anything at all, he'd snap.

Tommy was about to close the door on Corinne, who'd remained strangely quiet except for a couple of soft coughs, when Carl touched his upper arm.

"Say goodbye to her," Carl said.

His vision went red as he shook loose from Carl's hand, but Carl didn't flinch.

"I know it hurts. But sometimes you have to do the stuff that hurts if you're going to survive. If you're going to be a man, Tom."

Tommy wanted to haul off and punch his uncle for that—*who was he to give* me *advice, the unemployed lush? He wasn't even a blood relation*—but instead he bent down into the car. With the shocks squeaking under his weight, Tommy leaned in and kissed Corinne full on the lips. She tasted like formula and smelled like spitup. He let her presence overwhelm him as he breathed her in as best he could.

This is what I have to do.

"I love you, baby Corinne," Tommy whispered. "You will be a great woman someday. You are already an awesome, amazing little girl."

He swallowed hard, with a clicking sensation.

Corinne cooed at him and reached a fat hand toward his nose.

"Goodbye," Tommy said, pulling away before she could pat his face.

Like a quarterback placing the ball in a fullback's gut on third and short, Uncle Carl wedged the grocery bag of cash in Tommy's stomach. Tommy took the bag and stormed away from him. He took the steps to his place three at a time, not stopping until the bag was deep under his bed.

"Oh God," he muttered as he got back up to his feet, his head light from standing so fast. "They're fucking *leaving*."

He ran back outside and down the steps again, just in time to see the Town Car pull away from the parking lot, headed for Corinne's new life.

All Tommy could do was stand there and stare as they drove away.

When his heart continued beating inside his chest, instead of exploding with overexertion and misery, Tommy turned south. He'd been circling his territory for over an hour, but now he headed deeper into the woods at the far edge of the rough land. His clawed feet pounded over the rocky, root-clogged terrain.

He couldn't run fast enough to hurt himself as badly as he wanted to. As bad as he thought he needed to. He couldn't run himself to death.

So he simply ran. And with each passing mile in his wolf body, his mind cleared, and his sense of wrongness doubled, tripled, quadrupled.

Within minutes he'd reached the end of the Westhoff land, and he felt only the slightest shiver in the highly toned, furred body he now inhabited when he crossed over the boundary he'd created years ago when he was just a kid.

I was stupid to think this would work out. Corinne was blood. *Uncle Carl wasn't blood. He'd never know what it was like to be part of a pack.*

Somewhere inside the shrunken, human corner of his now-lupine mind, he recalled the way to Uncle Carl's house. His internal compass turned and righted itself. Eighty miles. He'd never run that far in one night, but as soon as he caught Corinne's scent, there'd be no turning back.

Uncle Carl is gonna pay for taking advantage of me like this. Because I'm getting my pup back.

Chapter Fourteen

Tommy caught her scent for good nearly seventy miles and four hours later.

He saved time and energy on his wild dash through the starlit countryside and the sleeping towns by latching onto the trailer of a semi for a good twenty-five miles of his trip. He rode on the underside of the truck when the lights of other cars grew too bright, holding himself inches above the concrete highway under him. And he lost half an hour in the confusion of lights and traffic in the small, manure-scented town where the truck turned east.

But now he was just outside Iowa City, and Corinne was maddeningly close.

Away from the choking diesel and burning exhaust of the truck, he smelled his daughter as clearly as a series of tiny dots stretching out ahead of him on the two-lane highway. He ran in the ditch next to the road, all four legs burning, a stitch in his injured side as he followed the markers. As tired as his body was from pushing so hard, his wolf mind was on fire, thinking only of his little girl, cursing himself for letting someone else *buy* her.

Her trail grew stronger as Tommy approached a neighborhood outside Iowa City. This wasn't the way to where Uncle Carl lived with Aunt Melanie and their two boys; Carl and Mel had a little house close to the river in Iowa City, nothing fancy like the big houses Tommy could see taking shape now in the gloom ahead of him.

Corinne's new wannabe parents lived in one of these nice houses, he thought. *The thieves.*

He ran harder even as his lips let slide a whimper from the pain in his injured side and his banged-up feet. Everything was starting to blur together now—the lights, the endless highway, the miles pounding away under his clawed feet—not to mention the crushing guilt and anger he couldn't stop tormenting himself with every step of his journey.

And high above, the full moon watched it all silently, like an open mouth laughing at him.

I don't need you tonight, moon. Turns out I never did. I was just too stupid to figure it out on my own.

A brightly lit granite entrance approached on his left. Rivercity Cliffs, the metal sign read from atop a closed gray gate. The gate connected to an eight-foot, wrought-iron fence that caged in the neighborhood. Tommy risked the blazing white light of the two spotlights aimed at the entrance and leaped up and over the gate.

The impact of landing sent a shockwave through his battered feet and up his aching spine. A mewling cry slipped out his gritted teeth before he could stop it.

On the other side of the gate, he caught his breath in the shadows and sniffed the air. He couldn't get an exact fix on the smell like he usually could in wolf form, thanks to his own mad panting. His chugging breath sounded like a freight train in his own ears.

But he could smell something different in the air now. A more pungent smell. Something that put a surge in his muscles better than six cans of Burt's caffeine-laced pop could have done.

Blood.

All thoughts of catching his breath forgotten, Tommy sprinted on all fours toward Corinne. His nostrils flared as he snuffled at the ground, as if he were eating every tiny trace of her scent. And the smell was growing like a police siren, stabbing at his nose instead of his ears.

If anything has happened to her...

He scampered past shining SUVs parked outside three-story houses set back on wide, carefully manicured lawns. He swung his big head from side to side, tongue out, tasting the air. Copper and salt and heat. He was close.

He ran down a tree-lined street and saw the big house at the end of the cul de sac, surrounded by oaks and maples.

There. Corinne was there.

He'd half-expected to see Carl's Town Car parked outside, but of course he was long gone by now. He was probably drinking his way through his cut of the blood money right now.

Thieves. Bunch of thieves.

Tommy shot through the trees and charged up to the front door, smelling nothing but his daughter now. He didn't care anymore how much noise he made, and he barely gave a second thought to his own inhuman appearance.

Let them think that a big wolf broke in and stole their new baby away from them. Let that haunt their dreams for the rest of their lives.

Thieves.

A scream from inside the house pulled him up short. He crouched at the front door, holding his breath, reaching a clawed hand for the door handle.

Surely they hadn't seen me? Not yet.

He pushed open the outer door and heard another scream, followed by a sound that made his hackles go up.

A small growling sound, like a tiny motor running. Then a snapping sound, teeth gnashing together.

That's not a dog, Tommy thought, hurrying silently down the front hall of the house. *But that can't be, can it...?*

He was so distracted by that low growling that he nearly tripped over a dark brown dog, a chocolate Lab, in the unlit hallway. He smelled it now, especially the pool of blood spreading out onto the hardwoods from under it, but he'd been too caught up in Corinne's overpowering scent. So close.

The dog below him wasn't moving, but the poor animal was still warm. Tommy passed around it and its ink-dark puddle of blood on his way to the rest of the house. The house had a rotten odor to it, like something gone bad in the fridge, mixed in with the too-clean smell of detergent and cleansers.

The growling grew louder, as if the animal making it was about to lash out. And then it stopped, cut off by a trio of sharp coughs.

Tommy knew that sound too well. But it made no sense, accompanied by the growling. He entered the big living room and turned right. A light was on in the kitchen, under the black microwave.

Someone was sobbing in the far side of the kitchen. A woman.

The house held a reek of blood and dog shit and death, along with a too-sweet smell of baby powder, all of it thick enough to make Tommy gag.

"My babies," the woman was saying, over and over again, each time a bit louder, edging into hysteria. "All my *babies.*"

The woman sat on the tiled floor, wearing a white robe, which was now soaked red. She was bent over another dog: a younger, smaller golden retriever male. He had four long slashes right across his belly, and the stench coming from his innards was sharp and septic.

The low growl pricked at Tommy's ears.

Tommy could barely turn to look at what was making that growling noise. He'd run all night to get here, to find her, but his fears now overtook him.

Was I too late? Would she take me back?

Tommy reached out a hand covered in his own blonde fur.

Even if she doesn't recognize me, she'll take me back. Blood and bone. DNA. This child was mine. *We're family.*

He bent down at last and looked into the shadows under the big wooden table in the kitchen nook, where the growling and coughing had come from.

In the murky darkness Tommy saw his baby Corinne, transformed into something *magnificent.*

Growling, standing on four short, shaky legs, she was the same size as the puppy that had died under her claws. She'd locked her gaze on the woman and the other dog in front of her. But Corinne, in her new shape, was no puppy; she was all wolf; the long snout and claws were a dead giveaway. She was unharmed, but her front paws left bloody tracks on the tiled floor under her. Her fur was a strawberry blonde color.

When she turned to look up at Tommy, she hissed in a breath and coughed, just once, and then she started keening softly.

The sound broke Tommy's heart. Oblivious to the crying woman off to his right and the thin, silent man rocking convulsively on their silent glider to his left, Tommy reached out to his baby awkwardly with his front paws and pulled her to him. He forced himself to relax and let some of his wolf features fade so he could hold her better.

He nearly screamed as her claws dug into his arms and his shoulders as she hugged him at last. She was a bundle of hard, quivering muscles. So scared.

"*I've got you,*" he rumbled, a soft and tender growl coming from his tooth-filled mouth. "*And I'm* never *letting you go.*"

Leaving behind the two dead dogs and the two shell-shocked humans, Tommy wrapped up his baby girl in his arms, rose up on his thickening back legs, and ran out the front door.

*G*et out, get away from here, to the trees, get—
A set of high beam headlights stopped him in his tracks.

He hadn't even heard the car drive up. He was too busy clinging to Corinne and gearing up for his final run of the night. Wherever that might take them.

His hesitation lasted only a frozen, stunned moment. Then he growled at the car and tensed up, ready to leap across the yard and out of that light.

But a clawed hand gripped him and pulled him down to all fours again before he fell over from exhaustion.

"Turn off the goddamn lights!" a deep voice said from next to his ear. Female. And familiar.

An invisible hand clicked off the headlights. Blinking in the sudden darkness, Tommy inhaled the musky scent of fur and sweat. He knew the scent of another wolf.

And this one—he could tell—was his blood.

"Mel?" he said, voice cracking. At last, the change was fading from him, and his body began to quiver. He felt cold all over.

His aunt, however, was trying her best to pry Corinne from his road-torn hands.

"Let go," she growled. She was now bigger than him, still in her wolf form, as he shrank back down to his normal size. He became painfully aware that he had no clothes on.

But he couldn't release Corinne. Not with Uncle Carl so close by.

"Don't let him take her again," he said. He couldn't unlock his clasped and bloody fingers, which gripped Corinne like a chain. He was moaning and couldn't stop it.

Melanie's dark eyes stared down at Tommy, then she flicked her narrow, dark-furred head at the car, as if shaking water off her ears.

"*Look* at him. Think he's taking anyone anywhere tonight?"

Huddled in the front seat of the car, Uncle Carl peeked over the dash with one hand plastered to his forehead. He looked like a man who'd witnessed three impossible things in the past three minutes.

"She might be hurt," Tommy began, looking down at Corinne.

His daughter's skin was smooth, pink, and hairless again. At some point she'd changed back without him even noticing. He hoped she hadn't broken any bones or injured herself in some way, attacking the dogs inside. Poor kid was just learning to *crawl*, for Christ's sake.

"She's fine," Melanie said, her own fur receding as she slid out of her change as well. Tommy had to look away as his aunt's pink, human bottom took shape, but he caught a glimpse.

Aunt Mel had really kept in shape even after having two kids, he thought, and then wanted to kick himself for being such a perv.

"Go inside and take care of them," she ordered Uncle Carl, pointing at the big house, "and make sure they tell no one about what really happened. It was *intruders*, Carl. Intruders with butcher knives. Any other story and I tell the cops all you told me tonight on the way over here, you messed-up, baby-stealing bastard."

Without a glance at Tommy, Carl scurried out of the car and scuffled up the steps to the house, following her orders like a scared servant. The door slammed behind him, making Tommy move at last. His battered feet sent out warning flares of pain. The pain traveled upward, fast, up his spine until every inch of his body hurt.

Back in the car, Melanie had gotten Corinne hooked into her car seat in the back and pulled a coat over herself. Tommy gladly wrapped Carl's jacket over his crotch, though he wished he had something to cover his belly with.

"Your side's bleeding," Melanie said, looking like Mom with the way she was appraising him, like a nurse. She handed him some baby wipes from a box under her seat. Then she started the car and backed out of the long driveway.

"What did—"

Melanie shook her head.

"No questions. Not right now." She put the car in gear and they began humming through the darkness toward town. "Let's get you home, first of all. Both of you. Then we'll worry about all the questions and consequences."

Tommy thought he could hold it in until they got to Melanie's house, but after taking one look behind him at Corinne's sleeping, peaceful face, he couldn't help himself. He put his hands over his face and cried—big, wet explosions going off in his chest, tears streaming from his eyes at what he'd done, what she'd done, and what could've happened tonight.

All my fault. All my fault.

His aunt didn't say a word all the way home. She just rested a cool, steady hand on his bare shoulder, and Tommy had no choice but to love her for that.

Chapter Fifteen

Melanie had said she'd be able to sense if anything went wrong while they were out.

Initially, Tommy didn't believe her, but after they hit the street on their first early-morning jog together, he quickly forgot his worries about Corinne and his aunt's two young boys sleeping back home, unattended. In the weeks after that first run, it was all he could do just to keep up with his aunt. She must've been running all her life.

Jogging in the morning that early spring, down paved city streets and concrete sidewalks, was a huge change from running under the full moon out in Westhoff's field. You had to watch out for cars and other pedestrians, for one thing. And the stink of garbage and exhaust from the city buses and the cars and motorcycles on the road next to him made him want to gag.

But other than that, Tommy was starting to get hooked on these early-morning runs with Aunt Melanie. He felt like he was getting close to being somewhat in shape again. He could at least do two miles in twenty minutes without keeling over.

The real challenge was trying to carry on a conversation with Melanie, who always wanted to chat as they ran.

"So tell me some more about this job interview of yours," she said as they jogged down the narrow pedestrian bridge crossing the Iowa River.

He tried to let out a laugh, but was too busy panting. The first mile of their big loop around her house was over, to Tommy's relief. But there was still over a mile yet to go. They'd be back home by six thirty, before the sun had completely risen.

"I wouldn't call it a job interview. I mean, it's a pizza place. I just walked in and asked to talk to the manager, and we sat down at a table. He seemed like a cool guy—" *huff, huff, huff* "—with his funky black glasses, all laid-back. He liked the resume you helped me put together."

"Told you!" Melanie was able to bark out a laugh, a happy sound mingling with the pounding of their shoes and Tommy's loud breathing. "They love that sort of thing, even if you don't have a whole pile of experience to list on it. Gotta look the part, sell yourself."

Tommy grinned at that, and then he felt his face grow warm as a pair of girls in tight black spandex pants and sorority sweatshirts came jogging toward them. He closed his mouth and tried to jog with more ease despite his fatigue.

My age, he thought with a thrill of amazement. *These girls are my age. They probably think I go to school here at the University of Iowa, just like them.*

Melanie elbowed him in the side after the girls had puttered past and gave him a knowing look. He saw a lot of Mom in Melanie just then, and for a few seconds he felt a sharp pang of homesickness for Dyersburg.

He hadn't spoken to Mom since that bad night in February, though she knew he was now living here in the city with Melanie and her boys. He still got texts from Burt every other day or so, apologizing or asking whether Tommy had visited this place or that place in Iowa City, or just texting to say "Wazzup?" The only person Tommy responded to back home was Dad, and his phone calls had been getting fewer and fewer as more weeks passed.

They were all convinced that we were never coming back home. And they might just have a point about that.

"The one on the left was totally checking you out, Tom."

Chugging down the path leading past the warehouse-sized art buildings at the edge of campus and the glass-sided performing arts complex coming up on their left, Tommy just shook his head at Melanie and rolled his eyes.

"Give me a break," he spat, the words coming out harsher than he'd expected.

He saw Melanie tense up next to him. Thinking about Mom and Burt and Dad had set him on edge, and they were both jogging faster. He tasted copper on his tongue as his lungs burned hotter.

"Sorry," he said. "Let's just say I don't need a woman in my life right now."

"Gotcha," Melanie said.

They left campus and started on the last mile of their run. Tommy exhaled and tried not to think about Suzanne and the scene she'd made back in late February. Back when she tracked him and Corinne down, after she heard they were both leaving. She'd threatened that she was getting a lawyer and would fight for custody, but Tommy hadn't budged.

"Save your money," he'd said to her, talking in his new calm and confident voice. "There's no way you're getting her back. Not after you left us like that. You didn't even *try*, Suzanne. You just took off and left me. Left *us*."

Already, the girl that just two years ago seemed like the perfect match for him—the answers to all his desires and needs, possibly the one he'd marry someday—was fading from his memory. He was having trouble remembering what her face looked like, what color her eyes were. How her voice sounded. What he ever saw in her to begin with, other than her interest in him, Tommy had no idea anymore.

"So anyway," Melanie said, wiping sweat from her forehead and wiping it on her shiny black pants, "when do you start delivering for the Pizza Pit? When you gonna start bringing home the big bucks?"

"Soon as next week. They have to do a reference check." Tommy swallowed hard at that. "Surely they won't find anything bad, right? Other than the fact they laid me off at my last job?"

"You mean about the Uncle Carl-dead dogs shit? Don't worry. Nobody's talked to the cops. I've been keeping an ear out for that kind of thing at my office. Not a word. Like I said before, your record's clean. Just don't muck it up now, nephew."

"I'm trying."

"I know." Melanie glanced at him again, a half-smile on her lips. "Six months ago, I never would've expected you to go up to a place you'd never even been to before and ask to talk to the manager. You would've just grunted and refused. I mean, we haven't visited you and your parents much lately, but I was worried about you going out to look for jobs. Turns out I was totally wrong. So, my bad."

Unable to stifle his smile, Tommy let Melanie's comments buoy him up for the last portion of their run. The air was cool on his sweaty skin as they hung a left, and he wished he hadn't worn a second shirt under his long-sleeved gray T-shirt. Only five more blocks until they were home.

Every now and then Melanie would cock her head to the side as she jogged, slowing just a bit. She'd sniff a couple times, then straighten up and get back on pace. Tommy figured it was just some weird tick she had, like the way Mom would clear her throat a lot if she was uncomfortable or nervous.

Ever since Melanie kicked Carl to the curb that spring, her place had been surprisingly calm. As calm as a house with three kids seven and under could be. Tommy and Corinne had to share a room (Carl's former home office), which was a bit of a pain, and Melanie's sons Trey and Tyler constantly fought with and tattled on each other. But they loved having their niece in the house to spoil and play with when she wasn't napping or crying.

At first, when Melanie was busy with getting the last of Uncle Carl's stuff out of the house and out of her life, Tommy hardly ever got a moment to himself, but he surprised himself by not minding so much. He liked having family around him. His pack.

"Ah shit," Melanie said next to him.

Her head was cocked again, but before Tommy could ask what was wrong, she put on a sudden burst of speed, shooting off toward her house.

Tommy let out a half-groan, half-shout and charged after her as best he could on his tired legs. But Melanie was a block ahead of him already. His hands balled up into helpless fists as he sprinted as best he could toward home, black spots flashing in his vision, lungs burning.

By the time he'd made it home, Melanie was at the front door, waiting for him with Corinne in her arms. The baby's face was red with crying, though she was quiet now. Melanie's oldest boy Tyler stood next to her, a hand on his mom's side. His eyes were still sleepy, and his light brown hair was sleep-bent.

"Look who Ty caught trying to climb out of her crib."

Tommy felt his heart do its usual flip-flop when he took in Corinne's scent. He wanted to take her, but didn't want to coat her new pajamas in his jogger sweat. Instead, he steadied a level gaze at Melanie.

"How did you know?"

Melanie gave him a toothy grin. "Didn't I tell you that I'd be able to sense if anything went wrong?"

"Yeah, but I thought you were just giving me a line."

Melanie nuzzled a jabbering Corinne. "Think about it. You know the answer. You just forgot to ask the question."

Standing there sweating and waiting for his pulse and his breathing to return to normal, Tommy thought about their jogging route from the past two months. He realized that it was just a big circle around Melanie's house. They never got too far from her house in that circle. And as they ran, she was always cocking her head—not a weird tick, he realized now, but Melanie using her wolf senses—clicking them on and off, almost, like a GPS or something. She was listening for, and maybe even smelling for, any trouble back home, where the three kids were still asleep.

"No way."

"Yes way," Melanie said. "There's so *much* you can do, Tom. You just haven't let yourself figure them out yet. But you will. Stick with me, and I'll get you up to speed, Wolfman Jack."

Tommy wiped the sweat from his face with the sleeve of his long-sleeved tee and reached for Corinne at last.

I have so frickin' much to learn. I'm ignorant as a hick from the country.

"Okay," he said, holding his squirming and giggling little girl in one arm. "All right. It's a deal."

Chapter Sixteen

Three days, seven and a half jogged miles, and two phone calls later, Tommy made his first delivery for the Pizza Pit.

At least, he was trying to get these three large Meat Fanatic pies with extra cheese delivered to the right place. Iowa City was the home of the University of Iowa, and all the roads close to campus felt like a maze of one-way streets and dorms, frat houses, and apartments. Too many buildings and cars in one place, all of it so different from Dyersburg that Tommy was immediately overwhelmed.

And if he didn't get these pizzas—overpoweringly fragrant with cooked beef and pork and all that cheese—to apartment 5B of the Hawkeye Apartments on Lynn Road, they'd be free. The maps on his phone became garbled on this side of town for some reason. And Tommy would be out his delivery fee of five bucks.

He rolled his window down to get the maddening scent of fresh pizza out of his nostrils. He was tempted to ask for directions from some of the college kids—the girls dressed in sleeveless blouses and tight pants or skirts despite the chill in the air, the guys in jeans and collared shirts and coated in cologne, all of them obviously heading to the clubs and restaurants downtown for a night of fun. But he couldn't ask. His pride wouldn't allow it. Not while he was wearing his bright red Pizza Pit baseball cap, and matching shirt one size too small for him.

He was about to call his manager Paul back at Pizza Pit HQ when he turned down a one-way street and saw the green sign for Lynn Road float up into view.

"Thank God," he whispered. He waited for a trio of giggling girls smelling of perfume and hair spray to pass in front of him at a stop sign.

"Pizza guy!" one of the girls, a blonde with amazing blue eyes and great figure, called out, waving at Tommy. "Hey pizza guy. How you doing?"

He tried to look nonchalant as he waved back.

"He's *cute*," said one of her friends—tall, dishwater blonde, and skinny. "For a pizza guy."

"Ugh, Pizza Pit," said the third girl, a chunky brunette with a raspy voice. "Nasty stuff."

Tommy fought the urge to flip her off before rushing down Lynn past the first of the eight blocky-shaped Hawkeye Apartments.

I don't need a woman in my life right now. No truer words had been spoken.

But he still checked his rearview to watch the girl with the eyes and figure recede from his life.

At last he made his way to apartment building B. As he walked up the steps to the second floor, his eardrums started throbbing from the thundering bass and screaming voice of the thrash music from one of the apartments. Just his luck, it was coming from the other side of the metal door labeled 5B. With a wince, Tommy gave five sharp knocks and stepped back from the door, the bag of pizzas dangling like roadkill from his right hand.

The music went from its pounding volume to a more manageable level, almost quiet. Tommy heard the clanging sounds of metal on metal, followed by grunts and a bestial roar that tickled his fillings. He tensed.

Pretty sure that was just the TV. Maybe a video game or—

The door opened before he could finish the thought. The pale guy with the ponytail who opened the door was skinny as Burt, holding a wireless video game remote in one hand and a wad of cash in the other. He pulled the door closed behind him on what looked to Tommy like an apartment full of college-age girls gathered around a huge TV. The synthesized video game battle sounds continued.

"Ah, Pizza Pit. We were worried you wouldn't get here on time."

"We were *hoping*," a female voice called out from inside.

"Only thing better than pizza is free pizza," shouted another female voice.

The thin guy grinned. "What do I owe you, man?"

"Twenty-two fifty," Tommy said, pulling the three warm boxes out of the insulated carrier. And then, unable to help himself, he grinned at the other guy. "You and your girlfriends playing 'Dungeon Crawlers' in there?"

"Ha! You're batting five hundred, man. Got the game right, but no on the girlfriends part. I don't have a death wish, now, do I? Anyhow. Keep the change."

His bony arms loaded down with pizza, the guy bumped his way back into the apartment, and the battle sounds from the game washed out over them from the gap left by the partially open door.

"Thanks," Tommy called as he pocketed the other guy's twenty and ten.

He was about to leave when he peeked into the apartment and saw the fierce battle taking place on the screen. A team of knights, wizards, and barbarians—all female avatars— battled an oncoming horde of black-furred beasts with flashing teeth and yellow scimitars. Grunts and screams accompanied the slashing and smacking sounds of battle, coming from what had to be Bose speakers positioned all around the living room.

Burt would've loved this setup, Tommy thought with a pang of sadness. *Feels like I haven't seen him in a long, long time.*

And then the screen froze when someone noticed the pizzas.

Tommy realized he was still standing in the hallway, peeking in at the scene through the door like a perv, but he couldn't look away. He watched the skinny guy with the ponytail drop the three big boxes of pizza on top of the cluttered mess of the coffee table in front of the TV.

"All right, ladies," the skinny guy said in a deep voice. "Feedin' time!"

Remotes clattered to the floor from the paused video game as the girls attacked the pizza. They elbowed one another as they tried to get more than one piece, licking grease from their hands, no longer laughing but deadly serious. There wasn't going to be near enough pizza.

"They were hungry," the guy said, back in the doorway again, his skinny body blocking the pizza carnage as best he could. He wore a sheepish grin that looked fake to Tommy, but he couldn't help but nod at the guy and grin. "Sorry you had to see that. Don't want to get in the way of women and their food, huh?"

Someone screamed behind him, and Tommy could tell it wasn't from the video game. The scream was followed by a couple dull thunks and a bout of cursing. The ponytail guy just grinned, and at last Tommy headed for the stairs and his next delivery. Tommy was smiling too when he heard the guy call to him.

"Thanks, Pizza Pit guy. See ya 'round."

That night and Saturday night as well, Tommy saw all sorts of interesting, and sometimes wild things as he dropped off pizzas. He delivered to shy college kids eating alone, a group of bookish kids playing what looked like old-school Dungeons and Dragons in their apartment, giggling sorority girls, surly frat guys, tons of kids who met him in the lobby of their dorm—all of them terrible tippers—and the occasional family in their home off-campus.

His favorite stop was the group of guys sitting around drinking beer and watching the end of a NCAA men's basketball game on Saturday night. They invited him in and told him to sit down and have a beer. Tommy couldn't say no.

He got to watch a couple dunks and sip half of the foamy beer in his cup before he begged off to go back to Pizza Pit HQ. All the guys slapped his back on his way out, as if he'd made the winning three-point shot at the buzzer.

And later that same night, he dropped off more Meat Fanatic pizzas to apartment 5B at the Hawkeye Apartments, though the group of girls on Saturday was different from the group there the night before. Tommy couldn't figure it out, but he was glad once more for the ponytail guy's seven dollar and fifty cent tip. The college funds—one for him, one for Corinne—that he'd been discussing with Melanie grew with each pizza and every tip.

By the time he got home from his shift, smelling of grease and cheese and car exhaust, Tommy was exhausted. At half past midnight, he'd kept himself awake on the drive home by thinking of the summer session classes he'd found at the University this week—some criminal justice classes that had caught his eye, along with an Intro to Computers course. He'd kept surfing back to those courses on Melanie's lightning-fast laptop.

Mel worked as a lawyer at an Iowa City firm as a public defender, and he'd always liked hearing her stories about the different people she worked to keep out of jail. It sounded like a much more rewarding job than selling magazine subscriptions.

"Maybe even better than delivering pizzas," he muttered to himself with a laugh as he closed his car door softly and got out his house key.

Once inside, he made his way through the now-familiar contours of Melanie's darkened living room. When he opened the door to the kitchen, he was surprised to see Mel sitting at the kitchen table with her cell phone and a plastic cup full of ice and what looked like whiskey in front of her.

"Pizza guy," she murmured. "I could smell you coming a mile off." Melanie rubbed her face and looked at him with red, puffy eyes.

Tommy felt a surge of panic. "Everything all right? Are the kids—"

"Kids are fine. Everyone's sleeping. Corinne had trouble going down, a little fussy, but nothing major."

Her cell phone buzzed in her hand, once. Text message.

"It's Carl," she said.

"Oh great."

Things start looking up, Tommy thought, *then crazy Uncle Carl pokes his drunk nose into things.*

"He in trouble?" Tommy asked. He wanted to reach over and pat his aunt's hand, but didn't know how to do it without making both of them uncomfortable. He did feel like he'd talked more to Melanie in the past two months than he'd talked to Mom in all his twenty years. He'd learned a lot from her as the past two months flew by.

"He's drunk-texting me." Melanie handed Tommy her phone. "And being a pain in the ass, 'cause he knows I won't answer the phone."

"Maybe it's time for a new phone number?"

"No way. I have clients using this number. My slack-ass, soon-to-be-ex-husband isn't going to mess up my job, just because he's lonely and feeling sorry for himself on a Saturday night." Her phone buzzed again. "Keeps saying how it's all my fault he had to set up that deal with Marty and Shari."

Tommy swallowed hard and felt a sudden urge to go check on Corinne.

What if her crib was empty, and she was being carried off again?

He'd been having bad dreams again lately, and that feeling of losing her, of being too late to help her, ran through them all like a bad theme in a homework assignment for English class.

I need to work with her more. I'm not spending enough time with my little girl. I'm getting as bad as Dad was with me— never there, too busy working or, in Dad's case, drinking. How'd that happen so fast?

"Marty and Shari," Tommy said. He put his hand over Melanie's phone when it buzzed again. He saw that she was about to grab it and read the text message from his drunk uncle. *My druncle.* "So that's their names, huh?"

Melanie nodded and sipped her drink.

"I was friends with Shari. She did some clerking with us a while back, before she stopped working and started doing all she could do to get pregnant. Marty was making good money at the software company where he worked, so they could afford it. She asked me all sorts of legal questions about adoption a while back. I guess they just got tired of waiting. I haven't spoken a word to them since that night. At least they never tried to get the authorities involved. They knew *they* were in the wrong just as much as—" her phone buzzed again "—Carl."

Tommy could almost smell the mixed stink of blood and death from that night, along with the unforgettable undertone running through all the odors like a high-pitched whistle: his daughter's scent. He saw the two dead dogs again, slashed through the bellies, and felt nauseous.

Corinne. I let that happen to you. And you were just trying to protect yourself. All my fault.

"Okay," Melanie said, sitting up and scraping her chair on the hardwood floor under it, "this is turning into a pity party from hell. Don't feel too bad about Marty and Shari. They knew what they were doing. We're lucky that your little girl was able to control herself that night and not go after either of *them*. I must've been hoarse for a week after yelling at dumb-ass Carl all the way over to their house that night. Still can't believe he set all that up and thought it'd ever *work*. Damn..."

Tommy's face burned as he remembered the horrible state his life had been in when he'd made that call to Carl. Sitting here now, with Melanie's support and Corinne safe in bed, he could scarcely understand how desperate he must've felt back then.

"Hey," he said to his aunt as her phone buzzed with yet another text message.

I really need to get her to turn that damn phone off, he thought.

"Yeah?"

"Got a question for you I've been wondering about for a while. How long did you know Uncle Carl before you let him know you were a—before you let him know what you were really like?"

Melanie gave him a slow grin, all teeth and slitted eyes. "Really like? You mean..." Her voice lowered, and her eyes gleamed at him. "A *werewolf*?"

Tommy rolled his eyes at her attempt to be dramatic and nodded. She took another sip of her drink, ice cubes clinking.

"Who says I told him?"

Tommy stared at her for a long couple of seconds, waiting for her to crack up or look away. Her eyes had lost some of their puffiness, but the redness seemed like it had spread.

"No way. You're messing with me."

"Totally serious." Melanie hadn't even blinked.

Tommy looked away first. She wasn't lying.

"Holy *crap*! How do you hide something like that? I mean, didn't you have to get out and... and... go wolf at some point?'

"I'd tell him I was working late, get a sitter for the boys so he could go drink at the bars. Win-win."

"But... how? Why didn't you?"

"You tell your little girlfriend back home you had it in you?"

Tommy felt his eyes go wide for a second. Then he shook his head. Suzanne's head would've exploded or something.

Melanie just smiled at him with her perfect, white teeth.

"There's a reason we pick up our so-called 'normal' spouses. Or girlfriends. Maybe we sense the kind of people who don't ask questions like that. People who don't look so deeply."

"But Dad knows about Mom, and I guess me, too. So are you saying that he..." Tommy chewed on his bottom lip as

Melanie nodded at him. He was learning all the wrong things about the people in his life, and it was making his head spin.

"So Carl never had a clue?"

"Nope."

Tommy's hand went to his forehead with a slapping sound, and his vision doubled. He felt unexpected tears try to fill his eyes as he remembered her bolting from their car, shedding clothes and growing taller, furrier, more powerful. Fast.

"Oh shit, Melanie. He found out that *night*."

She looked down at her empty glass and nodded.

"Freaked him the hell out. As you might imagine. No way I could explain that night with anything but the truth."

Melanie paused and cocked her head to the side, looking upstairs. Tommy heard it, then, too. One of the boys had cried out in his sleep. She was always listening for them. Always on her toes.

He nodded up at the second floor.

"Do you think Trey has it in him? Tyler doesn't, right?"

Melanie shrugged. "Poor Tyler. He's his dad's boy. That was him, crying out. Bad dreams ever since Carl bailed. I hate it. Need to go check on him soon. But yeah. Tyler's normal, but I'm pretty sure Trey's got it. He just hasn't presented it yet, like your little one was. It usually doesn't come out 'til they're about five or six."

"Unless something triggers it, right?"

Melanie nodded, and Tommy thought about Corinne lying naked on the frozen ground the night Tommy tried to see if she had it in her. Child abuse, really. But he'd just been going on instincts, guessing his way through the darkness with his gift. The family curse.

"How do you *know* all this?" he said at last, dropping both hands to the table in frustration.

"Your great-grandmother. My Gran. She had it in her, brought it over her from Germany along with her mother. It runs strongest through the women in our family, it seems."

"Oh, nice," Tommy said. "What's that say about *me*? Girly man."

Melanie ignored him.

"There's an unspoken rule that the history and insights of the previous generations get passed down from parent to child—sire to pup, you could say. But your mom broke the chain. For whatever reason, she didn't give you the history you needed. Maybe she had her hands full with her work plus two boys and a husband who liked to drink a bit too much. Maybe. But there's a reason Carl and the boys and I didn't come to Dyersburg to visit you much. I was mad at her, and have been mad at her ever since I learned that you had it in you, and found out she wasn't teaching you a damn thing."

Tommy looked down and saw that Melanie had rested a hand on each of his own outstretched hands. Her grip was warm and tight, but he hadn't noticed right away, thinking about chasing Mom through the woods on Westhoff's land, how she taught him to mark his territory and stick to it every month he went running there. How she'd left him on his own after that. Abandoning him, in a way.

"So the whole full-moon thing was just a crock?"

Melanie shrugged. "There's something to every myth, Tommy. The full moon is when we're at the height of our powers, in our wolf bodies. That just can't be explained away—it just is. But you know now that you could've changed whenever you wanted. Not just once a month."

"She was always so sure of herself," Tommy murmured. "Always so damn convincing."

"I can relate. She *is* my older sister, you know."

Tommy wriggled out of Melanie's grasp and stood up. His body felt suddenly tired, but his brain was swirling with too many thoughts at once. Mom and Dad, him and Corinne. Families and bloodlines. Secrets and enemies and lovers.

"I got to get some sleep," he mumbled. "Thanks, Mel. I'd love to hear more, but I'm beat. It's just... a lot to take in."

"I hear you," Melanie said with a smile. As they'd talked, her phone had buzzed a dozen more times, and she finally picked it up. "G'night."

Melanie looked at her phone and—with an apologetic look over at Tommy, who stopped on his way to the steps leading up to his and Corinne's room—began reading the texts they'd been ignoring for the past ten minutes.

"Oh shit," she said with a frustrated growl. "He's really going to try to do this."

Tommy stopped, his hand on the kitchen door. "What?"

"He says he's going to the Iowa City newspaper with what he knows about us. And if that doesn't work, he's going to set up his own website. He wants to tell the world about the werewolves living among his fellow 'normals' like illegal immigrants. Says he'll bring the smack down on all of us, unless I hook him up with some cash."

"What? He can't be serious. Mel, we should—"

Before he could finish, Melanie had gotten up from the table and wrapped him up in a hug.

"Hush. Don't worry about me. I've got my boys and you and Corinne now. We're family, Tommy. We'll take care of each other."

She let go of him and gave him a push that nearly knocked him off-balance.

"Now go wash that pizza smell off you and get some sleep, nephew. I've got a phone call to a drunk man to make."

Chapter Seventeen

In the past two months, Corinne had learned a lot. First it was crawling, now it was shape-shifting.

In the cool, moonlit grass behind Melanie's house, with the moon a day from being full above them, Tommy watched, amazed, as Melanie coaxed his daughter and nephew into changing from their human bodies into wolf form. Tommy was amazed at what you could get a kid to do with the promise of an animal cracker (for Trey) or a spoonful of applesauce (for Corinne).

And the kids made the change look *easy*.

Tommy kept checking to make sure the six-foot-high privacy fence enclosing Melanie's half-acre of backyard was enough to block any curious onlookers that night. But the fence and the line of trees and bushes inside it provided more than enough cover for the crazy activities taking place that night.

Out in the grass, Melanie in her wolf body wrestled with Trey, rolling him around and pinning him to the ground until he got frustrated.

She told him it was okay to get mad.

"But when you get angry," she said, her voice distorted and deep, "control it. Let it make you *strong*."

"Master Yoda," Tommy muttered, thinking about the night a few weeks back, when Trey had wept like a baby the first time the change came over him.

One moment he was a tow-headed five-year-old, all elbows and skinny legs. The next he was a foot taller, covered in light fur, his jaw elongated into a muzzle, his small hands now sleek and tipped with claws. He'd howled and dropped to all fours, reaching madly for his mother after the transformation was complete.

After that, once Trey's young mind understood what his body had known all his life, changing had been easy for him. No more panic, no more tears.

And Corinne had never had an issue with it. What Tommy and Melanie had to do now was control her changes on a minute-by-minute basis—she'd pop into wolf form when she got upset or too hungry or needed her diaper changed. More than once, Tommy had woken from a deep sleep from her cries, only to pick up a small wolf cub from her crib instead of the pink-skinned human child he'd been expecting.

There was a good reason Corinne wasn't going to daycare, and why Tommy had to do all his work at night, after Melanie got home from her job.

"We're going to have to do their training separately," he said as he watched the two young wolves chasing each other around—and up and down—the various trees of the back yard. They looked like a normal pair of dogs at first glance, playing and yipping with each other. Until you looked closer and saw the wolfish features and the eyes that seemed to almost glow, letting you know that these were *no* dogs.

Melanie began shifting out of her wolf form, rising up from all fours to her feet. Face burning, Tommy averted his eyes and went for her pile of clothes on the dew-tipped grass a few feet away. He kept his eyes on the kids as he held Melanie's blouse and jeans—her black panties inside—out to her. He knew he should be used to this by now, and his aunt certainly didn't seem to mind being naked in front of him, but he still felt embarrassed as hell when it happened.

"I know," she growled as she dressed. "He keeps setting her off, and she wants to play with him in her wolf form. She's going to start shifting all the time so she can keep up with the boys, 'cause they're so much bigger than her even in their human form."

"Are there ways to stop the change from happening?" Tommy realized he hadn't changed into wolf form all night, despite the training sessions with the kids. He'd felt distracted tonight, thinking about work and that odd ponytail guy with the apartment full of women.

"Not that I know of," Melanie said, touching a fresh pair of scratches on her arm where one of the kids had gotten her. "Not with someone so young. I could explain why regular people wouldn't understand how they can become a wolf whenever they want to, and Trey would probably get it. But Corinne? No way."

Two sets of paws thundered past as Corinne chased Trey, tiny teeth bared.

She's going to hurt herself, Tommy thought, *the way she's running all out like that. Or worse, she's going to catch Trey and hurt him.*

"We'd better stop them—" he began.

"Just wait. They have to get some of the wildness out of them." Melanie pointed at the fat moon with a long finger. The moonlight gave her skin a bluish tint. "That thing still has a strong pull over our people. Especially our pups here."

Tommy gritted his teeth and nodded. He tried to remember his runs back behind Westhoff's, guided by the white sphere overhead. How long it seemed like between each monthly run.

And I could've just gone whenever I wanted. Go figure.

"Man," Melanie said, watching the kids tear back and forth one more time, yipping with joy. "I really wish Gran was still alive to see this. Then I could cross-examine her, too."

"What do you mean?"

"There's so much I don't know about our past. Like where did the werewolf gene start? Who brought it over to America, and why is it fading on us? I thought for sure, the day I saw your big brother Burt after he was born, that *he'd* have it in him. He's got the look in his eyes, you know?"

"Burt?" Tommy asked. "Are we talking about the same guy? My brother, tall and skinny, glazed-over eyes from smoking too much pot?"

"Come on," Melanie said. "You know there's more to him than that. Burt's a tough son of a bitch. And I mean that literally and figuratively, nephew of mine."

Damn if I don't miss that skinny spaz, he thought, his eyes suddenly sore. *Even if he did always bring trouble with him. I hope he's not messing with those Callahan boys anymore. Surely they've gone back home by now. And the case about their dead brother has to be closed at this point. Couldn't the cops figure out something like that in three months?*

Tommy looked over at Melanie for a moment, and was about to say something else, but he stopped when he heard a hand brush the screen door behind him.

Melanie's oldest, Tyler was standing inside the back door. Ty watched the two cubs with an odd, confused look on his face, as if he still couldn't quite figure all this out, though Melanie had explained it to him more than once.

"Mom?" he said at last. "Isn't it past their bedtimes?"

Melanie was up on the back deck and at the screen door in just a few heartbeats.

"Hey, buddy. Sorry if we bothered you. I thought you were watching a movie in your room."

"It ended," Tyler said.

As Melanie opened the screen door to hug her oldest, Tommy felt something in his throat that made it hard to swallow. Ty was left out of it all, just like Burt.

The night air had turned cold. Tommy rubbed his bare arms and gave one last glance at the yellowish-white moon, so close to being full. It sported a halo tonight, and its brightness blurred and hid the stars around it. He looked for the profile of the face of lady in the moon Mom had shown him all those years ago, when he was about Trey's age, but he never had time to completely make it out.

A high-pitched squeal came from the other end of the yard. The instinctive panic of a parent took hold of Tommy, and he tore across the lawn to the far edge of the fence. Both Corinne and Trey had slipped out of their wolf forms by the time he got there. He was panting and asking over and over what had happened.

"She tried to bite me!" Trey said, hugging his knees and breathing heavily in the moonlight. "So I hit her on the nose."

Tommy stifled the angry growl he felt at the little boy next to him and scooped up Corinne.

Can't get mad at him. Not his fault.

She didn't seem to be hurt. Tommy knew from experience that the kind of blows and injuries that would've clobbered one of them while they were in human form usually only amounted to a bump or a scratch while they were in their wolf shapes. Corinne had a little bit of redness on her perky nose, but neither nostril was bleeding.

"*Don't* bite your cousin," Tommy told Corinne as sternly as he could while she was crying into his shoulder. She was coated in sweat, as was Trey, and Tommy took them both back inside as fast as he could.

"You two are a couple of wild childs," he said with a laugh. His laugh died on his lips, though, when he saw that Melanie and Tyler were already inside, and Ty's bedroom door was closed.

"Let's throw you two in the tub," Tommy said, and waited for the two of them to howl in protest. He didn't have to wait long.

Her name was Nina, and she worked dual roles as a chef and cashier at the Pizza Pit. Tommy had noticed her on his first day of work, with her short dreadlocked hair, piercing brown eyes, and her dark brown skin. He was amazed at the range of people he kept running into here in Iowa City—people of all colors, from all over the world. Back home in Dyersburg, everyone in town was white and familiar. Dull.

But here was a pretty girl his age who had her own look, her own style, and she didn't seem too worried what anyone else thought about it.

She was way out of his league, he knew, but he still found the courage to go up and talk to her anyway. Maybe it was the thought of his little girl last night—scrabbling up and down trees and leaping onto Melanie's back deck as a wolf, when she couldn't even *walk* in her human form—that gave him the courage to say hello and chat with Nina on that quiet Sunday night at the Pit.

"Hey, I got about a dozen more balls of dough made for ya," he said. When deliveries were slow, the pizza guys were expected to pitch in and make dough. "Want me to throw them in the freezer?"

He tried not to wince. As far as opening lines went, those weren't the greatest, but it was a start.

"You're the man," Nina said in a distracted tone, slicing onions and squinting at her spin rack of orders. "Just throw 'em in the fridge, 'kay? Thanks."

Tommy was about to turn on his heel and do just that, but he figured the dough could wait. Nina was holding up an order ticket in her hand and squinting at it.

"Now if I could just read these chicken scratchings so I knew what kind of pie to make outta that dough, I'd be lovin' life right now."

"Mind if I take a look?" Tommy held out a hand.

Nina laughed and gave him the ticket, one eyebrow raised. "Like to see you try. It's worse than a doctor's handwriting. Paul must think he's going to med school someday or something."

Tommy made a big show of turning the ticket this way and that as he read it. He felt Nina watching him, as if this was the first time she'd really seen him, though they'd worked four shifts together already. Luckily, he knew Paul's handwriting pretty well already from all his deliveries in the past two weeks.

"Large, thick-crust, pepperoni, mushrooms, black olives, onions and—ugh—anchovies. A Pit special, pretty much." He looked from the ticket at Nina with a triumphant grin, but the intense way she was gazing at him made his mouth go dry. His heart rate shot up. "Well, except for the anchovies. They're... extra. Right?"

Nina was nodding at him, as if she'd figured him out.

"You're a scholarship guy, aren't you?" She plucked the ticket from his hand and began sprinkling flour onto a large ball of dough. "Football? Surely not basketball. You're tall, but not that tall. And... you're kinda... white. If you don't mind me saying so—" she glanced at his pinned-on badge "—Tom."

The sound of his name in her voice kept some of the bite out of her dismissive words. Tommy felt annoyed, but also curious. It seemed like she was throwing down a challenge. The Tommy of three or four months ago would've backed down and just walked away. Instead he straightened up to his full six foot three, feeling an unfamiliar flush of pride at being thought of as a football player again.

"What, is that some sort of put-down? Being," he held up the first two fingers of both hands to do a pair of annoying air-quotes, "'kinda white'?"

Nina bit back a grin and slapped the ball of dough like she was smacking a baby's ass.

She hadn't expected much push-back, Tommy realized.

"Sorry. That was rude of me. You probably get shit about that a lot, with the blue eyes and blonde hair. Aryan Nation and all that."

Tommy fought the urge to slap the ball of dough himself. This girl was approaching rude, but she kept defusing her words with that sly smile. And by meeting his gaze each time. She had incredible eyes.

"Um, actually, no. *Never.*" He piled on the sarcasm the same way Nina applied the pizza sauce to the circle of flattened dough in front of her.

"Ah," she said with one last flicker of her eyes, lifting up to meet his.

They stood there for an awkward five seconds that seemed to last five minutes.

"So. I better see if Paul needs any pizzas delivered," Tommy said.

Nina nodded. "I'd better get this Pit special with anchovies made."

"Right." He began walking toward the office.

After three steps, he stopped.

"You have to admit you were impressed by my ability to read Paul's scribbling. Not bad for a scholarship kid."

Nina gave him a curious look. She'd already dressed out most of the pizza, her slender hands dancing over the round pie almost faster than Tommy could follow.

"Okay, that's not true—I'm not on any scholarship. I *used* to play football," Tommy added, and the words hurt him more than he could've imagined. "But no, I don't even go to college here. I just needed a job. You know? How 'bout you?"

Nina finished up the pizza and wiped her hands on her apron.

"Ah, I'm a student. And now I feel like a dog. Can I say I'm sorry again?"

Tommy tried not to smile. "Wouldn't hurt."

"I'm sorry, man. I mean, Tom. You just caught me at a bad time. My roommate Danica and I are fighting, and I don't wanna be here tonight, and there's this guy—a jock—who's been harassing me in one of my classes, and..." With both hands she picked up the big wooden spatula holding her uncooked pizza. "And I need to just shut up, right?"

Tommy watched her slide the pizza off the spatula and into one of the ovens with a practiced flick of both wrists.

"Wouldn't hurt," he said again, and then, without being able to help himself, he smiled at her.

To his surprise, Nina smiled back.

Chapter Eighteen

I can hardly feel the strings. But they move my arms and legs, while something else controls my jaw. The words come out in someone else's voice, a person pretending unsuccessfully to sound like me, though the rumbling comes from my own chest. I don't even know what the words are. They're mostly growls, anyway.

The strings pull me out of bed at one a.m. I pass Corinne's crib without even checking on her. Outside in the hallway, I let the change roll over me in the time it takes me to let out a breath. I'm suddenly coated in fur, lean and full of fast-twitch muscle instead of slow-moving flab. I fall forward and pant softly, paws clenching, four legs quivering. I need to run.

Evading the bright street lights and obstacle-littered sidewalks (bikes, garbage cans, discarded pop cans, broken glass), I charge across the front lawns of my new city. My claws dig into the cold dirt under the manicured grass. I give in to the urge to yip as I leap over fences, and night-time dew sprays behind me in tiny clouds.

Though my brain keeps scolding me—*No no no!*—I revel in the wildness and the wrongness and keep running.

I can't even lift my head to look for the moon. It's like I've lost all ability to tell right from wrong. I just run, controlled by the instincts of my ancestors and the power of the blood pounding through my veins.

I do things on that mad dash through the starless, moonless night that disgust me. Small animals, panicked by my fatally silent approach, fall prey to the slashing of my claws. I kill and don't even feed, wasting their lives in my madness. I knock limbs from trees and uproot bushes in my path. I break car windows and knock over mailboxes.

The blood drenching my paws and filling my nose makes me run faster. The houses blur past. I hear distant voices calling my name along with my own tortured breathing.

I ignore it all and just run and kill and run harder. If I stop, I fear my crimes will wash over me and drown me in guilt and retribution.

I turn a corner, silently, lethally, and find myself once more in the clearing on Westhoff's land. Dark trees wave an endless number of empty branches to welcome me.

It's all so familiar it nearly makes me cry out—the dusty scent of the trees and the musky odor of fresh dirt and worms and animal dropping, the cool breeze of night ruffling my fur, the hum of crickets and frogs, and the mad skittering of animals fleeing my approach for a mile in every direction.

Home again, I want to cry out, but my mouth won't cooperate.

Home.

And it's not just me out here.

I should've smelled the intruder five minutes ago, his—not *hers*, definitely a male, and big—his stink is so strong. But I was out of my head from running through the city. Now, out in the country—where I belong—I can function properly.

I smell his breath and his heat now, loud as a fire alarm blaring, but I also inhale the metallic smell of his sickness, too. He's burning up with fever. Sick, maybe even dying.

"Wait," I say, too late.

He charges at me.

In the long, extended second before we collide, I absorb every detail about the other wolf. Long black fur, matted and thick with blood on his left flank; a gray sliver of gravel wedged into his right forepaw along with clumps of black Iowa dirt; eyes red with a madness that seem to set his black coat on fire from his long muzzle to his tail—easily seven and a half feet away from his nose.

I am *dead*, I think, and then he hits me.

Pure impulse takes over.

I roll with the impact, falling onto my back. I kick upwards with my back paws as I drop, keeping his claws away from my neck with my front paws.

I look into those red eyes as he passes over me with a squeal, and I see my own fury and madness reflected back at me. I want to claw out those red eyes.

As he flies away from me, I notice something tearing into my side, but I'm almost completely lost to all thought or memory now. The sudden burning there just knocks loose my last remaining bit of human conscience, and I fall on my attacker.

Kill, a voice screams inside my head.

With blood filling my nostrils and rage coursing through my veins, I am all too open to the suggestion.

I fall on the other wolf and swing one clawed hand after another. The other wolf struggles underneath me, but only for a few more seconds. He just stares up at me, fur receding, his wolf body shrinking towards his original, weaker human form.

I have to stop. I *must* stop.

But I can't, because the red light of his eyes refuses to go out, though, no matter how hard I swing. No matter that his fur is gone, and just a ruined human body remains, crisscrossed in bloodied wounds.

Because whoever's pulling my strings like this—they won't *let* me stop.

Tommy woke with what felt like every muscle of his body locked up tight. For a bad couple of seconds, he couldn't even breathe, and he felt like his nightmare about losing the power over his own body had simply continued.

The nightmare. He'd been running like a maniac, and attacking... something. Mercilessly. Pretty awful.

Then he heard Corinne sigh in her sleep and fidget in her crib ten feet away, and he was able to relax and suck in a shuddering breath.

Haven't had one of those in a while, he thought, letting go of the pillow he'd nearly strangled to death. *I saw red eyes and everything.*

Dropping his head back onto his pillow, Tommy exhaled.

Just a dream. Doesn't mean anything.

Before he lost consciousness and dropped into a black, dreamless sleep, Tommy shuddered one last time. He had a bad, bad feeling that he'd *forgotten* something about that night in the clearing four months—four full moons—ago. Something crucial. Like a clue.

But he had no idea what it was. And a few seconds later he was asleep again, running no more, free of dreams.

So, Tommy thought the following night, *this is where my life has taken me.*

He sat at a table in a tiny Indian restaurant in Iowa City, a smile still stuck to his face—maybe permanently—after watching Nina excuse herself and walk around the seven other tables to the bathroom.

I did this. I made this happen.

He and Nina had worked two more shifts together after their first awkward chat on Sunday, and Tommy kept finding reasons to stop by her spot in the kitchen. Their conversations jumped all over the place, and they always left him thinking. He usually had one more thing to add to it later, after running through all the concepts and questions and never-ending challenges to the way he used to think as he delivered a pizza or mixed up yet another ball of dough.

And that topic would lead to another—from college life and roommates, to race relations and politics, to families and their own personal histories. They had quite a bit of time to talk after eight or nine on Monday and Tuesday, after the supper rush ended.

Last night, Tommy dropped the Corinne bombshell on Nina, and to his shock, it didn't blow up in his face.

"Okay," she'd said, instead of the shocked "Really?" or the disappointed "Oh, I see" he'd been expecting—his usual responses. The way Nina said okay had immediately untangled the bundle of nerves Tommy had felt bunching up in his neck and shoulders. She just *accepted* it, like the fact that he was white and chunky, or that she was black and curvy.

"I know it's kind of... different," he said, feeling the need to keep explaining despite her response. "But I live with my aunt now, and she helps out a lot with watching her at night while I'm working. It's tough at times, but it's working out, and—"

"It's *okay*," Nina said, and the smile she hit him with nearly knocked Tommy back a step. She'd smiled before at him, but never like this. Nina's smile made her look like someone who figured out the trick ending to a movie ten minutes before the end. She also seemed relieved, somehow.

"That was the thing I was trying to figure out about you, Tom. What made you different from other guys our age. You've been through it, haven't you? Having a kid will do that to you."

Tommy leaned on the metal table next to the oven. His legs felt suddenly weak for some reason.

"How do you know? Do you have—"

"No. No no no. No kids for me. Not yet. But my younger sister, though, back in Chicago. She has a two-year-old boy. Cute as can be, but quite a handful."

Nina set down the pizza cutter she'd been wielding over the piping hot triple pepperoni and onion pizza in front of her.

"Dude, don't look so *relieved!*"

Tommy felt a weird urge to simply start laughing out loud. At least that would keep him from crying like a freaking baby in front of this stunning girl. He'd never told anyone else about Corinne and gotten a reaction like this. She made him feel like he hadn't just mucked up his entire life for a change. Usually, after telling someone, the other person acted like they had to go do something else, fast, instead of actually stopping to talk to him about it.

So they'd discussed babies and kids and responsibilities, until Paul came out of his office with folders and receipts in his hands to yell at them about the smell of burning pizzas.

At the end of their shift, Tommy heard the words leave his mouth, though he never could've imagined saying them a week ago.

"Nina," he said. "We should go out for dinner sometime. So long as it's not pizza."

Nina nodded, as if his suggestion was perfectly logical and hadn't made his heart pound like a machine gun.

"I know this awesome Indian restaurant," she said. "You off work tomorrow night?"

Tommy could only grin and nod. He was afraid if he opened up his mouth to speak, he'd just start babbling.

And now, a day later, as he carefully picked at his eye-wateringly spicy masala chicken at the Indian restaurant, waiting for Nina to come back to continue their conversations, Tommy still could barely believe it.

"I'm awake," he whispered, just to hear the sound of his own voice. It still didn't make it any more real. But he could live with this feeling of lightness and bliss.

A flash of dark blue caught his eye—Nina on her way back, threading her way around the closely packed tables of couples lit by candlelight. Heads turned as the tall girl with the short dreadlocks and the dark blue sweater and black tights passed by each table. Tommy caught his breath when she caught his eye. Nina was smiling and shaking her head.

"What?" Tommy said, grinning at the sight of her smile.

"You'll never guess who I bumped into in the ladies' room."

"Hillary Clinton," Tommy said immediately. "Asking for some advice from you about the problems of the world, no doubt."

"Ah, nice. You know how to flatter a girl. But... no. It was one of the girls from the basketball team. Shelvia. We had a Rhetoric class together my freshman year."

"She taller than me?"

"Don't feel all threatened, Mr. Football. You may have an inch or two on her. She's a sister. Very nice."

Tommy paused, wondering if he should risk the good mood of the night by asking naive, small-town-Iowa-kid questions. Then he forged ahead with it anyway. So far he hadn't done any lasting damage with his curiosity.

"Did you really just call her a sister?"

Nina's eyes narrowed for an instant, and Tommy wanted to pull his words back out of the air.

"Yeah," she said slowly, eyebrows raised. "Black people tend to stand out a bit here in Iowa, you know. We have to stick together. Even if we're not best buds and all—I mean, I know her name, but I've never gone out dancing or drinking with her or anything." She pushed back her glass of water. "Why do you ask?"

"I just..." Tommy began, his face hot. He looked at her eyes, which blazed with intensity and maybe anger. He couldn't tell for sure. "I just wanted to know."

"Tommy Roling," Nina said with another look on her face like she'd solved another puzzle. Tommy wasn't as crazy about that look right now as he wriggled like a worm on a hook in her gaze. "Tommy—am I the *first* black person you've ever been friends with?"

He shrugged, and then nodded, feeling ashamed.

"I can't help where I grew up. It's a little town, and everyone there's white. Everyone's the same."

Except for my family, he thought.

"More or less," he added.

Nina squeezed his hand, making him lift up his chin so he could look at her again. She smiled at him, but he couldn't see any condescension or pity there. She kept her hand on his hand, her small, strong fingers hooked onto his fingers.

In his jeans pocket, Tommy's phone buzzed against his upper thigh.

"It's all right," she said. "I'm the only black person in this restaurant, now that Shelvia and her friends are gone. You just notice those kinds of things."

After three buzzes, his phone went silent. He was glad he'd switched it over to vibrate mode before his date. No way was he going to answer his phone right now.

"I bet you didn't even notice that," Nina continued. "But I also bet you didn't notice some of the older people in here giving us the evil eye, did you?"

"There are other people in this restaurant?" Tommy said with complete honesty.

Nina laughed so loud she had to clap a hand over her mouth. Tommy was glad it was the other hand, and not the one still holding onto his.

"This was a good idea, Tommy," Nina said as she sipped some water.

He nodded his head vigorously at that, feeling a thrill pass through him.

This is all happening so fast, he thought.

Tommy's phone buzzed again. He made no move to answer it, though a sliver of worry began to prick at his blissfulness.

What if something was wrong with Corinne? I can't leave the table to check voicemail now. I can have a date and not worry about being a dad for an hour or two, can't I?

They both sipped their water and fiddled with their napkins for a few more seconds. The pause was awkward, but not as bad as any of the awkward pauses he'd felt on any of his first few dates with Suzanne. *This* date just kept going in new directions, and he didn't want it to end. Even if all their food was gone, and their waiter was hovering over them, ready to pounce with the bill.

"Hey," Tommy said, thinking back over the tangents of their most recent conversation until he reached the origin. "Wonder if your buddy—Shelvia, right?—knows that chick magnet guy who orders all the pizzas? The one over at Hawkeye Apartments. I could swear that all the girls he has over are athletes—they're all fit and..." He trailed off as Nina squeezed his hand. "I mean. They *eat* like athletes—like it was a competition."

"Right," Nina said. "All the delivery guys talk about him. Guess they think he's living out their dreams, with all those different girls at his place every night. Shelvia never told me that he's a manager for a couple different women's sports. All the girls think he's the bomb. I don't get it—everyone always says he's just this skinny dude with a ponytail. I mean, does he look like a movie star or something?"

Tommy shook his head.

"No. He does have this voice that's sort of strange. Kinda hypnotic. But you should see the girls with him. It's like they're a bunch of guys, really. Playing video games, shouting, drinking. And eating the pizza like they were a bunch of starving—"

Tommy stopped himself. He was about to say "animals." But that didn't feel right. That felt insulting. There had to be more to it than that.

Nina didn't seem to notice. She was fiddling with her empty glass of water.

"Wish I could deliver pizzas, too, so I could see that. But it's against company policies. Stupid old-fashioned rules. I can take care of myself, you know. For a girl."

"Oh really?" Tommy said. He felt a tingle of protectiveness for her pass over his skin. "I wouldn't want my daughter doing that—too many weirdos out there. Predators. You know?"

Nina paused and looked at him a long time before speaking. Her head was turned to one side, just like Melanie did while they were running. Tommy felt his heart skip a beat once, then twice.

"What'd I say?" he said in a soft voice. "I'm just old-fashioned, I guess—"

Nina shook her head, her brown eyes still locked on his in a way that, once more, made his brain freeze.

"I *know* about you, you know," she whispered. "I called my mom last night. She knows your aunt—they went to school together here. Turns out your aunt called my mom a few weeks ago, and then my mom called me. They wanted to know if we needed help at the Pit. I didn't put it all together right away."

"Great," Tommy said, both hands now squeezed into fists on the table. "Melanie made it sound like I got the job on my own. But she just... pulled some strings."

"I don't know about that," Nina said, resting a warm hand on each of his numb fisted hands. "Just relax a second. I have something I want to tell you."

For the third time that night, Tommy's cell phone vibrated against his leg. Even though Nina was sitting just a few feet away from him, leaning towards him, mouth poised to say whatever it is she had to say, Tommy caved in to his own weakness.

"Ah, man, Nina. I'm sorry," he muttered, face turning hot. "But I have to get this. I'm worried it's something with Corinne. My little girl."

Extricating his hands from Nina's surprisingly strong grip was one the hardest things he'd ever done in weeks.

"I thought I heard your phone buzzing earlier," Nina said, giving him a hard-to-read smile. She looked disappointed. "That's fine."

I am such a dick, he thought, afraid to look across the table. *I bailed on her to answer my phone, as if I couldn't handle what she was about to tell me.*

He groaned internally when he saw the caller ID, wanting to punch himself in the face for not being able to control himself. And for not being able to cut the apron strings that connected him to a tiny town, eighty miles away.

"It's my mom," he said to Nina, hitting the Answer button. "Which means it has to be bad news."

Chapter Nineteen

As soon as he lifted his phone to his ears and gave one last glance at the prettiest girl he'd ever met, Tommy knew that his date with her was ruined. Nina sat watching him silently, arms folded across her chest, an inscrutable look on her face.

"Hello," he muttered into his cell, rubbing his eyes.

"Tommy," Mom said into his ear. No *Hello*, no *How are you and the baby*? Just dropping his name in that dead tone of voice that made his back stiffen. "I have some bad news for you."

"*Mom*," Tommy said with a final apologetic look at Nina. She was pulling her coat over her dark blue sweater and motioning for the waiter. "Can't this wait? I'm sort of in the middle of... something here."

"No, this can't wait. I'm calling from the hospital. There's been an attack."

Tommy almost dropped the phone. The red eyes from last night's dream flashed to the surface of his memory. Followed by the Callahan brothers jumping him.

"What?"

"An *accident*. Your dad and I were in an accident."

"What happened? Are you okay?"

Nina's eyes locked on Tommy's now. He felt like the rope in a tug of war.

"We'll be fine," Mom said after a pause, dragging it out to torture him, Tommy figured. He stared at the crumbs and bits of sauce on the tablecloth in front of him, where his plate of spicy Indian food once sat—food he'd never had anything like before in his life.

He didn't dare look up at Nina. He could almost smell her anger, mixed in with her perfume. Like burning roses.

"Was it a car wreck, or what?"

"Dad got into a fight downtown. Arguing about something with a stranger. I tried to help out, break it up when they went outside, and that made it all worse. That guy had friends waiting. The cops are trying to find the guys who did it—some out-of-town guys, young guys, cocky as hell. Came at us from out of nowhere. Dad has a couple busted ribs, and I broke three fingers on my right hand."

"A bar fight? Really, Mom? Not an accident, then?"

At the way Nina recoiled at his words—she couldn't help but overhear his side of the conversation—Tommy immediately wished he could take them back.

"Tommy," Mom said, the command in her voice making him jump. "We need you back home. Now."

Her words made his stomach fill with acid.

Home? Go back there, after all this time away? I'm not ready.

Across the table from him, Nina mouthed the words "Are you okay?"

The restaurant had mostly cleared out now, with just two other tables left with diners, along with the two waiters and the hostess watching them from the front, ready to close the place down.

After a long pause, with a wave of claustrophobia that made his breath come in shorter and shorter bursts, Tommy nodded at Nina.

He felt a tickle in his nose as someone in the restaurant's kitchen dumped some bleach into a bucket. He heard the waiters muttering to each other in their native language. The hair on his arms stiffened, like dog fur. All his senses were going into overdrive.

He smiled at Nina, hoping that would reassure her that things weren't as bad as they sounded.

"Why? What's going *on*, Mom?"

"Some things I can't talk about on the phone or in an email or a text. And you *know* what I'm talking about, Tommy."

So this, Tommy thought, *is what a dog feels like when it's being called.* Come. Now.

Already plotting out a plan to get back to Dyersburg that night, he wiped cold sweat from his forehead, hoping Nina hadn't noticed it there before now.

"I'll be there as soon as I can. Should I go to our house or to the hospital?"

Nina winced again.

What a complete bomb of a date for her, Tommy thought.

"Our house," Mom said, sounding distracted now. "Okay, they're almost done with us here. Come soon." Her voice went lower, softer. "And don't tell Melanie a goddamn word about this."

The phone went dead in his hand. Tommy stared at the tiny rectangular screen for a second, and then he killed the phone. He paid the bill with a wad of ones from his pizza-delivery money and walked Nina to the door, afraid to say anything until they got outside. He heard a girl at one of the tables whispering the word "black," but he couldn't make out the rest of the words. His nose now felt clogged up.

Outside, the cold wind slapped them both in the face, one last reminder that winter wasn't completely done with them yet. The narrow side street was quiet, and he wanted to take Nina's hand as they crossed it to his car. Instead, he kept both hands tight in his coat pockets.

"Nina, I'm really sorry," he said as he unlocked the passenger door to his car. "I shouldn't have answered the phone like that. Wasn't thinking."

She nodded without a word. He closed the door behind her and hurried over to his side, cussing out himself and his crazy family with each step.

"Everyone okay?" Nina said after he'd dropped into the driver's seat. "I mean, you said the H-word. Hospital."

Tommy felt a wave of shame wash over him from out of nowhere.

Dad's not the kind of guy who gets in a fight when he's drinking. He was friends with everyone when he was getting his drink on. Mom wasn't telling me the whole story. As usual.

"My parents were in some kind of—" he was about to say *attack*, which Mom had first called it, but then she changed it to "—accident. She wouldn't give me any more details. So I need to go back home tonight and make sure everything's okay, see if I can help out, somehow. Sounds like it's a big mess."

Nina nodded and glanced out her window. Students bundled in heavy jackets passed by, lugging their backpacks and leaning into the wind. Everyone headed back to their dorms and apartment after a night of studying. A normal night for them. The end of the semester was probably coming soon—it was almost May.

"Don't they live like an hour and a half away?"

"Yep."

"You won't get there until midnight, if you leave now."

"I know."

His phone started buzzing in his pocket again.

No way am I answering it again.

But the buzzing stopped after one short vibration: a text. Tommy fought the urge to drive faster through the narrow roads of campus. His ears rang with a strange echoing sound.

"I don't suppose," he said, glancing over at Nina, who was still looking out the window, "that you want to pick up where we left off, before the phone call? You were going to tell me something, right?"

Nina sighed, looking down at her hands. She wore a glittering ring with a ruby on the first finger of her left hand, and bronze bracelet wrapped around her right wrist. She set her hands on her knees, as if admiring her clear nail polish.

"It's nothing," she said. "I was just... talking. You probably noticed I tend to go on and on at times."

"Well," Tommy said, waiting for a pair of students to pass in front of them in the crosswalk. He risked a glance at her face. "It seemed kind of important."

Nina shrugged, meeting his eyes. She still wore the same hard-to-read look on her face as the one she wore at the table, when Tommy first grabbed his cell.

Just as he was about to follow Nina down that line of conversation and do some damage control for this date gone wrong, his phone buzzed again. He didn't dare answer it. He sighed in frustration and watched his breath plume out in front of him.

Nobody ever wants to talk to me until it's too late. Or an emergency.

The next three blocks passed by in an awkward silence. In front of the entrance to her dorm, Tommy put the car in park.

"Thanks," Nina said, already pulling open her door. "I had a pretty good time tonight. Sorry about the bad news about your folks."

"Nina, wait—"

"No, you have to get on the road. I understand. My family's had their share of drama, too. Just go, and be safe, okay?"

Nina was out of the car before he could respond. His phone buzzed again as she crossed in front of his idling car.

"Damn it anyway."

With a growl, Tommy fished the phone from his jeans. Instead of beating it to pieces against the steering while like he wanted, he looked down at the screen.

A three-word text from Burt: *Call me bro.*

Tommy stared at the words.

I should just go home now. Forget going to Melanie's. She'll have to take care of Corinne for a day or two. I'll make it up to both of them later.

"Tommy," Nina called from next to his closed car window. She was tapping on the glass, but he hadn't heard her until that moment. He rolled down the window, letting the cold night air snap him out of his reverie.

"Oh man," he said, fighting the urge to get out of the car. "I'm sorry. About everything. This didn't end the way it should've, Nina."

"It's okay. I just wanted to say—Well. Just... *call* me sometime."

"I will. Wait," he said.

I'm screwing this up all over again.

"Let me at least walk you in."

"I got it," Nina said, patting his hand and then prodding it back toward the steering wheel. "You need to go. Take care of your people."

And with that, she maneuvered around the hood of the car and hurried up the sidewalk, the wind at her back. He could still smell her perfume in his car, and he rolled up the window to trap the scent inside as long as he could.

Might be a while before I see her again. I don't want to forget a thing.

When Tommy looked back out his window to look at Nina, she'd already disappeared. After searching, unsuccessfully, for a last glimpse of her outside the five-story brick dorm, Tommy gave up.

He put his car in gear and tried pulling away. But his hands were shaking too badly. That disappointed look on Nina's face still burned into him, like a scar forming on the inside of his skin.

I didn't let her in. I didn't let her help.

He closed his eyes and rested his head on the cool, unforgiving steering wheel.

But she wouldn't understand any of this. Would she?

When he finally opened his eyes and pulled away from the curb, Tommy lifted up his phone again. He needed to call Melanie.

The hell with what Mom said, he thought. *I'm telling Aunt Mel* everything.

But as soon as he opened up his phone, it buzzed again. It was Burt, calling him this time instead of texting.

The last person I want to talk to tonight. Well, other than Mom, that is.

He waited for the call to go to voicemail, where he had five other messages waiting for him, and then he called Melanie.

"I'm going with you," Melanie said as soon as she answered, in a way that made Tommy nearly swerve off the one-way road he was on. Somehow she already knew what was up. Burt had gotten through to her, no doubt.

"Mel—"

"I won't let you go there alone. Not with all that's going on up there."

Driving away from campus and over the narrow bridge over the river, Tommy kept telling her that he couldn't ask her to come along, that she'd done too much for him already, that this was *his* problem.

"*No*," Melanie said at last, her voice cold as the late-winter air outside, "you're wrong. If it affects anyone in our family, it affects me. All of us. We're blood, Tommy. I'm going, and so are my boys. And Corinne, too. You can't split up the family. Never break up the pack. You got me?"

"Let's talk about this face-to-face. I'm almost at your place. Is Corinne—"

"Bye," Melanie said, hanging up before he could finish asking about his daughter.

"Great."

Tommy tossed his phone into the passenger seat, which had just minutes ago been taken up with Nina's presence. The car was way too cold and empty without her there.

"This night is full of suck," he muttered, crossing over the Iowa River and rolling into the quiet neighborhood where Melanie lived. Half the houses were already dark, while those with lights on were bathed in a warm, golden light. Tommy felt jealous of these people, safe and happy in their houses, free of the wildness that coursed through his veins. Normal people. The *lucky* ones.

He came to a stop in front of Melanie's house, where only the kitchen light in the back was on. From the corner of his eye, Tommy saw a flash of crimson.

"Son of bitch," he hissed.

Waiting in the darkness of Melanie's front porch were two wolves, flanking a tall, thin young man with skin so pale it glowed in the moonlight.

Burt, Tommy realized, hurrying out of his car so fast he forgot to shut off the engine. And the Wolf Brothers. Tommy could hear the tick of their pickup's engine, farther up Melanie's driveway—they'd just gotten here, too.

The two wolves, easily five feet high despite the fact that they had dropped to all fours, quickly closed the distance between Tommy and Burt, snarling and shaking long lines of drool from their fanged mouths.

Blonde fur sprouted down his arms and the rest of his body. A thousand smells filled his nose—sweat, Indian food, motor oil, bird shit, carrion, and, most of all, musky fur. The world shrank down as he grew taller.

Wish I had a baseball bat, he thought. *But I'll do what I need to without it.*

Chapter Twenty

Tommy *wanted* this fight. In his head, he'd been prepping for a fight with one or both of the Callahan brothers on a daily basis since the night he met them.

Just try *to stop me,* he thought, clothes dropping off his frame as he went from human and upright to wolf and all fours. He steeled himself for the collision of the Callahan wolves as they prepared to leap.

But the impact never happened. Something *else* got to him first.

A blinding white light filled his head, throwing him to the cold, wet ground. Searing pain tore at his eyes and filling his ears, clogging his nostrils. The sound was like a thousand jet engines roaring over him.

And then it stopped.

Tommy rolled to his knees, blinking hard until his vision cleared. He was naked and furless, just like the two burly Callahan brothers on the sidewalk next to him. As he gathered up his clothes, he tried not to stare at the scars carved into the arms, backs, and legs of the other two werewolves.

Burt tossed a duffel bag of clothes down to the brothers and held up a small silver whistle.

"Sorry to pull that on you guys," he said with a wicked smile, blinking fast. He didn't seem too apologetic to Tommy's eyes. "But we don't have time for that shit."

Melanie's front door opened just as the three of them in the yard had gotten their pants back on. Tommy had never been more glad for the big oaks in Mel's yard than he was at that moment.

"Let's go," she said, pushing open the screen door with her hip. She carried Corinne in her car seat in one hand and held the hand of a very sleepy-looking Trey with the other. Tyler was right behind her.

"You're seriously not taking these kids there, are you?" Mark said, pulling his sweatshirt back over his head.

"No way, Mel," Tommy said. He pushed past the grumbling Callahan brothers and reached for Corinne.

Melanie growled at him, her face darkening so fast Tommy retracted his hand as if he'd been stung.

"Remember what I said. You don't break up the pack. They're going to need all of us there, from the sound of it."

"Mel," Tommy said. "What's going on back home? Mom barely told me anything."

She nodded at Burt. "He knows. He can explain on the drive back. If we stay here much longer, it might be too late for us to do anything."

"Well, I'm taking Corinne with me in my car," Tommy said. He needed to find something he could do on his own, without being told what to do.

"Of course," Melanie said. "I don't have enough room in my car for three car seats, anyway."

Tommy took the handle of Corinne's car seat and swung it over to his car. He'd just gotten it strapped in with the seat belt when Burt got in the passenger side, and Luke Callahan slid in behind the driver's seat. The car bounced on its wheels as he dropped like a pile of rocks into the back seat.

"Just wanna keep you company," Luke said with a toothy grin.

"No." Tommy turned around in his seat, knocking his head against the roof. "You're riding shotgun up here, where I can see you."

"Don't start that shi—"

"Luke," Burt said. He brandished the whistle again, stopping the Callahan brother in his tracks. "Let's switch seats. Now. And don't slam the door and upset the baby, either."

"This is such bullshit," Luke muttered as he pushed his way out of the back seat. Like a little kid, he stomped around the rear of the car, and dropped into passenger seat.

"Happy now?" he said to Tommy, eyes blazing.

"Frickin' ecstatic," Tommy said, and then grinned. "Don't forget your seatbelt."

As his passengers got situated, Tommy checked on Melanie, but she'd already gotten her boys strapped in. She sat in her car, waiting on him. The roar of Mark Callahan starting up his truck behind them shattered the cool, quiet night.

Then the small caravan pulled away from Melanie's house, headed for parts north and east.

Tommy exhaled, hoping he'd be back in the city again, soon. This house felt more like home than anywhere else right now.

*W*aning, Tommy thought ten minutes later as he peered at the deep black sky, salted with stars and what looked like a shrunken moon. *The moon was waning.*

He checked his rearview and—to his relief—saw Corinne in her seat behind him, dozing away as the clock approached eleven. And the headlights of Melanie's Volvo glowed behind him like two giant white fireflies. Mark, on the other hand, had roared past in his truck and quickly disappeared ahead of them as soon as they got out of Iowa City.

The next time he glanced into the mirror, he met the gaze of his brother, lit up with the oncoming headlights of the highway outside of Iowa City.

"Tommy-boy," Burt began. Tommy shot him a dirty look in his rearview. "Sorry. Tom. Man, you have to understand how bad things have gotten back home. The town's all messed up. Like Baghdad, man."

"More like Afghanistan, really," Luke said with a chuckle next to Tommy. "But with fewer roadside bombs. And more predators."

Corinne sniffed loudly at his sharp voice, but didn't wake. Tommy shook his head slowly.

"Wait. Before you get going on Dyersburg—tell me about that whistle you used on us, and where you got it. And then tell me why I shouldn't confiscate that damn thing from you right now."

"Oh," Burt said with a nervous chuckle. "You noticed that, huh?

"Hard not to," Luke said with a snort. "About made Tommy-boy here cry like a baby."

"Come on, Burt." Tommy gripped the steering wheel harder and ignored Luke. "Spill."

"I picked it up at a sports shop. Dog whistle. With some, ah, enhancements. More of a coyote whistle. I needed it after all that's gone down in the past few weeks. You don't know, Tom. I've been trying to get in touch with you, but you don't respond to emails or texts or phone calls. You don't respond to anything. Well," Burt added with a chuckle, "except for that whistle, I guess."

"Very funny," Tommy said. The pounding of his car's tires on the two-lane road made the tension in his body grow with each passing mile. "So you need that whistle, huh? Are you saying there are *wolves* in town? More than just Frick and Frack here, visiting from up north?"

"I've seen a couple at night the past few weeks. Never really get a good look at them. They keep to the shadows and all that."

"You sure it's not just Luke and Mark messing with you?"

"Dude—" Luke began, slapping the dash.

"No—" Burt said at the same time from behind Tommy. "These are... different. They're smaller, and faster. More like real wolves."

Luke growled at that, making Corinne shift and moan softly in the back seat.

"And you don't know what these wolves are up to?"

Burt shrugged. "I have my theories."

Tommy shook his head. He felt himself getting pulled into the drama back home all over again.

"So you think Dad got into a bar fight with someone you think is really a wolf?"

"Is *that* what Mom said happened?" Burt said, looking at Luke again. "A bar fight?"

Tommy tried to catch Burt's expression in the back seat, but couldn't pin him down in his rearview mirror.

Corinne sniffed loudly in her sleep, then exhaled with a low growl.

"It was an *ambush*," Luke said in a low voice, all teasing gone from his deep voice. "Town's been crawling with these people claiming to be tourists, coming to see your big, fancy church."

"The basilica," Burt said, but Luke talked right over him.

"It's like its centennial or anniversary or something. Anyway. About half a dozen of them were waiting outside the Side Entrance for your mom and dad today, just as it got dark. Good thing half the town was there to break it up. 'Course, Smith and his cop crew were nowhere to be found until *after* they took your folks to the ER."

"I don't get it," Tommy said. "Dad doesn't get into fights. He's a happy drunk."

Luke laughed at that. "I think they thought your dad was—you know. One of us. The bad shit's only starting, guys. Trust me on this."

Tommy sighed. "Okay," he said, looking in his rearview again. "Tell me what I've missed from the start. Just *you*, Burt," he said with a glance at Luke next to him. "No interruptions."

People," Burt began, "have been talking in town for over a year now. Some of us," he said, sniffing with exaggerated pride, "keep an eye on things in town. We don't go through the day with our head down, just getting by."

"Okay, all right," Tommy said. "Some of us are responsible for other people besides just ourselves, too. Some of us have to act like adults, even if we don't wanna."

Luke sighed loudly in the shotgun seat.

"I think I'm gonna puke here from all this family therapy. Got a burp cloth or a bucket or something?"

Just trying to get under my skin, Tommy told himself. *Ignore him.*

"So people are talking in town," he prompted Burt, "and this all started before the strangers starting coming around, right?"

"Yeah. And these so-called town leaders have a couple of families they decided they needed to watch a bit more closely. People who've been acting a bit... different in recent years. Guess which family's name came up?"

"The Roling family, right?" Tommy squinted at a flash of red up ahead of them. Brake lights, probably. "Just get on with it, man. Quit dragging it out."

"Well," Burt continued, "they never mentioned us by name while I was around. But I knew it came up. What you're not gonna believe are the other names. People I thought were normal. The Schnellings, Jaegers, Kleins, Hoerners, and old man Lucas. Along with the suspicious Roling clan."

As Burt rattled off the names of people Tommy had known all his life, with kids he'd gone to school with for a dozen years, he found himself thinking about Nina.

Her smell was gone from the car now, pushed out by the collision of Burt's smoky aura and Luke's sweat and aftershave, along with Corinne's unmistakable smell underneath it all. Tommy wished she were still here, even if the story Burt was unfolding at his slow-ass pace would've driven her away for good.

If she's not already gone, that is. That hurt look in Nina's eyes was going to stick with me for a long, long time.

"Did you talk to your people in town about the wolves, then?" Tommy asked to try to get that image out of his head. "And the dead guy from back in January?"

"*Matthew*," Luke murmured. "That's his name."

"Matthew's death was just the start," Burt said. "In the past couple of weeks, three people from town went missing—Lisa Schnelling, Bill Hoerner, and his brother Steve. People claim that Lisa's been out of town with a sick relative, and that Bill's just on another bender over in East Dubuque. Bullshit. 'Cause someone slashed up Steve really bad two days ago. Mom told me Steve didn't make it. Died yesterday afternoon."

"What?" Tommy's foot came up off the accelerator instinctively, and everyone rocked forward. Corinne let out another annoyed squeak.

"How come I never heard about any of this on the news? It had to be wolves, right?"

"Quit slowing *down*, man," Luke rumbled, and Corinne sniffed loudly.

"Smith claimed it was a farming accident," Burt continued. "Power takeoff. More lies. Most people don't even know about Steve yet. The word on the street is that all the missing folks are on vacation somewhere. I tell you, people will believe any story so long as it doesn't muck with their cozy little lives."

"I still can't believe that—"

"Smith's got a pretty tight lock on town," Burt said, "and he's buds with old man Schindler and the guys at the paper, so nothing's making it into the news without his say-so. He learned his lesson back in January, with all the press and media coming to town for Matthew. Smith doesn't like that negative attention on his town."

"And the cops haven't figured out anything more about Matthew and—" he swallowed hard, seeing red lights flash in his vision from the darkness all around them, "and how he died?"

Luke exhaled next to him hard enough for Tommy to smell his beery breath. Burt continued with his story, shaking his head in answer to Tommy's questions.

"Matthew was just the first to get caught up in this. Mark and Luke tracked him here to try to figure out why here, and why Matthew."

Tommy's mind flashed on the faded remnants of last night's dream. How he'd lost control and fell on the other wolf. Slashing until there was just a dead shell—a human shell—left on the cold ground.

Tommy shivered. He wanted to lean forward, out of the reach of Luke's long arms, but his car wasn't big enough. That shell of a wolf had been Matthew Callahan. He knew that now.

"Can't figure out what made him come to your dinky little town," Luke said. Corinne took a shuddering breath and squeaked in response to his deep, grating voice. "But we know now it wasn't a woman, like Mark thought it was at first. Pretty sure it wasn't Matt's choice either, coming here. And now we're pretty sure something is drawing other people here, too. Your town's like a damn magnet for us wolves."

"But wait. Hadn't you guys been to town before?" Tommy glanced into his rearview once more and caught Burt's confused look. "Big Krunch said you were friends of the family the night I met you. Or am I not remembering that, thanks to the punches to the head you and your bro gave me that night?"

Tommy relaxed a bit when he looked over and saw the hint of a smile in Luke's dark eyes.

"Big Krunch is our uncle, though he hates claiming us. Through marriage, not blood—his first marriage, to our aunt, which I guess lasted less than a year. He bailed as soon as he found out Aunt Janie had a werewolf for a sister—our mom. All three of us boys came here once to visit for a couple days when we were kids. But we never met anyone here or did much. I think Big ol' Krunch was embarrassed by us, the wild nephews from his past."

"Really?" Burt said from the back seat. Obviously this was all news to him.

"So there's a connection for you," Tommy said. "Maybe Matthew knew something about town. Or some*one*. Like maybe Big Krunch introduced him to one of those 'strange' families, like maybe sweet old, dangerous Mrs. Jaeger and her rabbits next door to Krunch's house. And he was coming back to see them or something. He didn't say anything to you before he left? I mean, was there something bad going on with your brother before he came here?"

Luke's silence was the answer to both of Tommy's questions.

Corinne gave a soft groan. Tommy knew that sound. She'd be waking up soon, hungry, and he hadn't packed a bottle or any snacks for her. Didn't even pack a diaper bag. Good planning, Tommy-boy.

And here I am, bringing her into what was looking like a big shitstorm.

They turned onto X47, less than ten miles from Highway 20 and home. Through the windshield, the night sky opened up with the crazy panorama of stars that Tommy had missed in his three months away in Iowa City. You could almost see the dust of the Milky Way up there, with no city lights to obstruct the view. Tommy felt small and insignificant underneath all those other stars and hidden worlds.

"So," he said as the last few miles melted away under the tires of his Grand Am. "Who *can* we trust in town?"

"Give him the roster, Burt. Show him we haven't been farting around the whole time he's been off in the big city, acting like Joe College."

"There's Mom and Dad, and Big Krunch and his family, of course. Livy, the owner of the Side Entrance. She knows everyone too, including the people who don't go to church. Mom said she was gonna get in touch real soon with the other families on the list—the Hoerners, the Jaegers, the Schnellings, the Kleins. Even crazy old Mr. Lucas. Pretty sure at least one person in each family is a wolf."

"That's just... crazy," Tommy said.

"I know. We've been steering clear of Smith and the rest of the cops. They've covered up any news about the missing people and Steve's death, so who knows what else they're hiding from us. Probably some of the folks at the hospital are in on the cover-ups too, since they tried to save Steve there. And the cops have been hinting very strongly that Mark and Luke should be heading back home, soon."

Luke growled loudly at that, and that was the last straw for Corinne.

Like an engine revving up, her cry started low, then turned into to full-fledged scream within three seconds.

"Jesus," Luke said as Corinne kept right on screaming. "Can you shut her up?"

"She's hungry," Tommy spat, fighting the urge to reach over and slap Luke upside the head. "And tired. You woke her up, talking so loud, dumb ass."

And I don't even have a pacifier with me, Tommy thought as he rolled through the stop sign for Highway 20.

His pulse was racing, and he felt sweat tickling at his hairline. Her angry crying always made him a bit crazy. He pressed down on the gas pedal and shot out onto the highway.

"So freakin' *loud*," Luke groaned.

"Relax, we're almost there," he said, and then flashing red lights filled his rearview mirror.

A police car. Where the hell did *that* come from? The road had been deserted ever since they turned onto it, with no sign of Mark's loud-ass truck anywhere ahead of them. At least Corinne's screaming had stopped.

"Ah *shit*," Burt said. "We got a problem back here, guys."

"I know," Tommy said, not moving his foot off the gas just yet. "I see him."

"No, man, it's Corinne."

Tommy hit the brakes and grabbed the rearview mirror. He felt like his spicy Indian food was going to eat a hole in him as he tried to locate Corinne in her seat.

"What's wrong?" he said, but he knew the answer as soon as he spoke. Corinne's earthy and sweet smell now flooded the interior of the car, and as the car decelerated, Tommy could also detect the musky scent of fur. A soft, high-pitched growl echoed in his ears.

"Oh, shit," he whispered.

Red light bounced off the windows and windshield as they pulled over onto the gravel shoulder of Highway Twenty, no more than half a mile from the Westhoff farm. In that swirling glow, Tommy caught a glimpse of Corinne in the back seat with his rearview. A pair of small, furry paws waved madly in the air, tipped with tiny razor claws. Pressed up tight against his door, Burt didn't dare try and grab her.

She'd gotten herself so worked up that she'd changed into her wolf form. Tommy could sense a howl building in her little body.

And the town cop's cruiser just rolled to a stop twenty feet behind them, cherries flashing.

"Hey, man," Luke whispered in a raspy voice, looking at the chaos in the back seat, his face lit up red as a cardinal's. "Welcome home."

Chapter Twenty-One

Y ou know," Luke said a moment later, "we're gonna have to kill him."

He sounded like the idea appealed to him.

"Shut up, man!" Burt said over Corinne's growling. "Just stay cool."

"We'll have to do it, if she don't turn back now," Luke's voice grew deeper and rougher with each word. "Just give me the word, and it's done. Tired of Smith's crap, anyway."

"Calm *down*," Tommy said to his three passengers. His voice was sharp, but under control. Even the animal noises of his transformed daughter dropped a few notches in volume.

"I'll take care of this," he said. "Corinne, it's okay, baby. I'll be right back."

Tommy watched in his side mirror as Smith the cop stepped out of his cruiser. He wore a smile on his bearded face that didn't come close to touching his eyes. Not good. Tommy put the car in Park and reached for his door handle. Just before opening the door, he flicked off the interior light.

"*Tom*," Burt said, grabbing for him from behind, but Tommy had already opened the door and set his foot on the highway.

Smith stopped at that, his right hand automatically dropping onto the gun in his holster. He stood with one foot on the empty highway and the other on the gravel shoulder like a Wild West sheriff in the middle of a dirt street.

"Shit," Burt said right before Tommy closed the car door behind him.

High frickin' noon, Tommy thought. The cold wind took his breath away, and the tall grass in the ditch next to the highway rustled and swayed like waves.

Tommy concentrated on the steady thump of his pulse inside his ears and the muffled sounds his little girl was making in the car next to him. He made himself relax, despite the policeman staring him down, hand on his gun. He inhaled and, despite the wind, caught a calming series of scents from his own clothes—first Corinne's smell, then the fainter whiff of Nina's perfume.

He took three strides toward Smith, determined to keep him away from the car and the certain death waiting for him in the front seat.

"Hey Mr. Smith," Tommy called. "Heard there was some trouble today in town."

Smith hadn't come any closer, but his face was tight with anger, and something else. Maybe surprise, maybe uncertainty. Smith's cruiser was empty, and Tommy wondered if he'd called in some backup.

"Tommy-boy," Smith said, stepping forward again. "That you? Barely recognized ya. Look, just get back in your car. I'll come talk to you. Okay?"

No, it's not *okay. Not with Luke Callahan in there, ready to rip out your throat, and my werewolf daughter behind him.*

Tommy stood at the rear bumper of his car, cool wind drying the sweat on his now-hot brow. He moved a foot or two to the left to try and block any strange activity that might be visible inside.

"We really need to get home to see my folks, Mister Smith. I'm in a bit of a hurry. Can you just let us go on into town? You know I won't cause trouble. I just heard my mom and dad got into some kind of fight downtown today."

"They called you home for that? Heard you were down in Iowa City these past few months. People been wondering about you and your little girl."

I'm sure they have, Tommy thought, but he just nodded at Smith.

Out of the corner of his eyes he saw a familiar pair of headlights approaching. Melanie's car, carrying her and her two boys. Tommy hoped she'd keep right on going instead of stopping and making this worse.

Inside the car, Corinne gave a loud screech that turned Tommy's skin to gooseflesh. He risked a look down at his hands and saw—just for an instant—a fine covering of fur sprouting over his fingers and the backs of both hands. If you didn't know what to look for, you never would've seen it.

Calm down, he thought, aiming his words both at himself and his little girl. She just screeched louder.

"Guess who didn't like getting brought out in the cold and woken up," he said to Smith, with what he hoped was a fittingly sheepish grin.

"Little one ought to be in bed," Smith said, eyes going dead like they had the last time he'd pulled over Tommy. "I keep running into you two late at night. And who else you got into the car? Burt? Up to no good, I'll bet."

Tommy fought down the urge to leap at Smith and break the wrist of the man's hand resting on his gun. Smith was just toying with him right now. Cat and mouse. Boar and wolf.

As Melanie's car approached, headlights cutting through the dark, Smith stepped off the highway and motioned with his jaw at Tommy's car.

"Go sit back in your car, nice and slow," he said. "I'll be right there. Tell your brother and whoever else is in there to stay calm and not make any sudden motions. I'll keep this short for your sake, and your baby's."

Tommy stepped backward two steps until his left hand hit the cold metal handle of the driver's door.

Hope I stalled long enough.

He gave what he hoped was a calming nod as Melanie's car rushed past. He exhaled when she kept going, never once setting off her brake lights.

His exhalation was cut off when a strange feeling filled his head, making his eardrums throb like tiny balloons blown up too far. His eyes watered and his head spun, just for a split second, and he tried to cover up his moment of confusion by pulling on his car door.

He dropped into the driver's seat, and instead of the crying and howling he'd expected from Corinne, the car was strangely silent.

In the red glow of the cruiser's flashing lights, Luke was holding both hands to his head, while Burt in the back seat slipped something small and silver from his lips.

And next to Burt, Corinne gazed up in her mirror at Tommy, tears staining her hairless cheeks, her breath hitching and ragged.

The wolf whistle. Burt had blown it, just in time.

"Good job, bro," Tommy whispered. Corinne hiccuped behind them, and then gave a soft giggle.

He caught Burt's relieved grin next to her, and then he had to crank down his window to deal with Smith.

The cop stood a good three feet from the side of Tommy's car, and Corinne whimpered at the cool air blowing in from Tommy's open window.

"Your interior light not working?" Smith said.

"Nah, it's been acting up."

"Try the switch for me. Just humor me, huh?"

Tommy flicked the switch and white light filled his car's interior.

"Hey, fixed," he said with a grin.

Smith looked over at Luke, then Burt and Corinne in the back. He stepped forward at last.

"Right. Well, you didn't come to a full stop back there, you know, getting off X47. And you were going five miles over the limit after that."

"Oh. Okay," Tommy said, wanting to kick himself for not being more careful. Though Smith probably would've found another reason to pull him if needed.

Smith hunkered down to look Tommy in the eyes, hands on his knees.

"Look, son. You ain't been around here for a while. I stopped you for your own good, really. Some folks in town have been doing some rabble-rousing. Asking questions and looking for trouble. Might be that's what happened to your folks this afternoon at the Side Entrance. Not saying they *started* nothing. Just saying we got some new people 'round here, out-of-towners visiting, and they need to be treated with care. God knows this town could use the money from tourists. But in the end, there's only so much my men and I can do to protect you. If you cross 'em."

"What do you mean?" Tommy said. "You guys are the *cops*."

Smith's dark eyes went dead again, his face clear of all emotion.

"Some things we can't stop, once they start rolling. Your mom and dad learned that today. Bigger things are going on here, things you guys couldn't understand. I'm just doing my job, trying to keep the people safe who deserve to be kept safe. Don't make my job harder, like your folks did tonight."

"You've got to be kid—" Luke began, but Tommy elbowed him hard enough in the gut to send him recoiling back into his seat.

Smith's in over his head, Tommy realized. *He doesn't really know what's going on either. He's in total panic mode, and this is how he handles it—putting the whole town under lock and key. And blaming the people from town if they screw up the balance.*

"Just keep your nose clean," Smith continued, "and your eyes open. Give me a call if you see anything strange. I'll take care of it."

"Yes, sir," he said to Smith.

Smith nodded at that. He snapped his little notebook shut and headed back to his cruiser.

"Not even a ticket," Burt muttered. "Lucky."

"Let's just get out of here and get home," Tommy said. He reached back to check the buckles for Corinne's car seat. "She all strapped in, Burt?"

"Yeah. Let's go. Smith sure as hell isn't going to do anything. He as much as admitted that. Chickenshit."

Tommy flicked on his left blinker and got into the turn lane heading into town. He let out a small sigh as Smith's cruiser continued on down the highway.

"I dunno," he said as they entered town. He drove up the hill and past the familiar white and beige houses toward Mom and Dad's place. "I think he might be doing all he's able to do. Smith was never the brightest bulb in the pack."

"Pack," Luke said with a humorless chuckle. "Smith's never been in no damn pack. That's for sure."

"Burt," Tommy said, mouth suddenly dry as they made the last turn toward home. The driveway was empty, and only one light was on, in the kitchen. All the blinds were closed up tight. "Where are they? They said they'd be home."

"I thought so too, but—"

"Stop the car," Luke snapped, grabbing Tommy's right shoulder and squeezing hard. "Now!"

Tommy touched the brake as Luke's hand slipped off his shoulder. "What's wrong?"

Luke opened the back door, flooding the car with light.

"*Wolf*," Luke said in a guttural voice.

His door slammed shut, making Corinne cry out. And then, with a clatter of claws on pavement, Luke disappeared into the night.

Chapter Twenty-Two

Should I blow my whistle?"

Tommy jumped. With his car idling in the middle of the road behind him, he'd been staring hard into the shadows between the houses in front of him, trying to locate Luke in his wolf skin. The big guy had disappeared in a heartbeat, and it felt too convenient. Tommy hadn't registered his brother coming up behind him.

"No," he whispered. Instead of feeling comfortable back home, he felt exposed in the place where he'd lived most of his life. Like he was being watched.

"No," he repeated, checking on Corinne back in the car. She poked her head out of her car seat as high as she could, blue eyes wide. "That whistle might do more damage than good. And it'll draw way too much attention. Just keep it tucked away for now. But not *too* far away, you know?"

"Good. That thing gives me a nasty headache whenever I blow it. So. Shouldn't one of us go after him and try to help?"

Meaning me, of course, Tommy thought. *No way was skinny little normal Burt ever going to catch a fully changed wolf like Luke.*

"No," Tommy said. He looked over at Mom and Dad's empty driveway. "I've got to get Corinne somewhere safe. Luke can handle himself. We need to get home. If anyone's there. Not sure what happened to Melanie and Mark, either. Maybe Smith scared them off, too."

Once they were both back in the car, Tommy flicked off the headlights and drove as quietly as he could up to the big white house where he and Burt had grown up. The empty driveway and the lone light in the front window gave off a feeble glow that made the house seem abandoned.

He checked the time on his dashboard clock. Almost midnight, so it made sense that everyone would be asleep.

But Mom had demanded I come here tonight. The least she could've done was be there, waiting for me.

"Let's go in back," Burt said, "to the basement."

"Um, okay," Tommy said as he unlatched Corinne's car seat from the back. The cool night air seemed to have calmed her down in the past few minutes, though her round cheeks were still wet with tears. She smiled up at him and waved a pink hand in his direction.

Tommy dried her cheeks and followed Burt down the hill into the back yard. He felt a kid again, sneaking back into the house after running around all night with his little friends. Except this time he had his baby in his arms.

When Burt's key rattled in the lock to the sliding door leading into the basement, an explosion of noise erupted from the other side of the door. The heavy shades inside opened up a crack, and a pair of red-rimmed eyes, one almost swollen shut, peeked out.

Dad.

Tommy and Burt passed through the sliding door into the brightly lit basement, and the transition was like going from night to day. Some kind of party was going on, but without any music or laughter. At least a dozen people sat in a circle around the cracked fireplace of their big lounge room. People started talking and calling out Tommy and Corinne's names as soon as they walked inside.

Dad, with his black eye and swollen lip, slapped Tommy on the back and gave Burt a thumbs-up, while Mom grabbed Corinne out of her car seat without saying a word to her two sons.

Hello to you, too, Mom, Tommy thought, shaking his head at her.

Tommy recognized old man Lucas next to Dad's scratched-up bar, sipping a can of Coors Light and nodding at him. Three of the four Schnellings were next to him, along with Mr. and Mrs. Hoerner, plus Marv Klein and his wife and their grown daughter Kim. Big Krunch and Little Krunch sat next to the empty chairs where Mom and Dad had been sitting.

"Just in time for the show," Dad said, nodding at the big guy in the black cap perched by the computer table with his back to the room.

The image on the flatscreen monitor caught Tommy's eye, and he turned away from the crowd to see more.

At the top of the screen was a graphic of a wolf's head with a red circle around it, and a diagonal line cutting the circle— and the wild-eyed, furry face—in two. Below it was a grainy, YouTube-style video of someone chasing... *something* in the dark. Tommy could almost make out a figure, running low to the ground. Tommy crept closer to the screen, just as a flash of orange light shot across the image.

A flamethrower? No way.

He heard tinny laughter from the computer speakers even as the small figure on the wrong end of the burst of fire howled out in pain. That had to be a wolf.

"This some kind of faked video some kid put together on his laptop?"

Someone snorted next to him. Tommy pulled his gaze away from the screen and realized that the person at the computer next to him was Mark Callahan.

Somehow Luke's older brother had gotten himself invited to Mom and Dad's meeting.

Who knew how fast he'd been motoring to get here so far ahead of us from Iowa City. Crazy bastard.

"Antiwolf dot com," Mark said as he finished typing, not once looking over at Tommy. "About time you got here, slow-ass. Been here for about half an hour now, entertaining the locals with this."

"Messing with their heads is more like—" Tommy began.

"Hey," Mark interrupted. He'd finally peeled his gaze from the monitor, where the video kept running in a loop. The scuffle of someone running, the flash of fire, the sharp laugh and the pained whimpering. "What the hell. Where's my brother?"

"Chasing down a wolf," Burt said, stepping up next to Luke. That killed all conversation in the basement. Tommy felt everyone behind them lean forward, listening intently. Even Corinne was quiet.

"And you just *let* him go off on his own like that?"

Mark stood up, ready to head outside after his brother.

"He didn't give us any option," Tommy said.

"I have to go after him—"

"Wait!" Tommy said at the same time as Mom. He winced.

"Finish telling us about this website," Mom said, giving Tommy a cool look, "before you go off all half-cocked. We've been waiting all night for this. Come on."

"Yeah," Burt said, watching the grainy movie again. "Is this thing for real?"

"It's for real," Mark said, still standing. "Unfortunately. Word's spreading about us, somehow."

"*Us?*" Tommy said.

Skin prickling, Tommy looked around at the other people in the room. Mom and Dad stood a few feet behind him, while the rest of their neighbors remained sitting in the metal folding chairs spread around the room in a horseshoe shape. Nobody was saying boo, but most of them were smiling at him like he was slow.

"Looks like," Mom said with a steely look in her eye, "we weren't the only family with the werewolf gene, after all. How about that?"

Now that he knew, Tommy could tell which members of the gathered families had it in them. Something about the eyes and the way they sat—the tension in their shoulders. He could pretty much *smell* the difference in them, too, if he only took the time to give them a quick sniff with his wolf nose.

Old man Lucas was one, for sure (he had it in his eyes, and he'd always smelled like wet dog). Big Krunch and Little Krunch, definitely not (they had the same slumped shoulders and fogged-over look to their eyes as Dad). Yes to Mr. Schnelling and his son Larry, both seething with rage over their missing daughter and sister Lisa, but not his trembling and pale wife Amber. Sharp-eyed Judy Hoerner had to be, but chubby Dexter Hoerner? Not. A big no to Merv, but yeah to Debby and Kim Klein.

"He's getting it now," crowed old man Lucas as he crunched up his beer can and grabbed another from inside his coat. "Thought I'd seen someone running out at Westhoff's a year ago while I was out hunting squirrels. Light-colored fur."

Damn, Tommy thought. So that was half a dozen other wolves from town that Mom had hidden from us. *People who could've helped make things a little easier on me growing up. What had she been thinking?*

"I know, it's messed up," Burt said next to him in a soft voice.

"This site lists everyone in this room," Mark said. "Plus people from my hometown up in Minnesota. Don't know where they got this information, or why they felt the need to post it, unless they just want to make people turn against us. I mean, who's gonna take this shit seriously?"

Tommy let out a slow, shaky breath.

I'm taking this shit very *seriously right now, thank you very much.*

Tommy wanted to melt back into the shadows, but everyone was looking at him again, as if waiting for him to tell them what to do next. He could feel Mark tense up next to him, probably mad at getting upstaged again. Mark stalked off to the window to look outside, most likely for signs of his little brother.

"We interrupted your secret meeting," Tommy said, and then realized something. "Is that why there aren't any cars out front? Were you trying to make sure nobody knew you were all getting together?"

Mom pretended to be too busy fussing over Corinne to look Tommy in the eye and answer him. With a chink of ice cubes

Dad took a sip of his drink—whiskey and 7UP, no doubt—and nodded at the screen.

"This is the first time we've all gotten together like this," he said, touching his swollen eye. "But after today, we knew no one was safe, thanks to this damn website. They know where we live, 'cause of this site. It has the addresses and names of people that—" Dad gulped the rest of his drink " — are wolves."

A chorus of low growls answered Dad. Tommy felt the hair on the back of his neck stiffen at first, but then he found himself relaxing.

I'm not alone in this. I have others like me. Not a pack, but close enough.

He couldn't shake the feeling, though, that someone was missing. And not just Lisa Schnelling and the two Hoerner brothers.

Mark came back to the computer from where he'd been looking out the window, as if trying to force his brother back here through sheer force of will.

"Like I said before, all the families in this room are listed on the site," he said. "Someone in the know is trying to get us all outed as weres. Or, more likely, killed."

More growls from around the room.

"Some of us already lost someone, you know." That was Dexter Hoerner. "The doc wouldn't let us see him, but Tammy here saw his... his, ah. Steve's body."

Mom nodded, face tight.

"I'm so sorry, Dexter and Judy," she said. "I hated to have to tell you that. But you needed to know. Smith and the doctors wanted to cover it up. All of it. They're all in on the same damn scheme. Told me we couldn't let the media pick up the story."

"Don't forget Mrs. Jaeger," Linus Schnelling said in a dead voice, "and how the cops found her last week. Pieces of her, that is. Fucking animals."

Tommy fought the urge to snap his fingers. Mrs. Jaeger— she was the one he'd been trying to remember. Burt had mentioned her as one of the wolves on their drive back here. She was a wolf, too? Guess you had to be tough to teach middle school as long as she did before she retired.

The rest of the crowd was quiet now, and Linus' harsh words hung in the air like thunderclouds. Everyone in the room was hurting in some way, and they were scared and angry. That was easy enough to smell in this enclosed space.

"So," Tommy said, unable to stand the silence any longer. "How did the guy running the website know about us?"

"I think I know the answer to that," a familiar voice said. Melanie stepped up from next to the stairs leading up to the main floor. Ty and Trey clung to her as she moved closer to the front of the room. Tommy felt a rush of relief at her presence.

"*Melanie*," Mom said. "Who let you in my house?" She turned on Tommy. "Didn't I tell you not to tell her about this, Tommy-boy?"

Melanie gave Mom a cool smile and just shook her head, as if to say, "Not now, Sis." She looked out at the other families in the basement as if she were addressing a jury at her day job.

"I have a soon-to-be-ex-husband," she began, "who didn't find out about my, ah, werewolf condition, until quite recently. Let's say he didn't take it well. Anyway. He's been trying to blackmail me for a couple months now. I'm Melanie Heying, by the way," she continued, "and these are my boys Tyler and Trey. I'm Tammy's sister. And I think my ex Carl set up this damn website to get back at me. Knowing him, he got carried away with outing other people as well. I am so sorry..."

As everyone in the room stared at Melanie with a mix of shock, anger, and disbelief, Tommy saw Mark tense up next to him. An instant later, he sensed it too. He smelled someone approaching outside. Someone big.

"*Luke*," Mark spat, and then he was out the back door in a rush of dark fur.

"Let's go," Tommy told Burt as he rushed through the room to get to the sliding door. Mom and Dad's faces, along with a dozen others, flashed past him. "And bring your wolf whistle, bro!"

A s it turned out, no wolf whistle was needed. Luke came walking back across Mom and Dad's dark back lawn, limping a bit, but intact. He'd already switched back into human form, and his pale white skin, slick with sweat, caught the waning moonlight, making him glow slightly. Tommy sucked in his breath when he saw the two long scratches running across Luke's left leg.

I should've gone with him, he thought. *I let him go off on his own, into what could've been an ambush.*

A sharp, almost sweet smell struck Tommy as Luke trudged up the low sloping backyard in the dark. Apparently unbothered by the fact that he was naked, Luke waved at the crowd now standing on Mom and Dad's back patio. The smell came from the furry object Luke was dragging by its legs behind him. It looked like a dead gray dog. A *big* gray dog.

Mark tossed his younger brother his sweatshirt, which Luke caught with one hand and held over his crotch. But he never let go of the hind legs of the lifeless creature gripped tight in his other big hand.

As Luke came into the light coming out of the sliding door, grinning with pride at his catch, he nodded at Tommy.

"Thanks for the *backup*, partner," he growled, slightly out of breath. "Now let's get our friend inside before any of your normal neighbors get a good look at her."

Unconscious growls rolled out of the mouths of the wolf families standing on the patio as Tommy picked up the other end of the dead wolf—*this was no dog*, he realized soon enough—and carried it inside.

Melanie had already grabbed some towels from the downstairs bathroom, Tommy and Luke dropped the wolf onto them in the middle of the room. The wolf was big, about five feet from nose tip to tail, but she didn't have the thickness of a Callahan, or even a Roling. Tommy remembered his mom being much bigger and longer than this gray with the three big gashes down her side. Her muzzle was also beat up, with bone showing in a couple of places where Luke must've hit her, hard.

"Come on, get back in here!" Mark shouted at Burt and Dad, who were still lingering outside. Probably looking for more wolves or other predators.

At last everyone else was back inside, the sliding door was shut, and the blinds were drawn. Melanie had gathered up her boys as well as Corinne, and she was in the process of leading them down the hall to the spare bedroom there.

Tommy mouthed the word "Thanks" at her. She nodded back at him, and then she had to focus all her attention on the three overtired children in her care, two of whom were yowling like angry little dogs. They wanted to see the wolf, just like the rest of them. But Melanie herded them away with an experienced hand.

"So," Luke said, looking up at his older brother while he strategically wrapped the sweatshirt around his naked waist. Mom had already slapped a couple bandages onto Luke's leg. "You know what kind of wolf this is, don't you, Mark?"

From the middle of the room came a low wheeze.

Tommy sucked in a breath tasting of blood and bile. The gray wolf wasn't dead after all.

He had a sudden urge to hunt down a leash and collar for the creature, but it was obvious the wolf was too badly injured to even attempt getting up. The smell of approaching death made him think of the expensive tile floors of Carl's unlucky friends, Martin and Shari.

Mark stood in front of the screen still set to the anti-wolf website, his face dark as he looked down at the dying wolf. The red of the site's logo matched the blood seeping onto Mom's old towel from the injured wolf's side.

"This is a pure-breed were," Mark said, creeping closer toward the wolf sprawled on the floor. She was breathing shallowly, just once every ten seconds or so. "An offspring of two weres, which means no human blood ever touched her genetic line. And my guess is, since she hasn't reverted back to human form at this stage, she's one of those who's forgotten how to *go* back." Mark went to one knee in front of the wolf, but kept a safe distance from her glistening white claws. "She's all wolf now."

Tommy stared at the wolf, watching the gray-furred skin over her ribs ripple slowly with each ragged breath she took.

How could I be related to something as wild as that?

Mom pushed past Dad and Burt and hunkered down next to Mark. Luke tried to pull her back, but she slapped his hand away with a sharp smack. Her face was red, a shade Tommy knew all too well from his hell-raising days. Mom was pissed.

"But she can still *talk*, can't she?" Mom said in a whisper that made Tommy glad she wasn't aiming that question at him. "That's what I heard. She's got a lot to answer for. Can you make her talk?"

"Yep," Mark said, pulling out a pair of heavy winter gloves and flipping open a metal cigarette lighter. With the thick gloves on his hands, he had to crank the wheel three times before he could make a flame. "But it's not gonna be pretty."

Chapter Twenty-Three

Tommy couldn't get the stink of burnt flesh out of his nose. It felt permanently embedded in there, like a bloodstain or a tattoo. At first, when Mark started trying to get the wolf to talk, the smell was accompanied by a couple of thoughts that were just as horrible as the smell.

What if we've got the wrong wolf? What if she hadn't done anything other than try to eavesdrop on Mom and Dad's secret meeting? Or worse, what if she wasn't a female werewolf at all, but an actual wolf, wandering in from the woods on the other side of Highway Twenty?

At first, the wolf had tried not to talk at all. Then, in a thick, clotted voice, she started to speak. She claimed to be a lost soul, looking for her pack, which had migrated from their home, "innn zzuh norfff," she'd claimed. *In the north.*

"Right," Mark had said. "Why the hell would you come here?"

"Lost. Looking for... my pack."

Linus Schnelling dropped onto the floor next to Mark, tired of waiting.

"What did you animals do to my daughter? I know you took her. If you've hurt her like the others, I'll kill all of you." He reached for Mark's lighter, but Mark gently but firmly pushed him away. "Tell us where my Lisa is!"

The she-wolf started to laugh, and kept on laughing even as Tommy heard the flick of the lighter and smelled the whiff of fire. She stopped laughing.

"No," she said, in a voice that was smoother, less rough. More human-sounding. "Don't... burn..."

"I don't want to do this," Mark said.

"I'll do it then," Linus said, holding out his hand for the lighter.

Luke moved in from next to Tommy to take Linus by the shoulder and pull him away from the wolf.

Tommy looked around the room and felt sickened at the way everyone else was leaning forward, eager looks on their faces. They looked *hungry*. Old man Lucas had slipped into his wolf form—a majestic gray-white beast hunkered down on all fours, panting with his pink tongue dangling out. Even the non-wolves looked like animals.

"Okay," Mark said, flicking the lighter until a flame emerged. "Let's talk, then."

After ten minutes, two scorched front paws, and what looked like five pints of blood soaking into Mom's old towels, the she-wolf admitted that she wasn't a lone wolf, nor was she lost. She had shrunk, somehow, and her fur had thinned. She looked less wolf-like and more human. Which made it all even worse.

"Came here," she said, voice raspy and weak, but more clear, "to find... new blood. Our line... dying. Inbred."

"Why'd you kill my son?" Dexter Hoerner said, holding onto his wife Judy's now-furry neck as she changed in front of Tommy's eyes. "And where's my other boy? What'd you do to Bill?"

Linus Schnelling made a thick-bodied brown wolf with coal-black eyes. He hovered inches from the she-wolf's unmoving hindquarters, front paw poised as if aching to disembowel her.

"Want my daughter back," he said in voice that rumbled like an avalanche. "Dirty animals."

"Quiet!" Mark said, black fur sprouting all over him. With a grunt he stopped his own change and went back to the wolf sprawled on the floor next to him. He took off his winter gloves and touched her twitching, almost fur-less face.

"You're pure-breeds. Bet you heard about us on this damn website, didn't you?"

"Don't... burn..."

The she-wolf had lost almost all her fur now, turning back into human form. She was probably in her thirties, her skin pale under her thinning gray fur. Her jaw was broken and torn from Luke's attack. Mark moved the bloody towel to cover her nakedness and her gaping wounds. He didn't bother trying to hide her still-smoking hands.

"Just want... to live... carry on... our... line..."

Mark tossed the lighter to Tommy and shook his head.

"Goddamn pure-breeds. Don't care who you hurt or kill to get what you want."

"What do you mean?" Linus said as he started shifting back into human form as well.

Tommy shuddered as he fingered the lighter in his hand. It was still hot.

We're all wild creatures, deep down, living out each day by our instincts. Not thinking, just reacting. Trying to survive one day more...

"I think Lisa's safe," he said, surprising himself and everyone else in the room by his words. "I think they have her, yeah. She's definitely not on some kind of vacation like dipshit Smith claims. I think this wolf's pack wants to make her part of their family. They need," he stopped and swallowed, realizing he was about to say too much. He had a sudden urge to go check on Corinne.

Mark nodded at Tommy to continue.

"They need *babies*," Tommy said. "That's why they're here."

The arguments, shouting, and tears had lasted for a good hour after Tommy spoke his theory out loud. He wasn't even sure he was right about any of it at first, but the more he thought about it, the more it made sense. He felt bad for Kim Klein, especially, because she and missing Lisa Schnelling were about the same age as him. The right age for breeding.

Finally, exhaustion and the approaching dawn led the families to gather up their coats and shoes and head home at last. Mom had offered to put everyone up for the rest of the night, but nobody took her up on it. They all left, walking silently off into the early-morning dark, shaken by all they'd heard that night.

At a quarter to five, then, it was down to just the family— Tommy, Burt, Mom, Dad, and Melanie. They all sat in a circle around where the she-wolf had been lying on the floor.

Tommy had never seen anyone die. Even if she wasn't fully human. He never wanted to see it again.

When she died, she had reverted back to her wolf form. Tommy was glad for that—it made her death less horrific, somehow. Mark and Luke were outside now, hiding her in Dad's flatbed trailer in the back yard. They didn't even seem bothered by the fact that they were carrying a dead body. Said they'd take care of this, that they knew what they were doing, they'd done this sort of thing before.

"This is all so fucked up," Tommy murmured at last.

"Tommy," Mom said. "Language."

Tommy looked at Dad and then Burt. "Really? After all that happened? I'm supposed to watch my cussing? Don't you think we have more to worry about than that? Luke Callahan just killed her, and his brother tortured her before she died, and we let them do it. Don't you see anything wrong with that?"

Dad rubbed the side of his bruised face as he pushed open the sliding door a few inches to let in some fresh air.

"You don't understand," Dad said. "You ain't been around here the past few months. Those boys are on the up-and-up."

Mom saw her opening. "They've been trying to put things right ever since their brother got killed here. They didn't cut and run, like *some* people."

Tommy held his face steady, determined not to take her bait. Mom and Dad never knew what really happened that night in that fancy house outside Iowa City, and why he'd had to get away from Dyersburg. He needed to keep them in the dark.

Dad looked over at Mom, as if seeking permission from her to continue.

"You didn't see what they did to Steve. Your mom told me his parents barely recognized him. I don't even wanna think about what they did to poor Mrs. Jaeger. She'd been there so long in her house, dead, all torn up, that—"

"That's enough," Mom said. She held up the cast on her right hand. She'd done a good job of keeping it hidden from him until now. "They wouldn't have shown us any mercy yesterday outside the Side Entrance, Tommy-boy. And now thanks to Mel's sleazy husband, their job of tracking us all down just got way easier."

"I don't claim him anymore," Aunt Melanie said in a low voice. She gave Mom another dark look. "And why can't you heal yourself, Nurse Wolf?"

Mom slid her hand out of the plastic cast that went halfway up her forearm. A ragged half-circle had been removed from the meaty part of her hand, right below her right pinky.

"Just waiting for *this* to grow back. Not much I can do in my wolf shape about missing parts except wait. Hope I gave that four-legged shit-eater indigestion after he ate that bit of me."

"Did they say anything when they attacked you?" Tommy said. His stomach lurched at the sight of the bite hole in his mother's hand. "Give you any reason for what they were doing?"

"They were drunk," Dad said.

"We all were," Mom said. "Some of us more than others," she added, with a meaningful look at Dad. "I thought it was all a big joke, this young guy with the big-ass beard harassing your dad, trying to get him to arm-wrestle him at the bar, giving me the eye, anything to get him to go outside and start a fight. Then when Dad went out with him, he suddenly had five buddies out there. Only two of them were in their human shape."

"In the middle of the day?" Tommy asked.

"It was about six. Maybe six thirty."

"Damn," Tommy said. "You guys started drinking early. On a *Wednesday*."

"I'm ignoring that," Mom said. "They were pushing us, trying to get us to show our true form, if you know what I mean. They thought Dad was the wolf in the family. Guess I showed them."

Tommy watched Mom and Dad as she told the story. He could tell whenever Mom stretched the truth and Dad knew it, because Dad would squirm and stare down at his drink or his hands while she told the lie. But he sat next to her now, not moving a muscle, brow furrowed and eyes dark.

It really happened like that. No wonder they didn't have much sympathy for the dead she-wolf wrapped in the tarp and lying in Dad's trailer like a downed tree.

Mom gave him a hard smile.

"Starting to understand how truly messed up this situation is now, Tommy-boy?"

"Okay!" Burt said. "Let's just chill. Tommy's back, and we're all in this together."

The sliding door opened with a whisper, and Mark and Luke crept inside, faces flushed red from the cold and their unsavory labors.

"Done," Luke said. Back in his original clothes again, which were ripped at most of their seams, he sat on the couch next to Mark and leaned his head back against the wall. Within five seconds, Luke was snoring. Mark propped his chin on his fist and listened in with heavy-lidded eyes.

"We need a plan," Burt said. "First we need to get rid of the werewolf corpse out there. That's gonna attract all the wrong attention. I think we should take it to Westhoff's land and bury it a good ten feet down."

"Ah, man," Tommy said, hating to soil the land that he'd always think of as his territory. But he couldn't argue with the logic. Nobody would find the body there. "I guess. I'll see if the Callahan boys can help me do that later today. Damn."

Tommy looked over to make sure that was okay with Mark, but he was asleep as well.

"Good boy," Mom said. Melanie rolled her eyes next to her. Tommy looked down at the empty space in the middle of the floor, where a tiny drop of blood was turning black.

"By the time you boys get back from that," Mom said, "we should have everything cleaned up and locked down here, in case any more wolves decide to drop by. Then we need to start looking for our missing persons. I have a feeling in my gut that Lisa Schnelling's still alive. And I feel 50-50 about Bill. He was always a tough, wiry little sonofabitch. Not a soft and fat drunk like his older brother."

"Jeez, Mom," Burt said with a nervous laugh. "Tell us how you really think."

"No," Aunt Mel said. "None of us want to hear *that*." She stood up. "I'm gonna go check on the kids. And then I'm going to call that bastard Carl until he answers. I'll get that website of his shut down if it kills me. Then I'm sleeping 'til noon."

"Thanks, Mel," Tommy said, ignoring Mom's glare.

"We should all get some rest," Dad said. He stood up with a groan, then helped Mom up off the floor. "Go take care of your little one, Tommy. We'll hold down the fort and keep things safe while you rest."

Tommy wanted to do a double-take to make sure this was the same Dad he remembered from a few months ago—the guy who Tommy wouldn't dare leave his infant daughter with for more than a few minutes on his own. Now Dad was acting like he could fight off a werewolf invasion on his own.

As he trudged back to his old room in the basement, Tommy shook his head. Everything tonight felt like a dream, a bad one that had started off so perfectly with his date with Nina.

How could this have even been the same night?

He sniffed his shirt, but he couldn't find a trace of her scent anywhere.

I really could've used a kiss goodnight from her. Or a kiss goodbye.

He checked the time on his phone—6:41—before carefully turning the knob to his bedroom. Corinne's baby-powder scent relaxed him immediately, along with her soft exhalations. She was in the little portable crib Mom used back when she used to babysit her, and she was zonked out in her long-sleeved pink sleeper, butt in the air and cheek on the tiny mattress.

Tommy eased himself onto the bed and sprawled out onto his back with his phone still in his hand. He wanted to call Nina and apologize, and then tell her all he'd seen in the past few hours. Even if she'd never believe him, it would help to get it all off his chest and out of his head.

Instead, with the wind whispering through the oak tree next to his window just like it used to do every night while he was growing up, Tommy fell asleep with his feet hanging three inches off the end of the bed, phone still resting on his slowly rising and falling chest.

With a ragged gasp, he woke from a dream about running that had suddenly switched over into a nightmare about falling. In the dream, as always, were those red eyes, growing ever closer. He felt as if the mad chase had begun the instant he closed his eyes.

But now that he'd forced himself to wake up, he couldn't tell if he'd been the one getting chased, or the one doing the chasing.

He stared up at the ceiling, almost deafened by the pounding of the blood in his ears. When the roar died down, he checked the time on his phone. 7:12. He'd been asleep for just half an hour, and his head felt thick and sore, like he had a fever or a bad cold.

Something was wrong. He looked over at Corinne—still sound asleep. He relaxed, but couldn't close his eyes and get back to sleep. He sat up, waited for the room to stop spinning, and then snuck out into the hall. The door to the spare room where Melanie and the boys were sleeping remained closed. In the lounge room, the Callahan brothers were still out from where they'd sprawled out on the couch, both of them snoring like buzz saws.

Tommy sniffed. Smelled blood and something else. Something bitter and almost burnt, like strong coffee.

Outside. Something was outside.

Squinting in the harsh light of morning, stutter-stepping a bit as his head went light for a second, Tommy walked out onto the cold cement patio. This was where he'd gotten his first good look at the female wolf last night, when he realized this was no dog. Thinking of her, his gaze went automatically to Dad's trailer he used for hauling wood, propped up at the edge of their property.

Tommy scuffed in his bare feet through the cold wet grass, his suspicions growing until he got to the edge of the trailer. He could still smell her, especially the burnt smell from Mark's questioning, as well as the now-familiar tang of her blood. The smell of ruined coffee flooded his nostrils all over again, just for a second.

The blue tarp was still there, smeared with blood on one side. But other than the tarp, the trailer was empty.

The body of the gray werewolf had disappeared in the night.

Chapter Twenty-Four

Too tired and muzzy-headed to try and figure out where the female wolf—the pure-breed, as Mark had called her—had disappeared, Tommy stumbled back inside. His eyes hurt from the sun and lack of sleep. He thought about kicking the Callahan brothers awake to tell them about their missing corpse, but gone was gone. Her people had no doubt tracked her here and taken her away.

He tiptoed into his room and settled back into his lumpy old bed.

At least the baby's still asleep, he thought as he closed his eyes.

He felt like he'd just drifted back off to sleep when his cell buzzed on his end table like an oversized mosquito. He snagged it before it rattled on the table again and woke Corinne.

"Hello?" he whispered as he hurried past her crib and stepped out into the hallway. His head didn't feel as thick as before, but according to the time on his phone—ten a.m.—he'd still only gotten a precious few more hours of sleep.

"Hello," he said into the phone, louder this time.

"It's me," Nina said on the other end of the line. Tommy immediately stood up straighter.

"I was gonna call you today," he said. "I'm really sorry about last night. I just—"

"It's all right. No more apologizing. I wanted to check and make sure everything was okay there."

Tommy smiled.

Oh, the things I could tell you.

Down the hall, the couch that had held the two big, sleeping Callahan brothers was now empty. He walked down and sat down on the far end of it.

"We made it here safe last night," he said, trying not to look at the spot in the middle of the floor, "and everyone seems to be doing... fine. Healing up after yesterday's big fight and all. Are *you* okay?"

"I'm good. Why do you ask?"

"Well, our dinner ended on a bad note last night. I didn't give you a chance to let you talk much about yourself. Especially," he tensed up for a second, worried he was going to piss her off, and then he plunged on, "whatever it was you wanted to tell me, before my Mom called."

"Yeah. That was sort of why I'm calling."

I knew it, Tommy thought, slapping his forehead. *I am such a dick for not letting her talk. Damn it.*

Down the hall, he heard Corinne give a loud squawk. She'd be awake and hollering in five minutes.

"I'm glad you called," Tommy said, hoping she'd keep talking. She was being too quiet.

"I told you I knew about your family," Nina said, just as Corinne started calling out "Dada" from down the hall. Tommy plugged his left ear with two fingers and held the phone tight against to his right.

"Uh huh," he said. "Go on."

"There's a reason my mom and your aunt were such good friends, back in college. They had the same... *thing*. Mom would've called it a, um, a disability. I think your aunt would've probably called it a superpower."

"Nina," Tommy said, his jaw suddenly loose. He felt like he was about to start babbling. All the air had gone out of the room. Corinne's crying was like a distant echo as Tommy took a shallow breath.

"Nina?"

"I'm like you," she said. "A wolf."

"Get the hell out of here!" Tommy said, and started laughing like a maniac. He couldn't stop. He'd been convinced that she was going to tell him she was seeing someone else, or that she didn't ever want to see him again. That he wasn't good enough.

But another werewolf? *Shit. That was nothing. Hardly even headline news right now.*

He did his best to stop laughing, but he was too relieved to stop, even if Corinne had heard him and was calling out to him now even louder than before. Still laughing, he waved at Melanie in her rumpled clothes as she left her room. She looked at him from down the hall as if he'd totally lost it.

"I'm sorry," he said in a shaking voice to Nina, trying to pull himself together. "I just... Well, I was going to say I can't believe it. But I *totally* believe it. It's almost like I knew all along. Don't take offense, but I could sense it, like something about you, and your... smell. And the way you acted. You have those, um, wolf traits. The ones I lack, apparently."

Melanie had gotten Corinne out of her crib and was now walking with her down the hall. Corinne's fat legs wobbled as she tottered toward him with Mel's assistance. Tommy grinned big at both of them and motioned for them to come sit next to him.

"Wow," Nina said after a few more moments of silence. "I have *never* had that reaction the few times I've shared my little secret with someone. I guess uncontrolled laughter is better than screaming. Or complete silence. You really *are* something else, Tommy Roling."

Tommy grinned at Melanie and Corinne. "I'm just glad you told me, and I'm sorry I'm not there for you to tell me in person."

Melanie set Corinne at the edge of the couch.

"Need coffee," Melanie said, rubbing her puffy eyes. "Be right back."

Corinne, meanwhile, started cruising down toward Tommy, chubby hand over chubby hand, shuffling her feet on the bare floor. Tommy looked from his approaching daughter over at the black flatscreen monitor they'd all been staring at last night. His smile faded as all the nastiness of the last few hours flooded back over him.

"Hey Nina," he said. "Do you know a lot of people like us in Iowa City?"

"About a dozen or so personally. Mostly girls on the athletic teams. I've heard rumors that most of the football players and the soccer teams—male and female—are weres. But that's just a rumor. If so, those folks can really control their changes. Can you imagine watching a big game on ESPN and seeing someone *turn* in the middle of a big play, or after a big hit? Damn..."

He could hear the nervous tension in Nina's voice as she spoke. Something was bothering her. She was talking fast, like she didn't want him to ask any more questions. Tommy picked up Corinne and, balancing the phone against his ear, walked over to the computer. He woke it up and launched a web browser.

"No!" Corinne shouted when she saw the big wolf with the red line through it.

"Sorry," Tommy said. "That was Corinne. My little girl."

"Hi Corinne!" Nina said. "Tell her it's nice to meet her. That I hope to see her in person someday, too. If she and her daddy ever come back to Iowa City, that is."

"Ah, crap." As Nina had been talking, Tommy had done a search for Nina's name in the site's directory of werewolves. He found her name, along with about thirty others, in the University section.

"Do you have a computer handy?" Tommy said, bouncing Corinne on his knee. He held her a little bit tighter as he thought about all that had happened in the past day. "I need to tell you about this site. I have a feeling it's maintained by my pain-in-the-ass uncle who lives somewhere close to Iowa City."

Tommy could've sworn he heard a growl coming from Nina, and the sound both thrilled him and scared the living crap out of him.

* * * * *

Talking to Nina that morning made Tommy restless. He couldn't sit at home anymore, feeling caught up in the middle of some crazy battle here on the one hand, and so far away from her and the place he truly wanted to be on the other. He had to get out and do something.

So he gathered up Corinne, told Melanie he'd be back in an hour or so, and headed downtown for some lunch at the diner.

"Are you sure that's such a good idea?" Melanie had said before he left. She was fixing herself another cup of coffee, and Tommy could hear either Mom or Dad bumping around inside their bedroom, about to get up. He did not want to deal with either of them right now.

"I'll just do some scouting downtown," he told her with a smile. "You know, look for suspicious folks. People from out of town."

"Don't look in the mirror, then," Melanie had muttered. "You're as suspicious as they get these days, city boy."

For a weekday morning at almost eleven, the diner was surprisingly quiet when Tommy carried Corinne inside. The mouthwatering fried smells of bacon, eggs, and toast still filled the air after the breakfast hours, but all the tables were empty. Two white-haired old men in jeans, checkered shirts, and John Deere caps sat at the counter, talking politics and crops over cups of coffee. Their voices were almost drowned out by the country music playing over the speakers above the counter and the sizzling coming from the grill in the back.

With a wince, he waved at Keri, one of his high school classmates, as she refilled the two older men's coffee cups at the counter. Gritting his teeth, he dragged a high chair to a table against the far wall. Keri and Suzanne had been best buds, back in the day.

Suzanne. *I haven't thought about her in months. And nobody's so much as mentioned her in the past day—nobody had time to even think about the girl who'd done so much damage to my life.*

No, Tommy corrected himself as he combed back Corinne's wild, strawberry blonde hair with his fingers. *Suzanne was the girl I let do all sorts of damage to my life. Not hanging out with my friends. Quitting football. Becoming a dad at twenty.*

I could've stopped seeing her at any time and tried to make things better. I'd just been along for the ride back then. I was stupid, thinking with my—

"Heya, Tommy," Keri said, interrupting his pity party. "What can I get you and your cute little date here?"

"Hi Keri," he said. He watched her sharp blue eyes taking him in, then Corinne, as if she were recording all this to tell Suzanne later, all the while smiling. "Can I get some milk in a cup, with a lid and straw, for the little one here, and some ice water for me."

"Pie's half-price today," Keri said, tapping her notepad. "And the bacon burger's on special."

She stood over them for a few more awkward seconds, as if waiting for Tommy to say more. Tommy just smiled at her and waited her out.

"Let me get those for you, then." Keri walked off, throwing one last, dark look back at him before she went to get their drinks.

I don't need this drama today, he thought, remembering Suzanne's last words to him back from that awful week in February: "You do *nothing* for me, Tommy!"

"She may have had a point," Tommy whispered to his daughter, who was waving at one of the old men at the counter—his friend Mickey's grandfather, Tommy realized. The old guy nodded at Tommy and waved back at Corinne.

"I didn't do much of anything back in those days. Just did whatever your mommy told me to do." He caught himself before he started talking in a baby voice to her. She was getting too old for that. "What the heck was I thinking, huh?"

In front of Corinne he spread out some Cheerios he'd snagged from Mom's kitchen to tide his little girl over until he ordered their food. Thinking about Suzanne had made him lose his appetite, but Corinne was always game for a snack.

I'll order her a grilled cheese and go back home, he figured, just as two new customers walked into the diner.

At first Tommy thought it was Joe Breitbach from the furniture store across the street with his latest girlfriend, but this guy had darker hair and a much less friendly look on his face. Joe never scowled like this lanky dude with the goatee and dark eyebrows was doing at the guys at the front counter.

Tommy tried not to stare at the woman next to the scowling guy. She had long black hair, shot through with a couple streaks of grayish white, that flowed down past her shoulders, and movie-star cheekbones and blue eyes. Despite the cool weather outside, both of them wore shorts and sandals, and her legs were, as Dad would say, as long as a summer day.

Just his luck, they sat down at the table right next to him and Corinne, between them and the door.

Keri came out of the back at last, carrying Tommy's water and Corinne's cup of milk. She said goodbye to Mickey's grandfather and his buddy on their way out.

"Be right with you," she said in a cool voice to the new customers before she plunked down the drinks at Tommy's table. Her face looked flushed, like she'd just run up a couple flights of steps. She took Tommy's order for two grilled cheeses and fries and headed back to the kitchen, giving the new patrons a wide berth.

"Good to see you again, Tommy-boy," Mickey's grandpa said on his way out the door. Tommy saw the angry-looking guy at the next table swing his head toward the older man, listening in. "You should stop by the farm sometime. I know Mickey would love to see ya. You back home for good?"

Tommy sipped his water. "For a little bit."

He hated that the two strangers sat so close to his table. The woman's perfume was strong, and it filled his head with a swimming sensation. And he itched to reach out and touch that long black hair to see if it was as soft as it looked.

"Hope your folks feel better," Mickey's grandfather said, casting a dirty look at the table next to them. Neither the man nor the woman reacted, though his elderly friend tugged at his shoulder. "Crying shame that our town has come to this. People getting attacked in broad daylight. Wouldn't you say?"

Keri was walking up to the other table slowly, pen tapping her notepad, when the lanky man spoke up in a sharp, commanding voice.

"Run along home, old man. Lock yourself up in your home like the rest of the sheep here in town. We'll be out of your hair soon enough."

"*Hush,*" the woman with him hissed.

Keri stepped back, face pale, while Mickey's grandfather took a faltering step toward the door. Corinne let out a loud giggle.

"What did you say to me?" the older man said, almost shouting. His face was red now. Tommy was worried he'd stroke out right here in the diner.

"My apologies," the woman said. "My friend here was making a joke that was only between us. He spoke out of line, my friend."

"Come on," the other old man said to Mickey's grandfather. "We've got to get to the feed store."

The woman chuckled at that, and then cast a look at Tommy and Corinne. Tommy jumped when he realized he'd been staring, watching the strange scene unfold like he was watching TV. Her blue eyes were cold, and for just a second, they seemed to flash red as they caught the light of the fluorescents overhead.

Instead of looking away, though, Tommy met her gaze. He felt like what her friend said had been as much for *his* benefit as for the two old men now shuffling out of the diner. Keri, in the meantime, had slipped back behind the counter as if remembering some important task back there.

Something about the shape of this woman's face reminded Tommy of the gray wolf from last night. The dead woman. He thought about how Mark had claimed that these wolves had lost the ability to turn back to their human form. And how after she took her last breath as a human, she reverted to her wolf body.

The woman nodded at him, just a tiny flick of her head, as if she'd been following every single one of Tommy's racing thoughts. His mouth went dry, and he inhaled her sweet scent of flowers and something earthier, underneath.

Glad you went out for lunch today, Tommy-boy? he asked himself when the woman turned back to her companion.

He heard the door to the diner slam, and Tommy assumed that was Mickey's grandfather and his friend finally getting around to leaving in a huff. At least Corinne hadn't started fussing through all of this.

"Mama!" Corinne said, clapping her hand and sending Cheerios flying.

Tommy looked sharply over at his little girl, eyes wide. Corinne's blue eyes were bright with excitement, and her chubby fingers were splayed as she reached her hands into the air, as if wanting someone to pick her up.

"Oh crap," Tommy muttered as he saw a shadow fall on their tabletop. The woman at the other table gave another sharp laugh.

As his daughter clapped her hands together madly, Tommy turned to look up at a young woman with strawberry-blonde hair, now cut short, who had just walked into the diner. Keri must've called her while she was getting their drinks.

"Hello," he said with a sigh, followed by a near-growl as he said her name out loud for the first time in months, "*Suzanne.*"

Chapter Twenty-Five

Heard you were back in town," Suzanne said, inching closer, her red-rimmed eyes sliding from Tommy to Corinne. "With my baby."

Something smelled crazy about Suzanne today. Crazier than usual. Like she hadn't showered in a few days, or she'd been sick. Her jeans were stained in a couple spots, and there was cigarette ash on the sleeves to her sweater.

"So *now* you want to see her, when it's convenient to you."

"You've been out of *town*," Suzanne spat, her voice growing louder. "How am I supposed to get to Iowa City without a car of my own?"

Again, the guy at the next table tilted his head in the direction of Tommy's table. Tommy looked from him to Corinne, who gave him a two-toothed grin, and then back up at Suzanne. Looking at her made him feel tired and somehow sad, all at once.

And a weak part of him wanted to just give in and let her have her own way. Just like the old days.

"Sit down, then. Let's talk like grownups. Then Corinne and I have to get back to Mom's house. Family stuff."

Suzanne's nostrils flared, as if she smelled something sour, too. Or maybe she just felt like she was walking into a trap.

"Don't be all cute with me, Tommy-*boy*."

"Sit," Tommy said. "You're embarrassing yourself, standing there yelling."

To Tommy's surprise, Suzanne obeyed. She lowered herself into a chair next to Corinne, her hands shaking.

"You sure got here fast," Tommy said when it became obvious she wasn't going to say anything more. "Where you living now?"

Suzanne's lower lip trembled, and then she bit down on it.

"Keri and I share the apartment upstairs. She called me when she saw you two come in."

"That's good," Tommy said in a cool voice. "Least you didn't have to move back home."

Suzanne gave him a long look. Tommy felt another spine-weakening sensation roll through him, like he wanted to abandon all his plans and take care of Suze. He returned her gaze, not speaking until the last of the feeling drained from him.

Corinne giggled softly next to him, and Tommy exhaled.

"What's *happened* to you, Tommy-boy?" Suzanne pulled back, wiping a stray lock of reddish hair from her forehead. "You used to be so sweet. Now you just say and do these mean things, like you don't care about my feelings."

"Guess I grew a backbone," he shot back. "Got tired of being walked on."

At that Suzanne turned to Corinne. Tommy had been wondering when she'd pay their little girl some attention. As Suzanne handed Corinne some Cheerios, which Corinne promptly flung onto the floor, Tommy realized that it was completely over between him and Suzanne. She'd tried to win him over with a flutter of her eyes and a pouting of her lips, but that hadn't worked. She had no hold on him anymore.

Part of the reason staying in Iowa City had been so easy and so comforting was that he knew he'd never have to worry about running into Suzanne—or anyone else he knew—there. That was his new life, but he couldn't truly move forward there until he closed the book on his life here.

Slam, he thought, looking at the girl he thought he loved just a few months ago. *That book is now shut. What the hell was I thinking?*

Suzanne kept messing with Corinne's hair and trying to hold her hands, and Corinne was getting annoyed with her.

Tommy could tell by the sound of her voice that she needed that grilled cheese soon, or there'd be trouble.

"Aw. She misses her mommy," Suzanne said, looking over at Tommy with tears in her eyes. "Let me keep her this afternoon. I'm off work the rest of the day."

"Sorry," Tommy said as tenderly as he could, which for Suzanne wasn't much. He'd seen the pack of cigarettes in Suzanne's bulging purse next to her, along with the two bottles of prescriptions in there. Even if she wasn't smoking again and doing who knew what else, there was no way he was letting her take Corinne anywhere.

Keri tiptoed over to them with their grilled cheese and fries. Tommy saw the look pass between Keri and Suzanne.

"Don't make me get the law involved," Suzanne said in a loud voice as Keri plopped two plates in front of Tommy. The man at the other table cleared his voice, loudly.

"We're good, Keri," Tommy said. She was hovering again. "Thanks. I think that fella over there is ready to order."

"They can wait," Keri spat, her eyes narrowing as her voice dropped to a whisper. "Those folks've been killing business for a couple weeks now. Musta lost fifty bucks in tips every day since—"

"Really, Keri," Tommy said, as sweetly as he could, "you can *go* now."

"So rude," Suzanne said as Keri hurried off to the other table.

The woman with the long hair looked up at Keri, and then she glanced in Tommy's direction. Tommy met her gaze, just for a second, and he knew then, without a doubt, that she had it in her. Big time. She was a wolf. A "were," as Mark or Nina would've called her.

I should've noticed this right away. But Suze had me all distracted.

Suzanne was gazing at him as he cut the crusts off the piping hot sandwich and cut the toasted bread with its melted cheese into rectangles for Corinne.

"Blow on it," he told his little girl. "It's hot."

"Hot!" Corinne said, and immediately touched a steaming square of cheese. She squealed and tossed the bit of sandwich in Suzanne's direction.

"It's okay," Tommy said, kissing Corinne's fingers automatically and fanning her food with his hand. "Have some milk, sweetie."

"This isn't right," Suzanne said. "Not natural. A girl *needs* her mother."

"But you left her with me. You gave up that right."

"I wasn't in my right mind back then. I was... scared. We were gonna lose everything, 'cause of you."

Tommy had to laugh at that. He let her talk on.

"You never cared about how hard I had it. You were too busy being the... the martyr. All bummed out about having to go to work selling magazines and take care of the baby. Making me feed her and bathe her and spend all day in that nasty little apartment with her on my days off."

Tommy remembered that cabin-fever feeling all too well from earlier this year, when he'd been doing it all on his own. After Suze had run off.

"I know how that is..." Tommy began. He stopped when he saw Suzanne once more reaching for Corinne.

"Suzanne!" Tommy hissed.

"I can't take it, Tommy-boy. I've gotta hold her, just for a minute."

"*Don't*," Tommy said. But it was too late. Suzanne had her hands under Corinne's armpits, pulling up and trying to wriggle her free of the high chair.

Corinne struggled and started to cry. And then her cry became a growl.

"Knock it off—" Tommy began, and then he was on his feet, standing between Corinne and the table where the two strangers sat.

"Oh my God," Suzanne whispered. "Oh, my baby. Oh God..."

Tommy grabbed Suzanne's soft upper arm and squeezed until she stopped babbling.

"Quiet," he whispered as they looked down at Corinne. "She's okay."

Corinne gave a soft growl with a mouth now filled with jagged white teeth. Her pink skin had disappeared under a thick layer of strawberry blonde fur. Even the tips of her ears were pointed. Her eyes were small as raisins as she glared at her mother.

"Corinne," Tommy whispered in as calm a voice as he could manage. He would've killed for a whistle like Burt's. "Hush, baby. *Hush.*"

"What'd you do to my girl?" Suzanne said, knocking over two chairs as she jerked away from Tommy's table. "What's wrong with her?"

"She's fine," Tommy said. He stroked Corinne's cheek, calming her. The fur had disappeared, along with her mouthful of teeth. Her ears were pink and round again.

That's my girl, Tommy thought. *Back in control.*

"But she... I saw..."

"*Don't,*" Tommy said to Suzanne. "Do *not* make a scene."

He let go of Corinne and picked up the overturned chairs. He hoped he'd been able to block most of Corinne's transformation from the people at the other table.

Suzanne stood there for a moment, backed up against one of the other tables in the diner.

And then, without another word, she simply fled. The door leading outside slammed behind her.

"Buh-buh?" Corinne asked, holding up her arms for Tommy to pick her up. He got her extricated from the high chair and sat down for a moment with her on his lap.

"Yep. She went bye-bye, sweetie. That lady went bye-bye."

When Tommy looked up, the couple from the other table had both turned to look at him.

"Sorry 'bout all the noise," he said. Keri was nowhere to be found, so he dug a ten and a couple ones out of his wallet and set them on the table. "She's a bit of a handful sometimes."

"Your little one is very well-behaved, though," the woman said with a sly grin. Her teeth were so white they almost glowed.

"You *ought* to put the other one out of her misery, though," the man said in the same joking tone of voice.

Tommy saw the sense in that statement, and he found himself nodding along.

I could do it with just one hand, choke the life out of Suzanne. It'd be easy. Wouldn't even need to change. I really should—

"He's *joking*," the woman said in a sharp voice. She wasn't looking at Tommy now, but her companion. Her eyes glittered with anger.

Tommy sat back in his chair, heart pounding.

Funny. I never got worked up the whole time I was talking to Suze, but now I feel full of adrenaline. And was I really actually thinking about killing her? With my bare hands?

Tommy drank all of his ice water at once, and the cold liquid brought him back to reality. Time to get back home.

"I apologize for my friend," the woman said as Tommy stood, Corinne on his hip. "He's not used to how things are in small towns."

The man refused to look at Tommy, but Tommy could see him smiling at something.

Probably me, he figured.

"Um, okay," Tommy said. "See you later."

The woman nodded.

"I hope so, Tommy. I definitely hope so."

A s far as lunches go," Tommy said to Corinne once they were both strapped into his Grand Am again, "that was a pretty shitty one, wouldn't you say?"

Running back through the conversation with Suzanne, and the way their talk had ended, Tommy had to laugh.

What must've gone through that poor girl's brain when she saw her nine-month-old sprouting fur and fangs? That'll probably send her to the nuthouse. Or at least to a bottle of liquor. I'd almost feel sorry for her if she hadn't made such a scene in there. Almost.

And thanks to the big mouth of Mickey's grandpa, the strangers who had to be werewolves both knew his name now, too. Tommy shuddered, thinking about the way the man's casual suggestion had made him start thinking like a crazed murderer.

"Maybe your daddy needs some therapy," Tommy said with a nervous laugh. He didn't like the way his words or his laugh sounded.

He also didn't like how nobody seemed to be out and about today—the streets were empty of cars and trucks. Even the elementary school next to the basilica seemed dark and closed. But summer vacation wasn't for another month or two. It was like the whole town had gone on vacation.

He was thinking about something else the lanky guy back at the diner had said to Mickey's grandpa, how everyone in town had locked themselves away in their houses or something, when his phone buzzed in his jeans pocket.

He fished out his phone and nearly dropped it when he saw the name on the little screen. *Nina.*

"Hello again," Tommy said in as calm a voice as he could muster.

"This is so crazy," Nina said. Her voice sounded tight, like she was on the verge of busting out laughing. Or screaming. "So crazy. But tell me your address back in your hometown, would you?"

"What's going on, Nina?" Tommy said as they pulled into the driveway to his parents' house.

"Tell me their address so I can punch it into my GPS, okay? Then I'll explain what I can."

Tommy rattled off the address he'd known since he was five. He shut off the engine and listened to Corinne cooing in the back seat with one ear and Nina muttering under her breath on the phone with his other ear.

Surely she wasn't...

"Okay. Got it. Thanks. Oh my God, I can't believe I just did this. You are not gonna believe it."

"Are you making a road trip, Nina?" Tommy asked, hands shaking.

"I'll be there in eighty-two minutes, according to my roommate's GPS here."

"Nina! I don't think that's such a good—"

"Oops. My turn's coming up. See you soon," Nina said, and then she hung up.

"I hope so," Tommy said into the dead phone. He felt like he was smiling like a fool. He looked up into his rearview mirror and confirmed it.

"This is going to be one of those days," Tommy muttered as he got out of his ticking car.

Corinne giggled from her car seat behind him. She seemed to agree.

Chapter Twenty-Six

The loud conversation at the dining room table was on the verge of becoming a domestic disturbance when Tommy walked inside the house.

He heard Mom and Melanie arguing about something one of Melanie's boys had done, while Dad and Burt were trying to calm down Luke. The big Callahan brother was pounding on the table and repeating that they had to go now and find someone, or else he was gonna lose it.

Big Krunch and Little Krunch stood in the hallway connecting the kitchen to the dining room, peeking in at all the commotion.

"What's going on?" Tommy asked Big Krunch on his way past him.

"Mark's gone missing," Big Krunch said.

"Wolves attacked old man Lucas' house this morning," Little Krunch said.

"And something's up with your little cousin."

"Shit's hitting the fan," Little Krunch added, unnecessarily.

Tommy stepped into the dining room and nearly tripped over Melanie's youngest, Trey. The little blond-haired boy was sitting on the floor, Indian-style, rocking back and forth with his hands over his ears.

"Hey buddy," Tommy said, resting a hand on his nephew. Trey's back and shoulders were taut with tension. "It's okay. I don't think they're mad at you. We'll make things okay."

"But Tyler's *sick*," Trey whispered. Tommy set down Corinne and hunkered down next to Trey to hear. Corinne tried to worm her way into Trey's lap, which made him giggle.

"What's Ty got, a cold?" Tommy asked, just as a chair scraped over the hardwood floor.

Luke Callahan was headed for the door leading outside, with Mom right on his heels.

"Get back here!" Mom yelled. "You can't just run off again. Look what happened when you did that last night, boy!"

Luke growled, but stopped a few feet from Tommy.

"Oh *great*," Luke said. "Look who decided to grace us with his presence."

Burt slid between Tommy and Luke and managed to get everyone sitting back around the table again. Corinne and Trey were happy for the moment, playing with some Matchbox cars Trey had pulled from his pants pockets.

"Just chill the hell out for a second," Burt said as soon as everyone stopped talking and growling at one another. "Like I said last night, we need a plan."

"Tell me what I've missed," Tommy said, ignoring Luke's glare.

"Well, first off, and you won't believe this," Burt said, eyes wide with wonder and his face flushed, "but *Tyler* has it in him, too. He turned this morning while he was playing with his little brother. Frickin' unbelievable, man! He makes a kick-ass little wolf, too, just like his little brother. The two of 'em were running around the backyard, barking and rolling around until we were able to stop them."

Tommy exhaled and looked over at Trey and Corinne playing together on the floor. He couldn't handle the slightly blissed-out look on his brother's face. He knew what Burt had to be thinking—if it could happen to Tyler, why not *me*?

But surely it would've *happened* to Burt by now, right?

"Tore up my couch and half my yard," Mom muttered. Melanie growled at her.

"Anyway," Burt said, tapping his fingers on the empty dining room table, "there's that. And old man Lucas called up this morning to say that he and his neighbor had taken some shots at some wolves just after dawn today. Then Smith went over there and mucked things up, as usual."

"Is Lucas okay?" Tommy asked with a catch in his voice. Old man Lucas lived at the edge of town in the big, rambling farmhouse that'd been in his family for over a hundred years. If they'd gotten to that old cuss, they could get to *any* of us.

"He's fine. Pissed as hell, but not hurt. He's taking credit for blowing a hole in one of 'em. The crazy old fart was sitting up in his barn all night with a shotgun and a bag of shells, guarding his house."

"Damn," Tommy said. "Did anyone get a hold of the other families? I wonder if they had any visitors last—"

"Come *on*," Luke interrupted, hitting the table with the palm of one meaty hand. "Time's wasting..."

"And the last bit of news? Our man Mark took off this morning," Burt said. "Said he wanted to track down the dead she-wolf from last night. On his own."

"The idiot," Luke said.

"Agreed," Melanie said.

Tommy looked over at Luke. "Why'd he go off on his own?"

Luke gave him an exaggerated shrug of his shoulders and threw his hands in the air.

"Beats the hell out of me," he said in a surprisingly calm tone of voice.

"So we need to find him," Tommy said. "And we have some other folks to find, too, don't we?" He turned to his parents, who both flinched as if they'd wanted to slip out of this meeting without having to deal with anything. "Where do you think we can find Lisa Schnelling and Bill Hoerner?"

"Beats the hell out of me," Mom said, lip curling as she looked right at Luke Callahan. Tommy guessed she was pissed at him for bringing all this mess into her house.

"No," Dad said. He scooted his chair closer to the table, wincing and holding his ribs. "We heard 'em talking about this at the Side Entrance the other night. How folks had seen some wolves out by those new houses they were building north of town. The big ones that they had to stop building when folks ran out of money from the economy."

Tommy nodded at Dad, thinking about the two dozen fancy houses on their two-acre lots. Only four or five actually had people living in them, and the rest were just empty shells—finished on the outside, but still plywood and two-by-fours on the inside.

"Sounds like a good place to start," he said.

Down on the floor, Corinne was slapping at Trey, trying to get him to give her a mini fire truck. Trey grunted at her, refusing, and soon both of them had changed into wolf form. They rolled around on the floor until Tommy reached in to snag Corinne up in his arms, careful to keep her clawed paws under control.

"*That* just freaks me out," Dad muttered with a nervous laugh.

"Me too," Tommy heard Mom whisper.

"Thanks a lot," Tommy said to them. "Real supportive. She just needs a nap, that's all. She's getting wild."

Everyone around the table laughed at that. Tommy looked down at the furry little wolf pup in his arms, slowly morphing back into his daughter. He thought of Corinne turning on Suzanne at the diner and grinned down at her, shaking his head.

"I think we should split up," Burt said. He had his game face on, like he was buckling down for a long afternoon of playing strategy games on his PlayStation. "We can't all fit into one car, and it'd look suspicious anyway, all of us poking around. Don't want Smith tailing us, or one of the wolves getting wind of us."

"I want to check out those houses," Tommy said. "Burt, you wanna come with? Melanie?"

"I don't think Mark's there," Luke said, standing up and looking around the table. "I want to get down to the Side Entrance and get the word on the street from Livy down there."

"We'll go with you," Mom chimed in, elbowing Dad in the side. He gasped in pain from his injuries. "Sorry."

"Us too," Big Krunch said from where he and his son had been lurking in the doorway. "We could use a beer."

"Don't get in trouble down there," Tommy warned his parents. "No more fights. Call my cell if you hear anything." He gave Luke a nod. "And call me when you find your brother. He's probably there already with a pitcher of Bud."

Luke gave him a half-smile and nodded back. Everyone got up from the table and started heading for the door. Tommy picked Trey up off the floor and balanced him and Corinne in his arms.

Our little wolves-in-training, he thought.

"Let me go get Ty," Melanie said, as if reading his mind.

Just as they were walking out the front door, a rusty, dark blue Toyota Tercel rolled up into the driveway behind Tommy's Grand Am.

"Who's that?" Dad asked, sipping from a plastic cup. "That girl has *got* to be lost."

"Oh man," Tommy said when he saw the face of the driver. Dark skin, amazing brown eyes, short dreads. "*Nina.* I'd almost forgotten."

He set Trey down next to Burt and carried Corinne over to the still-idling Tercel, which smelled of burnt oil. She'd gotten here in record time.

Tommy felt like laughing again when he drew close to Nina, with surprise and relief.

She's here, he thought, *in my hometown. She came all this way to see me.*

"Nina!" he said as he pulled open her door. "You're really here. Want to shut off the car now?"

"Oh," she said. She looked frazzled, and not just from an hour and a half on unfamiliar roads. A storm was brewing behind those big brown eyes. "Right."

The big GPS unit mounted to the right of the dash gave a loud beep as she killed the engine. The bumping sounds he'd thought were coming from the engine continued, though.

"Nina," Tommy said as she popped out the car and stepped away from it, like it was about to explode. "What's going on? What's making that noise?"

Tommy knew he should be introducing Nina to his family and Luke—they were all coming toward them and gathering near the hood of the car, listening in and staring at the pretty black girl who just showed up out of nowhere.

But that wild look in her eyes made him forget his manners. Nina took a deep breath and waved at their spectators.

"You folks might want to come back here and take a look at this," she said, jangling the car keys together.

"Buh-buh?" Corinne asked as the three of them walked to the back of the car. The thumping sounds grew louder, as if someone was kicking weakly to get out. Mom and Dad, Luke, Mark, and Melanie followed them at a safe distance.

"This is my friend Nina," Tommy said as she fumbled to get the keys in the lock to the trunk. "From Iowa City. It's all right," he added, and then he nearly dropped Corinne as Nina opened the trunk.

Tied up, gagged, and folded nearly in half in the tiny trunk of the Tercel, lay Crazy Uncle Carl.

"Son of a bitch," Aunt Melanie said, coming up fast next to Nina. "I *thought* I could smell his cologne."

Tommy was glad they were back in the dining room again, and not down in the basement where they'd been interrogating the gray she-wolf last night.

Mom kept giving Nina the evil eye. Tommy wondered if Nina was the first black person to step foot inside their house. Probably.

Wait 'til I tell them she's more *than just a friend.* Tommy swallowed. *At least I hope she's still more than a friend.*

"How'd you get him into the car?" Melanie asked Nina.

Carl sat in the chair next to Melanie, with big Luke Callahan sitting nice and close to him on the other side.

"He thought I was the pizza guy," she said, grinning at Tommy. He was glad to see that most of the crazy light in her eyes had gone away. "Then I used some of my, um, persuasive skills to get him to come along for the ride. I made him pull the plug on his damn server before we left, too. No more Antiwolf dot com."

"Don't know what you got yourself into, girl," Carl muttered. He wore a dirty white T-shirt and baggy brown cargo shorts, and he looked like he'd lost about twenty pounds since Tommy last saw him.

"Hush," Luke said to Carl. "Don't interrupt. Rude."

Melanie snapped her fingers. "Persuasive skills, huh? Guess you inherited your mom's genes, huh?"

Nina nodded and gave Melanie a sly smile. "She said you need to give her a call and come to Chicago to visit."

"You know," Tommy said, "I didn't tell you about that website and Carl so you'd go over there and make a citizen's arrest."

"I need a drink," Dad said, getting up and heading to the liquor cabinet.

"I know," Nina said, talking only to Tommy now. "But I started reading some of the nastiness on that site. Bad enough he was calling out people like us. But I felt like I was reading a white supremacist site, talking shit about blacks and Jews and Mexicans. I kinda lose it when I see that kind of ignorance."

"So what're we going to do with Uncle Carl?" Burt said.

"He and I are going to have a talk," Melanie said, her voice low. Tommy shuddered at the sound of it. Uncle Carl was so screwed. "I'm so glad you brought him along for this visit. And Tommy, you and I are gonna talk later about how you never introduced me to your friend 'til now."

"I just—" Tommy began. "I mean, I would've... I mean..."

Luke laughed and got up from the table. "I'm going downtown, then. I got a brother to track down before anyone else gets to him. My folks will never forgive me if anything happens to him, too."

"Can we ride with you?" Dad asked, and he and Mom followed Luke outside.

Tommy picked up Corinne and looked over at Melanie.

"Want us to take your boys with us? I mean, do you think they should be seeing their dad like this?" He nodded at Carl, tied up and duct-taped to the dining room chair.

"I'll handle it, Tommy," Melanie said, patting him on the shoulder. "Carl and me and the boys have a lot of catching up to do. Plus, someone has to mind the fort while you're off saving the day."

I hope *that's what we're doing,* Tommy thought.

He clapped Burt on the shoulder. "What do you say we give Nina a tour of Dyersburg, bro? Sound good to you, Nina?"

Nina gave him a smile that made Tommy shake in his boots.

"Shotgun," she called.

Chapter Twenty-Seven

"Figure we got about two hours 'til it starts getting dark on us," Burt said from the back seat, where Corinne dozed in her car seat next to him. "Seems like the wolves always get more active at night. You know, like vampires."

"Oh man, don't go there," Tommy said. He gave Nina a nervous look. "I mean, there aren't *vampires* out there, too, are there?"

Nina raised an eyebrow at him, looking like she was about to give him a hard time, then she must have noticed the worry on his face.

"Nah," she said. "No such thing. At least, as far as I know. Most of the werewolves I know are like the only kid in their family with it. My mom said there used to be tons of us. But we're fading out. Guess it's evolution or something."

"Yeah," Burt muttered. "Don't remind me. Hey, maybe the werewolves killed off the vampires, back when the wolves were everywhere."

"Huh," Tommy said, not liking the thought that vampires *may* have existed once upon a time. He almost preferred the days when he and Mom were the only werewolves he knew. But then again, he never would have moved to Iowa City and met Nina if that were the case.

"So I'll give you a quick tour as we go," he said to Nina. "This is Dyersburg. My folks and Burt live at the south edge of town. It's Highway Twenty and then cornfields everywhere you look to the south of us. There on the left's the hospital, where Mom works, and the elementary school's coming up on the right."

"Ah man," Burt said in the back seat, "you call that a tour? You suck, bro." Burt leaned forward, pointing a long finger up toward the windshield. "See the two steeples up there? That's the basilica, one of only about a hundred big-ass Catholic churches like it in the country. Our town's claim to fame. More priests and nuns visit here than you can shake a stick at. Though not many of 'em been coming 'round to do the tourist thing these days. Thanks to our friends the wolves."

As they passed over a short bridge above the muddy creek and rolled through downtown, Tommy could count on one hand the number of people he saw out and about that afternoon.

Burt continued his tour guide routine with Nina, sharing stories of his misadventures at various locations along the way. Nina laughed along with him, and Tommy felt some of the tension leave his shoulders. Burt had really taken to Nina, instead of giving her the cold shoulder like Mom and Dad had, most likely due to her skin color. His big brother was full of surprises.

Just a few minutes later, they were outside of town, heading north on a ruler-straight two-lane. Corinne stirred in her sleep, but not from Burt's loud voice.

She must've felt what I just felt, Tommy thought with a shiver. *A weird chill in the air. And that smell, coming from that sub-division up on the right. Like the too-sweet smell of flowers at a funeral, trying to cover up the smell of death and rot.*

"Here's the neighborhood that never was," Burt said. "Hang a right, Tommy."

Tommy slowed for the turn, and then he drove past the unfinished, barely three-foot-high stone wall that was supposed to surround the entire neighborhood like a fancy gated community. The bit of wall now looked like a kid's pile of Legos.

Inside the neighborhood, the houses weren't much better. Most of them had finished exteriors, but Tommy could look through the dusty, paint-spattered windows of almost all the houses and see bare wood on the inside.

For some reason, his hands were unsteady on the steering wheel. And he couldn't get the smell of too-sweet flowers out of his nose. It was giving him a headache.

"I thought Dad said some folks still lived here," he said, peeking at Burt in the rearview. "I don't see any cars. No signs of life here at all."

Burt rolled down his window and stuck his head halfway out of it. "Maybe they moved out? Or just walked away when they couldn't afford the mortgage any more. Some of the folks were from out of town, so they probably didn't care what folks thought if they bailed."

Tommy nodded and kept driving, skin crawling, nose itching. The road curved around to the left and forked off to the right onto a non-existent road that would probably never get built. It ended in a cul de sac with just three houses on it.

Corinne sniffed loudly in the back seat and woke herself up.

"Mama?" she said in a curious, almost surprised voice.

Tommy pushed his right foot down on the brakes, keeping himself from slamming them, but just barely. The chills he'd been feeling ever since entering this neighborhood reared their ugly heads and took multiple bites out of his composure.

"What's that, baby?" Tommy asked, hating the high pitch in his voice. "Mommy's not here." He looked over at Nina to explain. "We ran into her mother at lunch today. Not a good scene."

"That would be Tommy's *ex*-girlfriend, by the way," Burt added in an overly helpful tone of voice. "A real loser. I tried to tell him not to date her, but he—"

"Shh!" Tommy hissed. In the shadow of the old oak trees that had once marked the edge of the Offerman's fifteen-hundred-acre farm, he could've sworn he saw something moving.

"I think," he said, taking a deep breath and parking his car right in the middle of the road, "we need to get out and take a look around."

Part of him was tempted to ask Burt to stay in the car with Corinne, but he didn't want to let her out of his sight. She was part of this, too, and he needed her close. Her little meet-and-greet with Uncle Carl's friends in their big house in Iowa City told Tommy that his little girl could handle herself.

Tommy lifted her out of her car seat, and the four of them walked up to the first house on the left without speaking. The sun was sinking too fast, filling the long, overgrown backyard with shadows stretching to the wall of trees that stood right before the cornfields started up again. A cool wind rustled the leaves, almost replacing the too-sweet smell stuck in Tommy's nose with the earthy smell of leaves and wild grass.

The front door was locked, so Tommy peeked into one the windows off to the side.

Should've brought some flashlights, he thought, squinting to see anything on the dusty, uncarpeted floor. Just plywood and a stack of broken-up drywall in this room, which was probably going to be an office or library. The room looked like it could hold all of Tommy's old apartment, with room to spare.

"Guys," Burt said from off to the other side of the house. Tommy hurried after Nina, who'd been peeking in another window, and found Burt about to crawl through a window he'd managed to wedge open.

"Burt, hold up," Tommy said, but he'd already wriggled his way inside.

"I'll get the back door for you guys!" Burt called out, and then there was a sickening, cracking sound, followed by the thud of something falling to the floor.

"Burt!" Tommy and Nina cried out at the same time.

"Oh man," Burt muttered in a slightly muffled voice, "that frickin' *hurt*."

"Burt," Tommy yelled, eying the tiny dimensions of the window with a sinking feeling. "What happened? What'd you do? Stay there. I'm coming in."

But before Tommy could even stop talking, something dug into both of his arms, scratching him, and then the weight in his arms was gone. Corinne had shifted, just like that, into her wolf form. All Tommy saw was a blur of her strawberry blonde fur as she shot through the window after her uncle, and he was left holding a pink sleeper with a dry diaper inside it.

"Corinne!" Tommy shouted, reaching for the window frame. But Nina was already halfway inside the window.

"I got this, big guy," she said. "Meet me at the front door. Hurry. And I know, I'll watch my step."

Tommy ran to the front door, feeling the change coming over him as well, but he tamped it down.

Pace yourself, Tommy-boy. Don't overreact.

After what felt like an hour, but was probably closer to ten seconds, Tommy heard the deadbolt pop out of the locked position, and then Nina opened the door.

"Hey, Furry," she said, grabbing his hand—covered in a now-receding layer of blonde fur—and leading him inside. "Your brother fell through the damn floor. Corinne's down there with him, keeping him company. She must've jumped right through the hole in the floor to get to him. Relax. Everyone's okay."

The interior of the house felt a good fifteen degrees cooler than outside, and it was full of drywall dust and a musty, moist smell that canceled out the too-sweet smell from earlier. They tiptoed down the creaky long hall and found the sinkhole that Burt had made. Tommy looked up and saw the hole in the roof high above them that had rotted the floorboards and plywood.

"You guys okay down there?" Tommy called down through the hole. He could see only gray shapes ten feet down in the darkness. "Burt, you got Corinne down there with you?"

"We're okay. And I think Corinne's got *me*. Come on down."

Before he could say a word to stop her, Nina leaped nimbly over the four-foot gap and landed without a sound.

"Show off," Tommy muttered, walking around the hole with his back tight against the wall. They found the steps and walked down into the murky basement, which felt another ten or fifteen degrees cooler.

Corinne, still in her wolf form, was busy licking her uncle's face when Tommy and Nina stepped onto the cool concrete floor. The walls were rough and moist with condensation. From somewhere in the distance, a siren sounded.

Burt got to his feet, still holding onto Corinne in her muscular wolf form. Tommy couldn't help but pat her head and rub her furry back. Corinne nipped playfully at his hands.

"She sorta freaked me out when she jumped down here on top of me," Burt said, sounding like he was apologizing. "I've never seen her like this. She's like a fox on steroids. Crazy."

Bite me, Tommy remembered Burt asking him a few months ago. He realized how scared and vulnerable Burt must feel, not having the ability to switch over into powerful wolf mode like Corinne, Nina, and Tommy all could.

"Did you hurt yourself? Can you walk?"

"Think I just sprained an ankle. Hurt like a bitch when I hit, but Corinne took my mind off the pain." He stood up and put weight on it. "Huh. Not bad at all."

With a low, soft growl, Corinne suddenly tensed and leaped out of her uncle's arms. Nina had slipped off to the room on the other side of the basement steps, where a rustling sound emerged. Corinne padded into the room, and Tommy followed, with Burt after them.

"Would you look at this mess?" Nina said.

Down on one knee, she patted Corinne's head and gazed at the far end of the rectangular room. A jagged hole had been cut into the concrete, leading to a muddy, root-lined tunnel.

Tommy stared, trying to comprehend the existence of that tunnel. It just didn't look possible. And he couldn't tell how far it went, because it ended in darkness after about ten feet. And the light coming in from the two narrow windows behind them grew fainter by the minute.

Why didn't we bring flashlights? Tommy asked himself again, hands fisted in frustration. *What was I thinking?*

Something rustled from deeper inside the tunnel, and Tommy felt himself shift into wolf form so he could hear better. He was so keyed up, the change happened almost instantly.

He held his breath and listened, and he recognized another sound. A *human* voice. Female.

"Let's go," he growled, plucking off the last bits of his ripped jeans and shirt. Nina had changed as well, and in the graying light, Tommy took a second to admire her wolf form, with its black fur and the chiseled muscles underneath it. He felt big and clumsy as he dropped to all fours next to her.

"You guys *suck*," Burt panted angrily from behind them as they plunged into the tunnel, with Corinne in the lead. Tommy could see much better now, thanks to his wolf eyes, and he saw Corinne shoot around a bend in the tunnel.

Gotta catch up to her before she charges right into a bad situation.

The female voice ahead of them was yelling now.

"Get away from me!" she cried. "You're so damn lucky I can't turn."

Tommy knew that voice. Lisa Schnelling.

This was the place, just like Dad had promised.

Faint yellow light now filled the tunnel, and he tried to catch Corinne, to snag her in his mouth and keep her safe, but before he could, they were at the end of the tunnel. Corinne, then Tommy and Nina, charged into a room lit with a small fire below an open window.

Five feet from the fire stood a struggling Lisa Schnelling, wearing torn and muddy clothes. She was chained to a big metal ring embedded in the concrete floor, and the chains around her wrists were a bright silver color. Surrounding her were half a dozen growling wolves.

A low growl came from behind Tommy as well. He spun and saw a big, brown-furred wolf pad out of the tunnel on all fours, eyes glittering in the firelight. The beast must've gotten Burt already.

Tommy felt nausea fill him along with a growing rage at himself.

"Oh *great*," Lisa said, her silver chains rattling. She was looking at Tommy, Nina, and Corinne with disgust. "More of your damn pack."

Just like Lisa, they were now surrounded. They'd walked right into a trap.

Chapter Twenty-Eight

Tommy had time to gather up Corinne in one paw before the other wolves reached them.

He saw her tense up, about to attack the lanky wolf that had come up behind them—the one that must have attacked Burt. That wolf would've torn her to pieces.

Except...

This new wolf still waited in the rough half-circle of the tunnel opening. Not advancing on them. He was long and thin, almost malnourished-looking, and something about its lanky brown hair made Tommy want to go up and sniff him.

The wolf's eyes were wide as it looked from Tommy to the other wolves in the room, and then down at its own paws. Awkward and uncertain, like a young, freshly changed wolf, though this beast was way too big for that.

The other wolves in the room, however, had turned on them. They ignored Lisa's desperate taunts and curses as she swung her chained-together hands at them. Their growls grew louder, and Tommy nudged Nina, letting her know he was there. She was growling too, teeth bared, eyes focused on the biggest one, a grayish-brown male.

"Buh?" Corinne said from underneath Tommy. Her furry little body was hot against his as he tried to keep her safe. She kept saying "Buh" over and over again. When Tommy looked down try and shush her, she wriggled free of his grip.

She shot across the basement floor and leaped onto the tentative brown wolf standing in front of the tunnel.

"Corinne!" Tommy roared, chasing after her. "No!"

The brown wolf—instead of peeling Corinne's little wolf-body off his with a swipe of his claws—went clattering to the concrete. Corinne's unexpected attack had taken out all four of his long, thin legs.

"*Buh!*" she yipped, now sitting on the brown wolf's stomach as he lay defenseless on his back.

Tommy took a big sniff of the other wolf, still struggling to get up with Corinne on him, licking his face.

Buh?

The wolf smelled of fur and musk, but also a trace of cigarettes and something distinct and familiar. A scent he'd known all his life.

Tommy stopped two feet from the other wolf, too shocked to move closer.

Burt.

This wolf was his brother.

"Tommy-boy," a garbled voice said. The brown wolf at the door got to all fours at last, with Corinne still nuzzling him in the side. The wolf looked at Tommy and spoke like he had five ice cubes in his wide, toothy mouth. "I got it *in* me!"

"Hell yeah," Tommy rumbled.

The stress of the situation must have finally forced the change in Burt. The guy had run from any conflict in his life for so long that he'd never had to dig deep and find his wolf side. Or maybe Burt was just a late bloomer.

"I don't know how you did it," Tommy added, "but your timing was perfect."

Burt put his new wolf body between Corinne and the approaching wolves.

"Let me do this, bro. There's more of them, but we're bigger. The brown and gray one's the leader, right?"

"Yep," Tommy said, about to say more, but Burt was already off.

His claws clattering on the concrete, Burt shot past Nina, who'd been busy snapping at the approaching wolves and keeping them away. Burt tackled the biggest wolf, the brownish-gray male closest to them.

"*Stay,*" Tommy told Corinne, and then he entered the fray, helping Nina pull the smaller wolves off of Burt as his brother bit and kicked at the other wolf. The brown-gray male was already on his back, whimpering from Burt's furious attack.

"Don't kill him!" Tommy shouted, just as a frothing Burt opened his jaws like a pair of huge scissors and leaned in on the defeated leader of the other pack. "No, Burt! Otherwise we'll have a war on our hands. Plus we need information."

"Go ahead and kill 'em," a female voice said from the other side of the room. "They deserve it, the bunch of inbred freaks. Half of 'em can't even change back into their human shape. Worse than a pack of wild dogs."

"Lisa," Tommy said, looking over at her. "Don't encourage him, okay?"

"I can tell you what you need to know," Lisa said. "That's you, isn't it, Tommy Roling? And that's your baby girl, and Burt? You guys all have it, too, huh?"

"Yep," Tommy said, "it's me. Burt and Corinne, yep, and my friend Nina here."

I must be nuts, Tommy thought. *Making introductions at a time like this.*

But the other wolves now cowered in the corner, next to the closed door leading to the rest of the house. They eyed the tunnel as if they wanted to make a run for it, but Corinne was there to guard it. She growled and yipped at them.

Bring it on, she seemed to say. That's my girl.

"What should we *do* with them?" Tommy asked.

"If you're not gonna put them out of their misery, then just let 'em go," Lisa said. "They can't think for themselves. Bunch of inbred idiots."

"Come on, Corinne," Tommy said. "Say bye-bye to the other puppies."

Corinne gave the cowering wolves one last yip, and then she came bounding over to where Tommy, Burt, and Nina were standing around Lisa.

The other wolves saw their chance and charged out of the room and into the tunnel with a loud clatter of claws on concrete.

"Bill Hoerner's in the next house over," Lisa said, pulling at the chain wrapped around her wrists. The skin was rubbed raw where the metal had touched her. "There's another tunnel on the other side of that door. We need to get him, too.

"So he's *alive*," Tommy said, exhaling. He felt the change starting to drain out of him like a fever breaking.

"Careful," Lisa said as Nina reached for the chains. "It's silver. With it wrapped around me, I can't change into a wolf. Pull it off fast."

"All three of us," Tommy said, noticing that the chains were simply wrapped around her wrists, "at the same time. But wait. We don't want to touch it."

He glanced around and saw an old wooden chair on its side next to the blanket that must have been Lisa's bed for the past week or so. He shattered the chair with one paw and handed chair legs to Burt and Nina. He kept one for himself.

"Touch the silver with this," he told them, then he looked at Lisa. "Will pulling it off hurt you?"

"Oh yeah. I've tried. Just do it fast, like ripping off a Band-Aid. I can heal myself later."

"Right," Tommy said, looking at Burt and then Nina. Nina nodded at him and held up her chair leg. "One, two, three—"

Lisa screamed as they pried the chains off her wrists with the shards of wood, but by the end of her loudest scream, she was free. Her healing had already begun before her scream ended—she'd shifted right into wolf form as soon as she was free of the chains.

Lisa shook the remnants of her filthy clothes off her muscular body, which was now covered with dark blonde fur. Corinne rubbed against Lisa's side with a small mewling noise.

"Thank you, guys," she said, looking at all four of them, though Tommy could've sworn her gaze rested longest on Burt.

"How'd you get stuck down here?" Tommy asked with a sick feeling in his gut.

"They snagged me about a week or so ago, when I was walking to my car after closing up at the grocery store. I knew I should've told Dad to fix the lights back there. They overpowered me, even though I was much bigger than any of them in my wolf form. I changed when I got overwhelmed, and that's when they slapped that damn silver chain on me. They never hurt me, just talked about how happy their people were going to be when I started having litters for them."

"Ew," Nina said. "Did they try to..." she paused, shook her narrow wolf's head, "mate with you?"

Lisa growled, and even in her wolf form, Tommy could see her shudder.

"No. Thank God. They kept saying they wanted to wait 'til the right time. Maybe they needed more females—they were always asking if I knew anyone else who was a werewolf. Or maybe they wanted to time it with the full moon. Then they got all pumped about some website they found a couple days ago—"

"God damn that Uncle Carl," Burt said, pacing back and forth. "Um. Sorry, Corinne. I mean darn that Uncle Carl. He just made their job real easy."

"At least the site's down now," Nina said. "Your uncle bawled like a baby when I made him delete it and shut off his server."

Tommy rubbed Corinne's head, thinking it all through as his pulse returned to normal.

If the wolves didn't learn about our town from Carl's site, then how did they find it? Was it Luke and Mark's brother, trying to find someone he knew down here? And if these wolves needed to reproduce so badly, why didn't they just have their way with Lisa and be done?

Too many questions. And they were down here in the middle of at least two wolf's nests. Not a good place to turn into an investigative reporter.

"Hey," he said. "We need to *go*. Those wolves are probably telling their entire pack about us right now. And we still have to get Bill from next door."

"Yeah," Lisa said, her eyes flicking toward the other room and most likely the tunnel it held. "Good luck with that."

"What do you mean?" Tommy said.

"You'll see. Let's go."

With Lisa in the lead and Burt just a step behind her, followed by Nina and Corinne, Tommy and his pack walked through the door and into a small room with stairs leading up on the left, and another tunnel on the right.

Inside the other tunnel, Tommy blinked a few times, eyes adjusting. He was back in his wolf form, one hundred percent, and it felt good.

Hope this next rescue mission is as easy as the first one was, he thought. *Though I doubt it will be.*

L ess than half an hour later, as he drove south back into town with a sick feeling in his gut and an ache in his head just behind his eyes, Tommy realized he was both right *and* wrong about how easy it would be to free Billy Hoerner.

"I feel nauseous," Nina said from the passenger seat.

Like Tommy and everyone in the back seat, she was back in her human form and wearing her torn clothes again. Tommy barely remembered backtracking through first one dark tunnel, then the second one, to get their clothes and leave the three connected houses in the aborted cul de sac. At some point everyone had turned from wolf back to human, but when that happened, he had no idea.

"It was bad," he agreed. Corinne and Burt had both stopped crying in the back seat, but Lisa was still muttering to herself and cursing every fourth word about what had just happened.

"I can't get that image of him, doing *that*, out of my head," Nina continued.

Tommy wanted to reach over and touch her knee or her shoulder to console her, but there was too much smooth, bare skin sticking out of her torn jeans for him to dare. Even after all that had happened tonight, he was still too timid to risk that.

"Try not to think about it."

"No," Nina said. "I gotta get it out of my head and talk about it, otherwise it'll get stuck there like it was glued."

"Okay," Tommy said, glancing into the mirror. Night had fallen while they were down in the tunnel, and he could just barely make out his passengers in the back.

Corinne was now snoring softly in her car seat. On Corinne's right, Burt stared out the window and rubbed his eyes with a quivering, dirty hand. Lisa was now silent, but she leaned forward to hear what Nina had to say.

"I think it was the way he snapped at us like that," Nina began, hand fisted under her chin. Tommy ached to touch that hand and open it up, squeeze it with his own, but again, he didn't dare. "He just screamed. No words. At least not that I could understand."

"'Get the eff out,'" Burt said, his voice flat and emotionless. "It all ran together, he was so mad. I mean, yeah, we interrupted him and those women—"

"His *bitches*," Lisa said, laughing sharply. "Literally."

"—But he and I were friends. *Used* to be friends. He looked like he was about to frickin' kill me. He didn't care that I was a wolf, too. Can't believe it..."

"Even if he was in his wolf form, just like those two, um, women he was with," Nina said. "That's still just wrong. And they just kept going at it, even with us there."

Tommy nodded along with Nina as she recounted the details of the basement room where the other pack of wolves had been holding Billy Hoerner. The place had smelled like a sewer, littered with clothes, garbage, boards and other bits of construction. And a moldy mattress thrown down in the middle of the floor. That was where they found Billy as an oversized brown-furred wolf, with two of the females from the other pack—Tommy knew them by their smaller size.

"Rutting," Nina was saying. Tommy cringed, feeling his stomach turn. "Rutting and—" she lowered her voice after a quick glance back at the baby "—fucking. That's what they were doing. Plain and simple."

"I think they were supposed to *wait*," Lisa said, tapping on the back of Tommy's seat for emphasis. "They kept saying someone was coming, then the real crazy shit was going to start."

"Really?" Tommy hung a right and started heading toward downtown. Once more, no other cars were on the road, and most of the houses were dark down Second Street. Maybe the lady from the diner today was right about all the normal people in town hiding out from the wolves.

"Hey," he said. "Do you know who the wolves were all waiting for? Was it a guy and a girl, in their thirties or early forties, maybe?"

As soon as he said, Tommy knew it was them. The two of them had the smell of kings and queens. Royalty.

He shivered again at the memory of how that dude had made him drool at the thought of killing Suzanne. That thought was way worse than thinking about walking in on Billy sexing up the two wolves and then taking a swing at Burt afterward.

I'd really wanted to do it, he thought, still feeling queasy. *Like he was* ordering *me to do it.*

"Maybe," Lisa said. "They always said *him* or *her*. Like, 'Not yet, he's on his way,' or 'Wait 'til she gets here first before we start.' That kind of talk made me feel *real* comfortable, you can imagine."

Nina took in a deep breath and let it out slow and shuddering. They were two blocks away from the Side Entrance, and Tommy wanted to stop and check in on Mom and Dad before heading home.

"What're you thinking about over there, big guy?" Nina said as they sat at a red light at the town's only stoplight.

"I think I should've never gone to the diner today with Corinne," he said, and then they were in front of the Side Entrance.

Tommy parked the car and heard Burt's grunt of disgust from the back seat.

"Looks like Mom and Dad are up to no good again," Burt said, pointing. "Wait'll they hear what I can do now."

At a table next to the window, with two pitchers of beers and four mugs in front of them, Mom and Dad sat across from a younger couple. The four of them were deep in conversation. Mom was waving her hands and laughing as Dad poured more beer into first his, then Mom's mug.

"Ah shit," Tommy said.

"What?" Nina and Burt said at the same time.

Tommy looked closer to make sure he was seeing clearly. Unfortunately, he was. Mom and Dad were talking to the woman with the gray-streaked black hair as well as the harsh-faced man with the dark hair and hypnotic voice.

"I think tonight's the night everyone's been waiting for. And my parents are right in the middle of it."

Chapter Twenty-Nine

The jukebox at the Side Entrance usually blasted the latest country-pop crossover loud enough to make the bubbles pop in your beer. But tonight the music was off and the TVs were muted. The place smelled like burgers, fried onions, and beer, with just a tiny undercurrent of stale cigarette smoke tonight. Tommy's stomach growled loud enough for five people.

What was left of the usual gang of hard drinkers that usually lined the bar, love handle to love handle, were all sitting around a small round table. That table was as far away from Mom and Dad's table as they could get without going outside onto the sidewalk.

Livy, the eighty-something owner of the bar, her white hair in a ponytail that hung halfway down her back, stood behind the taps like a gunslinger eying her enemy. She nodded at Tommy and Corinne as they walked up, and she gave them a bright smile. Her smile quickly changed to a scowl when she saw Burt; they had a history of bad blood from the days when he tried to sneak beers here when he was underage.

"Careful," Livy said, handing Tommy a mug of beer from the tap and nodding in the direction of his parents. "They been there for hours now, talking like old friends. I never seen those two sharp-looking folks before. And you know what *that* means."

Tommy took a big gulp of the beer, keeping the frosty mug free of Corinne's quick, swinging hands. He was tempted to drink it all down, but then he handed it to Nina. She took a quick pull on it and handed it to Lisa. Burt watched Lisa drinking it closely, thirstily, hands reaching for the mug, but Lisa finished it off.

Livy gasped.

"Lisa?" Livy had slipped out from behind the bar, moving with deceptive speed despite her advanced years and slightly hunched back. She grabbed Lisa and wrapped her up a big hug. Lisa's defenses finally broke down, and she burst into tears in the bar owner's thin arms.

"They found me, Auntie Livy," Lisa whispered, looking from Livy's shoulder to Tommy, Corinne, Nina, until her gaze came to rest on Burt.

"I, um, could really use a sip of beer, too," Burt muttered.

If this had been a normal night, the blasting music and the noise of the crowd would've drowned out the reunion next to the bar. But Livy and Lisa's voices had carried, and everyone else had turned to watch, including Mom and Dad and their new friends.

"Yes," the woman with the streaky black hair was saying in a fake-friendly voice, as if answering a question asked by Mom, "I do remember the two of them. Tommy and his little girl Corinne. Strapping fellow, isn't he? I think he's just what the doctor ordered, dear. Just what we need."

"Even if he and his little gang of mutts did take our Lisa away from us," the thin man with the goatee and dark eyebrows said, not even trying to pretend to act nice. "That wasn't so... *cooperative.*"

Looking over at the four so-called grownups over at their table with its empty pitchers and mugs, Tommy felt the same feeling come over him as the one he'd felt in the diner.

He *did* want to help the strangers. To cooperate. Maybe they could start by giving Lisa back to them...

Then Corinne squirmed in his arms, and her fist grazed his chin. Tommy jerked, as if waking up after being splashed with water.

"Gamma!" Corinne squeaked, fighting to get loose of Tommy's grasp and cruise from chair to table over to Mom. No way was Tommy letting that happen. Mom still sat at the table with Dad, as they couldn't be bothered to get up to greet their only grandchild.

Meanwhile, the two strangers now stood next to their table, arms crossed, watching Tommy approach with knowing smiles on their too-perfect faces.

"Mom," Tommy said, avoiding the gaze of the woman and her companion, "aren't you gonna introduce us to your friends?"

The too-sweet smell of funeral flowers filled Tommy's nose again when he was a few feet from the black-haired woman. She was tall, and she seemed annoyed to have to look up to meet Tommy's eyes.

"That's *funny*," Mom said in a laughing, happy voice that Tommy barely recognized. "I don't think they ever told us their names."

"You never asked, you silly thing," the woman said, an edge to her voice now. "I am Gwen, and this is Lance. No King Arthur jokes, please."

Dad cracked up at that, slapping the table and spilling beer all over himself. He held his sore ribs as he laughed, and he looked ready to fall out of the booth any second. They must've been drinking non-stop all afternoon. Luke Callahan must've gotten tired of waiting around and left.

Nina put a hand on Tommy's back, stepping up next to him. Gwen looked at Nina with a scowl, as if trying to figure out who Nina was and where she'd come from.

Mom and Dad are useless, he thought, *so it's up to me. And Nina's my backup, along with Corinne and Burt and Lisa.*

And Livy, too—Tommy knew the old woman kept a sawed-off shotgun and a tazer in a drawer under the bar.

"Well, welcome to Dyersburg," he said to the two newcomers standing in front of him. "I hope you won't be staying *too* long."

Gwen laughed sharply at that.

"Lance," she said. "We've crashed head-on into the town's Welcome Wagon."

"Tommy!" Mom said. "Don't even piss me off in front of my new friends, boy."

Tommy felt a moment's hesitation, wondering if he was making a huge mistake, getting it all wrong with these two strangers.

No, he thought. *I have to trust my instincts, for the first time in a long time. Go with my gut, just like I did when I was playing football.*

"Billy Hoerner says hi, by the way. He's up in one of the abandoned houses you guys set up outside town, where we found Lisa. He was a bit too busy to chat, though."

"I'm afraid I don't under—" Gwen began, taking a step closer to Tommy.

"I guess," Tommy continued, "Billy doesn't know what your... people did to his brother Steve. You know, the guy they tore to pieces. That would probably make him lose the urge to breed with your ladies. Probably."

"Lance," the woman named Gwen said. "I think I need you to set our friend Tommy straight. He's talking a bit on the crazy side."

"I was wondering when you were going to ask," her friend said, giving her an angry look before turning his gaze on Tommy.

Tommy wanted to step back from those dark eyes, but Nina's unwavering hand on his back helped him keep up his courage. He instinctively turned his left shoulder toward Lance, keeping Corinne, still perched on his right hip, as far from the man as possible.

"*Relax*, big guy," Lance said, and Tommy felt the tension leave his shoulders so fast he nearly dropped Corinne. "This is going to be a long night, and we need you—all of you—to work with us and do what we *say*."

That made sense, Tommy thought. The world bounced as he nodded his head vigorously. *These are good people. Doesn't matter that we don't really know them. We should help 'em.*

He looked over and saw Nina nodding too, along with Burt behind them, like a pair of bobbleheads. Even Lisa and Livy over by the bar seemed more relaxed, completely unworried about the two newcomers.

"That's more like it," Gwen said, eyes flashing red for a split second. Her smile was wide and full of perfect white teeth. "We were just discussing what to do about our Callahan problem. Tommy, come have a seat. Bring your little one, but leave your loser brother and that black bitch. Tell them to get *lost.*"

Tommy nodded and turned automatically to look at Nina, who didn't seem to have registered what Gwen had just called her.

He opened his mouth to tell Nina to get lost, but the words stuck in his throat when he saw the slightly glazed look on her beautiful face.

I could never tell this girl to get lost, he thought, even as the words formed in his mouth.

"Dada!" Corinne shouted, accompanied by a sharp slap on Tommy's cheek.

The slap seem to wake up Tommy's wolf-instincts. Time slowed as his brain rifled through the details of the situation. The urge to get rid of Nina evaporated, though he still felt the strangers' eyes on him.

Something about the guy's voice did this to all of us, he knew now. *Like a hypnotist.*

Tommy didn't have time to think more on it, not with everyone else watching. He swallowed hard, hoping he hadn't shown any of these rapid-fire thoughts on his still-stinging face, and looked down at Nina.

This sucks, he thought, and then he said to Nina, the girl who'd captured a large piece of his heart in the past few weeks, "Go on. Get lost."

Nina just nodded and stepped back obediently, which hurt Tommy even more than having to say that to her.

"You too, Burt. Go wait at the bar."

I'm going to kick that guy's ass for this, Tommy thought, and then he turned back to the strangers with what he hoped was a suitably glazed look on his face.

"Dada?" Corinne asked, rubbing his cheek.

"Shh," he said to her. "It's all right, baby."

"Tha's my boy," Dad said as he poured Tommy a mug of beer, sloshing more onto the table in his enthusiasm. "Finally got off his high horse and came 'round."

Mom put her elbows in the fresh puddle of beer on the table and didn't even flinch. Gwen and Lance, in the meantime, had slid back into the booth.

Tommy pulled up a chair and sat at the end of the table, between Gwen and Lance and his parents, with his back to Nina and Burt, waiting obediently fifteen feet away next the bar.

"Now, about these Callahan boys," Gwen began, pushing away the empty mug in front of her with a look of disgust on her face. "We were hoping to get them to see the error of their ways and help our people, for the good of all our kind. Virile young men, those Callahans. But they're also too damn stubborn. We have the middle one locked up, but the youngest continues giving us all sorts of grief. He killed one of our women last night, you know. And today he attacked two more of our people. Then he disappeared."

She moved in on Tommy, eyes blazing, and Tommy struggled to keep his face zombie-like.

"Any idea where we could find him, Tommy?"

"Westhoff's land?" he blurted out, the first thing that came to mind. "That's where they found his other brother. Matthew."

The second place he thought of—the ethanol plant—he kept tucked away in a corner of his brain.

If these freak wolves can read minds, we're hosed.

"Good boy," Mom said, sipping her beer. "Good boy."

"Ah yes, Matthew," Gwen said, ignoring Mom. "The meth-head. He was the one who told us about this place. After Lance here had worked on him for a few hours. The guy did *not* want to talk, but when his meth high wore off, he was surprisingly pliable. Always a shame when a wolf gives in to the weakness of his human side. Said he couldn't stand the changing anymore. Wanted to stay human, for God's sake. The meth helped with that, I guess."

It was all Tommy could do not to get up and run from the table, but he kept himself calm with the reassuring weight of Corinne on his knee. She was busy playing peek-a-boo with Mom and trying to tip over the empty mugs on the table.

"But in any case, we do have Matthew to thank for bringing us here. He may have given us the key to my people's continued survival. He told us of the old lady he knew who helped him with his first change back when he was a child, visiting this town. What was her name again? A schoolteacher, I believe."

"Eveline Jaeger," Lance said, without hesitation. "From an old were line from eastern Germany, going back at least twelve centuries. No children, though. Last of her line. Fine lady, even if she was a mutt. Left this world back in February. Matthew lost control while visiting her, apparently. A pity."

"Okay," Gwen said, rolling her eyes for Tommy's benefit. "You're bringing me down, already."

"Yeah," Dad said as he rested his head on the window next to him, eyelids growing heavy. The night was black through the window, the streets empty.

Tommy felt a strong urge to bolt from the table, turn, and just go running wolf-wild into that dark and quiet night.

Instead, he listened to Gwen ramble on.

"Don't know why his brothers cared enough about him to come here, to tell you the truth. He was weak and sickly from the drugs. Not good breeding material. But his younger brothers still might do."

"Even if they are mutts, too," Lance said with a sneer. Gwen's face tightened the tiniest bit at that, and then her mask of calm and control returned.

Tommy nodded along with them, keeping his face blank as he absorbed all that Gwen had told him about the oldest Callahan—*had Matthew killed Mrs. Jaeger back in February? And why'd he come after* me, *too, after killing her? Was it drugs, or something else? Had Lance been pulling Matthew's strings the whole time?*

After a few moment of silence, Tommy realized that Gwen had stopped talking. She was smiling at him, though it was slowly turning into a smirk as her face tightened again. She reached out a hand with long, bright pink fingernails to try to touch Tommy's face.

"And *you*, Tommy Roling. You'll do quite nicely yourself to help save our line."

Corinne kicked over Mom's half-empty mug of beer before Gwen could make contact with Tommy. Gwen jerked back her hand, though Mom and Dad just sat there as a river of beer flowed over them and onto their legs.

"Little urchin," Gwen spat, and then her face softened. "I mean, what a sweet, sweet little girl. So filthy, but very sweet."

"That's my girl for you," Tommy said in a dull, expressionless voice, though he wanted to throttle the woman for calling Corinne such things.

Gwen just stared at him all over again. Tommy felt sweat break out on his forehead and in his armpits.

"*Yes*," Gwen said at last, with a glance at Lance next to her. She seemed to be carrying on some sort of conversation with herself, and now that internal chat was over. "How long has it been, Lance?"

"How long what?" her friend said, and then Tommy realized who the Lance guy reminded him of—the ponytail dude at the apartment with the roomful of female athletes. The guy Nina said was the manager for the different sports teams. It was the guy's voice that reminded him of the manager guy; it was almost hypnotic.

"How long has it been since our friend Tommy here has been *faking* it?"

"What?" Lance said.

Outside the window, next to a snoozing Dad, Tommy saw two small, wiry gray wolves trot past on the sidewalk.

Reinforcements. We've wasted too much time here. We're about to get surrounded.

"Losing your touch, Lance. And me talking my damn fool head off."

And that's my cue to go, Tommy thought, standing up so fast he knocked over his chair. Another three wolves joined the other two wolves outside.

"No, no," Gwen said, voice sharp and biting. "I didn't say you could leave, Tommy-boy. Lance?"

"*Stay*," Lance said.

Tommy barely even felt that one.

"No thanks."

Gwen looked up at Tommy, tapping her fingers on the only dry patch of the beer-soaked table.

"I'm not sure you understand the situation here, Tommy-boy. My people *need* people like you. Yes, we're pure-breeds, but we have reached the point where we don't care if our blood mingles with half-human weres like you and the other weres in this town. We need our line to continue. Our women can't have any more litters—babies—from the few pure-breed men left. We need fresh blood, literally. Are you going to deny us that?"

Tommy felt his lip curl at her story, thinking of the chains around Lisa's wrists and the mad scene with Billy Hoerner. A guy who'd just lost his brother. And then there was Mrs. Jaeger, left for dead months ago. Even Matthew Callahan, sick and out of his head, attacking me that night. All those lives ruined by this woman's plan.

"So you thought it was okay to just take what you wanted? To rape innocent women?"

"Not women," Gwen corrected him. "Wolves."

"Hey, we haven't started the breeding process yet," Lance said. "We were still gathering suitable bitches."

"Language," Mom mumbled from where she was fiddling with her empty mug. She stared down at her hands, eyelids drooping just like Dad's. "Watch... yer language, mister..."

"Right," Gwen said, turning her glare from Tommy to Mom for a moment. She sighed and looked over at Tommy again as she got up out of her chair again.

"So you don't want to help us keep my people from dying a miserable death, is that it? You don't care that we're going extinct?"

"I'm sorry your people can't have more babies," Tommy said, holding tight to Corinne. "But the way you're going about this is all wrong."

Gwen growled, blackish-gray fur sprouting across her face and bare arms for just an instant.

"We don't have *time* to be diplomatic," she said in a low, angry voice.

"*You*," she said to Mom.

Mom sat up straight, and her empty mug slid out of her hand and off the table. Gwen reached out a hand with a blurring motion and caught the falling mug without a shred of effort.

"Show your foolish son what happens to those who disagree with my methods."

She pointed at Dad sitting next to Mom.

"Kill that weak mutt-lover. *Now*."

With a growl of her own, a sound was equal parts eager and terrified, Mom slipped into wolf mode. She changed so fast her clothes ripped and went flying around her in a cloud of tattered material. Her eyes went red. Tommy was too shocked to even inhale.

An instant later, a blonde-furred wolf that was easily six feet long leaped onto Dad, knocking him out of his chair. Wolf and man hit the floor with a sickening thud.

And then Dad started screaming as Mom's claws hit home.

Chapter Thirty

After a moment of stunned shock at witnessing his transformed mother in her fury of swinging claws, Dad's screams finally sent Tommy surging into action. He just hoped he wasn't too late.

He half-threw, half-pushed Corinne toward the bar, away from the cackling strangers watching Mom attacking Dad. In the same movement, he dove onto Mom's wide, furry back before she finished tearing Dad apart.

By the time he laid his hands—now clawed and fur-covered—on Mom, Tommy was completely in his wolf form. He was much bigger than Mom, but that didn't stop her from pivoting off Dad and catching him hard on the side of his head with a paw slick with Dad's blood.

Tommy's vision exploded with white light and shooting pain, but he rolled with the hit and grabbed Mom's paw at the same time. He used his momentum to pull her off Dad and carry her halfway across the bar with him, away from Dad.

Unable to complete Gwen's orders, Mom threw herself on Tommy in a red-eyed frenzy. It was all he could do to hold onto her arms and move behind her as she kicked and snapped at him.

"Snap out of it!" he shouted through his muzzle at her. Mom tried to shake free of his grasp, but Tommy wouldn't let go. She switched positions then and turned toward him, teeth bared and eyes glowing an even brighter red. Tommy slipped on the wet floor and went down hard on his back.

"Mom!" Tommy screamed as she leaped on top of him, her pointed teeth inches from his throat.

"Gamma!" Corinne yelled in her high-pitched voice. She sat on the floor just three feet away from Tommy and Mom.

Tommy used his back legs to try and push Mom off of him. She wouldn't budge. He clipped her across the face with his right paw as hard as he could. He hated to admit it, but that had felt good.

Mom's eyes still glowed red. She'd lost all her humanity as well, it seemed. She clawed and bit and kicked on top of him, trying to kill him. There was no Mom in there anymore.

I'm going to have to kill her, Tommy realized, grabbing Mom by her thick, furry wrists. *She won't stop until she does the same to me.*

But just as he was reaching up to bite into Mom's throat and Mom was biting a big chunk out of his left shoulder, another blinding explosion of white exploded inside Tommy's head. This time the pain came along with a deafening, high-pitched roar that nearly split his ear drums in two.

For a painful few seconds, he couldn't take another breath. The world went gray.

I'm dead, he thought, and then his airway opened and he could inhale again.

Tommy blinked and looked around the tavern. Mom was a few feet away from him, naked, her hands and the side of her face bloodied as she struggled feebly to cover herself.

I know that sound, Tommy thought. *Burt...*

Something glinted in the bar's neon lights off to his right, and Tommy looked over to see none other than Burt coming over to him. Burt held Corinne in his arms, and Corinne, whimpering, held her hands clamped to her ears.

Burt gazed at Tommy with clear eyes, a silver whistle in his hand.

"Thought you could use a little help," he said as he handed Corinne to Tommy, "once Corinne here snapped me out of my weird funk, that is. Let me check on Dad. And Mom, too."

Burt nodded one more time at Tommy and hurried over to Dad.

"You okay?" a soft voice said next to him. Nina handed Tommy what was left of his jeans.

"I am," Tommy said, torn between wanting to hug Nina as soon as he saw she was also clear-eyed and no longer under Lance's nasty control, and checking on his parents. "You?"

"Yep," Nina said, looking down at Mom. "I am now, thanks to Corinne. "

Corinne slid out of Tommy's grasp and crawled over to Mom. Tommy almost reached out to grab her, but Nina stopped him.

"It's okay. Just watch."

As soon as Corinne touched her, Mom burst into tears and hugged her.

"Where'd our two friends go?" Tommy said. The table with the spilled beer and overturned chairs was now vacant.

"They tried to make a run for it," a familiar voice said from the other side of the bar, accompanied by a clicking sound. "Didn't get too far."

Livy stood over Lance, who was quivering on the hardwood floor. She held her tazer in one gnarled hand, and the sawed-off shotgun, pointed at Gwen, in the other. It was just her against the two strangers—all of Livy's regulars had fled the bar.

"Nice work, Livy," Tommy said. He pulled on his torn jeans, sucking in his gut. He really wanted to get his shirt, but there wasn't time for being insecure.

"We got your back, ma'am," Nina told the bar owner as she and Tommy walked closer to Gwen, who was hovering over Lance and keeping an eye on the exit. More wolves had gathered outside, as if drawn to their leaders like moths to light.

"Burt?" Tommy called out, the pulsing ache in his head from his brother's whistle slowly fading. "How's Dad?"

"Ah man," Burt said. "He's bleeding bad. Mom cut him up good. Can't believe we just stood there and watched it happen."

Tommy was relieved to see that Mom had pulled herself together enough to gather up strips of clothing to bandage up Dad. She worked feverishly, with Corinne at her side, to stop Dad's bleeding.

"But he's breathing," Mom said. "I already called 911. Good thing he's had so much beer. Doubt he feels much of this right now. Just... hang in there. Hear me?"

Tommy let out a shaky breath of relief at that. But he couldn't help but give Lance a kick in the ribs as he and Nina approached Gwen.

"You *caused* that," he said to the groaning man on the floor, "you sick, hypnotizing bastard. You also made me say shit I didn't ever want to say. I should just kill you now. But that'd make me just as bad as all of you."

"Don't judge us so hastily," Gwen said. She nodded at the red-eyed wolves peering in at them through the windows. There had to be at least two dozen of them out there now, surrounding the place. "We have no other options. Put yourself in our place, Tommy. Imagine life without your daughter. An empty life, without offspring. That is the fate of my people, unless your pack here can help us."

"But you can't just take what you want," Tommy said. "And kill people who resist. Don't make this out to be all our fault.'

"We're talking about people here," Nina said, "not breeding factories."

As they were talking, three wolves pushed their way into the bar through the glass front door. Tommy immediately recognized the scent of the biggest as the brown-gray male from the basement of the house outside town. The male gave Tommy a long, low growl, teeth bared, nostrils flaring.

"Tommy?" Livy said, aiming the gun at the wolves. "Want I should shoot 'em?"

"Wait," Tommy said, holding off his own change, panting for air, struggling to control his instincts as well as this situation.

And then the tavern exploded.

Chapter Thirty-One

Shards of glass. Screeching metal. Burnt oil and gasoline fumes. Yipping wolves. A bone-jarring crash. A sour taste in his mouth.

And the screaming. The screaming didn't seem to ever end.

It all ran together in Tommy's heightened senses from where he'd dropped onto all fours, covered in fur, the instant the explosion hit.

Nina! Corinne!

He found Nina to his right, also lifting her furry little wolf head. Deeper inside the glass-strewn, smoky interior of the tavern, he saw Burt and Corinne waving at the air and coughing.

Alive. Okay. But what just hit the place?

"Danica's car," Nina said, answering his unspoken question. "But how?"

As the smoke cleared and the ringing left Tommy's pointed ears, he saw something impossible—a battered blue Toyota Tercel wedged halfway into the doorway of the Side Entrance.

And peeling himself off the steering wheel was none other than his uncle.

"Carl!" Tommy screamed, scrambling over broken glass and scattered tables and chairs. He moved past the unmoving body of Lance on the floor—the guy must've caught the bulk of the flying glass, he'd been so close to the entrance.

"My bar," Livy said. Nina hurried over to help her up and away from the debris.

Tommy, meanwhile, made it to within two feet of the mangled front bumper before pulling up short. In her wolf form, Gwen had worked her way into the passenger seat of the now-windowless car. Somehow the car's engine was still running from where it sat wedged into the entrance.

"Back off," she shouted, holding a clawed hand up to Carl's pale neck.

"The hell?" Carl mumbled through his blood spattered mouth and nose. "I'm on *your* side here." He quickly stopped talking as Gwen pressed her white claws against the skin protecting his jugular.

"Don't—" Tommy began, then stopped.

He was about to tell Gwen to not hurt Uncle Carl, but he had to actually consider that.

How much suffering had his druncle Carl caused in the past few months, starting with me and Corinne and his deal with his child-less friends?

Gwen laughed from inside the idling Tercel. The engine popped, missing a few beats, and more red-eyed wolves gathered outside.

"You sure you don't want to join our pack, Tommy-boy? Most of you mutts lack the killer instinct us pure-breeds have. But you've got something of us in you."

Barking out a harsh laugh, she pushed Carl out of the car and slid into the driver's seat. With a roar of the little engine and a series of backfires, she reversed the Tercel out of the tavern. The front bumper pulled loose with a horrendous screech, and then she was free. Tommy wanted to give chase, but her wolves blocked the door the instant she left.

Gwen and the Tercel, however, barely made it ten feet before hitting a roadblock.

Mark Callahan's truck took the worst of the impact, but the Tercel bounced and also hit the Volvo that had been parked nose-to-nose with the big truck as a roadblock.

"Melanie!" Tommy shouted, running out on all fours into the street, where he was jumped by a dozen of the other wolves.

Main Street was a riot of wolves of all sizes and colors for a good three minutes after that. Tommy saw Melanie in her wolf skin, fighting off three smaller wolves, while her changed boys stood back-to-back and paw-to-paw on the hood of Mark's truck. Both Callahan brothers fought to keep the other wolves away from them. Mark was already limping and hurting.

Charging through the smaller wolves like a four-legged nose tackle on the hunt for a quarterback, Tommy battered his way next to Aunt Melanie. He had to trust that Burt and Nina would protect the others inside the tavern. He had to find Gwen before she got away.

"Where'd she go?" he shouted, but Mel couldn't hear him. The interior of the Tercel was empty, though three small wolves stood on its hood, snapping at him.

Just as Tommy was feeling overwhelmed and approaching exhaustion from fighting off the smaller wolves, the Dyersburg reinforcements arrived.

Tommy recognized old man Lucas by his white muzzle and limp. Judy Hoerner was the gray wolf next to Debby and Kim Klein, both reddish-brown wolves with yellowed teeth bared at the other pack of wolves gathered around them.

And inside the Side Entrance was Linus Schnelling in his slick, dark-brown coat inside the Side Entrance, nuzzling his pup Lisa after her long disappearance, along with a younger version of Linus—his son Larry.

The other wolves were now backed into the corner created by the crashed Tercel and Mark's truck. Without their alpha female Gwen, the other wolves quickly lost their will to fight. A few darted around the edges of the car, but a quick bark from Tommy brought them closer, obedient as dogs.

They're lost without their leader, Tommy realized. *And probably just following orders, like Mom attacking Dad on Lance's command.*

Luke Callahan approached the crowd of scared wolves, panting and licking his blood-flecked lips.

"Stop!" Tommy yelled. "They're beaten, Luke. Let it go."

"Tommy-boy," Luke rasped. "They ain't beaten yet. Not 'til I'm through with them they ain't."

"Luke!" Mark said. He hobbled up to his brother, his fur matted with dried blood. "Stop. The woman got away. Their human whisperer is dead inside the bar. You're wasting time. Go ahead, Tommy."

Tommy let his wolf form recede just enough to allow him to talk more clearly, though he left a healthy coating of fur to keep his confidence from flagging.

He glanced back and saw Nina nodding at him and giving him a wide, toothy smile, with Burt and Corinne next to her in their wolf form as well. Mom was supporting Dad with Livy's help. And Melanie and her boys were out here alongside Tommy.

Everyone was there, even Uncle Carl, cowering on the sidewalk and watching the chaos he'd caused with stunned shock. The whole pack was here.

"Your leader has abandoned you," Tommy told the quivering mass of wolves in front of him. "We know why you're here, and I'm guessing a lot of you are here because they forced you to come here. You need to leave, tonight, and never come back. And we'll be watching, so don't try to come back here or try this any other place. We'll know."

Even before he was finished talking, the other wolves had started to disperse with a loud scrabble of claws on asphalt. Within seconds they had melted into the darkness, leaving behind the stink of defeat and desperation.

Tommy opened his mouth to say something to Melanie when the street lit up with flashing red lights. Smith and his deputy Bobby pulled up in their cruisers and parked behind Melanie's dented Volvo.

Tommy couldn't imagine what the scene must've looked like to Smith's eyes—three wrecked cars in the middle of Main Street, with a handful of oversized wolves around them, and more wolves crowded inside the trashed tavern next to it.

"Don't even try to explain," Smith said in an unsteady voice. "Just clean all this up before anyone else from town sees it."

259

* * * * *

And so the battle for Dyersburg ended, with mostly a bunch of whimpers instead of a bang.

Smith had directed the EMTs first to Dad, and then to Lance. The EMTs couldn't do anything for Lance other than carry him off in a bag and pack him into the ambulance, but Dad was doing surprisingly well for the series of gashes across his chest and arms. Maybe Mom had pulled her punches, finding some control deep down inside her despite Lance's power of suggestion.

After an hour of everyone cleaning and moving damaged cars, Smith gathered everyone inside the Side Entrance. Tommy had gotten most of his torn clothes back on and in place along with the rest of the town wolves. Everyone had returned to their human form. It looked like a late-night prayer gathering instead of a group of weres after a pitched battle.

"You're going to have to make a deal with me, right here tonight," Smith said. "You people," he said, and then coughed. "You, uh, all have to zip this up tighter than a tick. Nobody talks about what happened here. Not even to each other. Most folks will think you're nuts if you even try talking about it, but... People died here in the past few months. If what Mark and Livy and Tommy here have told me is accurate, and I have no reason to doubt 'em, then these intruders are finished here."

Tommy hoped he was right. He surveyed the crowd and felt himself relaxing. The town was in good hands with these people on the lookout. His fellow weres.

"So here's the thing," Smith continued, taking off his hat and running his hands through his graying hair. "You can't be turning into wolves like this again. My men aren't trained for that kind of thing. Plus, I don't want one of you getting shot by a hunter or a farmer. If you can't do that, well, you'll have to leave."

Tommy saw most of the other heads nodding to this, as if accepting his verdict like they deserved it. Some folks almost looked relieved.

"What if there's trouble like this again?" Tommy said as Smith put his hat back on.

"You let me know about it right away."

"And you'll handle it like you did tonight?" Burt piped up. "Coming in after all the fighting's over?"

Smith didn't even blink at that.

"Those are my requests. Take 'em or leave 'em. Or leave town. G'night."

Smith and his deputy beat a hasty retreat, boots clacking on the concrete sidewalk outside the tavern loud enough to wake Uncle Carl from his beer-aided sleep.

"No way he can enforce that," Burt said, draining the last of his beer. "I mean, really, what's he gonna do? Are he and Bobby gonna use silver bullets?" Burt paused and stifled a belch. "Um, Nina, does that even work?"

Nina just smiled at Burt and touched Tommy's hand. He gripped it tight.

"I can live with that," Mom said in a soft voice at the table next to them. She turned to Tommy and Burt. "Are you boys okay with that, too?"

Burt looked at Tommy, who just shook his head. Tommy looked from his brother to the bandages covering Dad's chest and arms.

He sighed as his gaze came to rest on Mom. He thought of how he'd used all his strength to keep her from ripping out his throat earlier.

"I understand, Mom," he said, and then he gathered up Corinne from where she was napping on some blankets on the pool table. "I understand everything."

Feeling a tiny piece of him break off and remain behind in the bar, Tommy took Nina's hand, and the three of them walked out of the hole left in the Side Entrance.

"Shit," Burt mumbled. "Wait up, guys." Melanie and her sleepy boys followed them out as well.

Soon the bar was empty, and the only people left other than Livy resting her head on the banged-up bar were Mom and Dad, sitting at the same table where they'd shared beers with Gwen the Alpha Female and Lance the Wolf Whisperer.

Sitting in the bed of Mark Callahan's truck with Burt and Nina next to him and Corinne in his arms, Tommy looked through the smudged window at his parents inside the otherwise-empty bar. He wished he hadn't.

"Hope that's not the last time I see the two of them," he said, and then Mark gunned the engine, and Tommy left downtown Dyersburg for good.

Chapter Thirty-Two

May and June were gone in a blur. Before Tommy knew it, July was half over, and he'd thrown himself into his new life in Iowa City. And on the seventeenth of July, he had a birthday party to attend. A first birthday.

He left the police station at eight that morning, still buzzing from the extra-strong coffee officer Attix always had in his Thermos. They'd been close to finding the guy who'd set fire to three of the trailers outside Coralville, one town over from Iowa City. What had started out as a night of shadowing a cop for his criminal justice class at the local community college had turned into an ongoing freelance opportunity for Tommy.

Guess it helped that on the first night of shadowing Attix I helped him find the guy who snatched that lady's purse on the University of Iowa's campus.

"It's like you followed the guy's scent right to his dorm room," laughed Attix. He was a forty-something black guy, light-skinned, with sharp, dark brown eyes. He didn't laugh for long. Just gave Tommy a look and gave him his business card.

Since that night, Tommy had helped Attix find eight suspects in less than five weeks. Attix was thinking promotion, so he didn't want to let Tommy out of his grasp.

Tommy, meanwhile, loved the job and doing something other than delivering pizzas to make money to help pay down his health-insurance debts. He and Melanie had a babysitting deal for Corinne—she'd watch her when he had class and his night shifts with Attix, and he'd help watch the boys and Corinne while she was at work.

Melanie had been able to cut her hours way back after Uncle Carl ponied up his share of child support with the money he'd made from ads on his Antiwolf website. Tommy hadn't seen Carl since that night in Dyersburg, and he couldn't say that he felt bad about that.

Any other hours of child care the kids needed got picked up by their newest housemate, Burt.

Driving back to Melanie's place with the summer sun slowly heating the streets and interior of his car, Tommy had to laugh at how happy Burt was to be out of Dyersburg for the first time in his life. Burt loved exploring the campus and finding new bars downtown, where he'd sit and sip his beer and make new friends almost instantly. And he was going to get a good job any day now, he kept promising Melanie.

Tommy's smile widened when he saw the battered blue Tercel parked on the street in front of his new home. Nina's roommate Danica had made Nina pay for the damage to her car, and then Danica claimed the car stank of dog fur, so she just gave it to Nina. Melanie knew a good mechanic who fixed it up almost good as new, except for the dents, and Nina never complained about any kind of smell in it.

"You made it!" Tommy said to Nina as soon as he'd made it inside and into the kitchen. "I missed you!"

He wrapped Nina up in a big bear hug, glad to have her arms around him again. She was living back home in Chicago, taking the summer off, as she called it. They'd been keeping up with each other, texting and emailing and calling, but it just wasn't the same.

"Anyone else coming?" he asked Melanie as he peeked in on the kids in the living room. Burt was fighting off Corinne, in her wolf form, as she tried to get to her pile of presents. A furry Ty was on Burt's side, but Trey, on all fours, was helping Corinne.

Melanie shook her head. Nina caught the look passed between them.

"I'm sorry," Nina said. "Your folks will come around. They *have* to."

"I know," Tommy said, and then gave both women a smile. "We'd better get in there. Burt's about to go down, I think."

"I'll get the cake," Melanie said. "Nina, can you grab the camera?"

"Happy birthday, Corinne!" Tommy said as he entered the living room. Corinne leaped up into the air as a wolf but landed in his arms as a naked little one-year-old girl. "You wore your birthday suit, too! How nice!" He gave her a big kiss on the forehead. "I love you, Corinne."

"Lub you!" Corinne said back, and then she was gone the minute she saw her opening and started tearing into her presents. Tyler and Trey joined the fun, until the air and floor were filled with confetti from the wrapping paper.

"I should get a diaper on her, at least," Tommy said.

"Don't worry about it," Melanie said, pushing him toward Corinne and Nina. "Go have fun already!"

Ten minutes later, after the presents were opened and the cake was sliced, Melanie sat down next to Tommy and slapped his knee. He was just thinking about his absent parents again. His aunt must've sensed it.

"You did good," she said "You didn't break up the pack. You know what I mean, don't you? *This* pack right here. This is what matters. You did this, Tommy. Get it?"

Tommy smiled in spite of the tinge of sadness.

He knew Mom and Dad had gotten the invite and his emails. They'd probably never leave Dyersburg after that crazy night at the Side Entrance.

Then he looked at his daughter, who Burt had wrestled back into her diaper and bright yellow dress. She was now sitting on Nina's lap, and both of them were slowly getting covered in pink frosting and chocolate cake. Nina looked at him with a mock exasperated look on her face, and then she gave up and let Corinne go wild with the cake and frosting. Tommy let out a long, deep breath.

"I got you, Aunt Mel," he said, feeling completely comfortable for what felt like the first time ever in his own skin. "I got you."

About the Author

Michael Jasper loves to explore the places where the normal meets the strange. In pursuit of this fascination, he has written and published over a dozen novels, three story collections, sixty short stories, and a digital comic with artist Niki Smith.

In the past he attempted bartending, teaching junior high, painting houses, being a secret shopper, working construction, and many more jobs; he prefers fiction writing. For his day job, he works as a technical writer.

He lives with his family in North Carolina, and his website is **michaeljasper.net**.

www.ingramcontent.com/pod-product-compliance
Lightning Source LLC
Chambersburg PA
CBHW030329200626
46816CB00006BA/1981